Havin

the gods and goddesses presented her with gifts befitting an Amazon Princess. Hera gave the child pride; Aphrodite gave her grace. An assembly of deities granted the newborn beauty, intelligence, strength of body and character, courage, compassion, and humility. Only Ares, the God of War, declined to present the child with a gift.

Also available from Pocket Books

Justice League of America

Batman: The Stone King
by Alan Grant

JUSTICE LEAGUE of AMERICA™
WONDER WOMAN™

MYTHOS

CAROL LAY

WONDER WOMAN CREATED BY
WILLIAM MOULTON MARSTON

POCKET BOOKS
New York   London   Toronto   Sydney   Singapore

An *Original* Publication of POCKET BOOKS

POCKET BOOKS, a division of Simon & Schuster, Inc.
1230 Avenue of the Americas, New York, NY 10020

Copyright © 2003 by DC Comics. All Rights Reserved.
Justice League of America, Wonder Woman, and all related titles, characters, and indicia are trademarks of DC Comics.

Wonder Woman created by William Moulton Marston

ISBN: 0-7434-1711-9

First Pocket Books printing January 2003

10 9 8 7 6 5 4 3 2 1

POCKET and colophon are registered trademarks of Simon & Schuster, Inc.

For information regarding special discounts for bulk purchases, please contact Simon & Schuster Special Sales at 1-800-456-6798 or business@simonandschuster.com

www.dccomics.com

Cover painting by Alex Ross
Series cover design by Georg Brewer

Printed in the U.S.A.

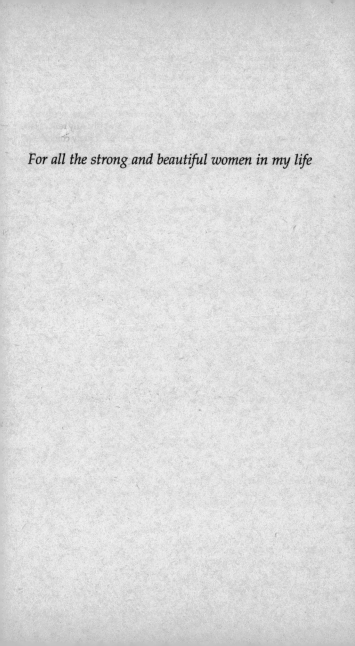

For all the strong and beautiful women in my life

Acknowledgments

I wish to thank several people for helping me write this, my first novel:

First, my editor at DC Comics, Charlie Kochman, for wondering out loud if I might be interested in tackling Wonder Woman. He kept me on the right path as I fumbled around in unfamiliar territory.

Thanks to Mark Evanier for saying the words "orb" and "island" in the same sentence, which somehow inspired 75,000 more words, give or take a few.

Thanks also to Rich Thomas at DC for supplying me with half a ton of comic books and information so I could read up on who's who in the world of flying people.

I also wish to thank Marco Palmieri at Pocket Books for his patience and skill, as well as Scott Shannon and Keith DeCandido; Allen Murdock for laughing out loud at the funny parts; and Joey Cavalieri for being a pal.

Lastly, thanks to everyone who gave Wonder Woman life, especially George Perez, Phil Jimenez, and her creator, William Moulton Marston.

MYTHOS

CHAPTER 1

Mysterious Island

Somewhere in the Bermuda Triangle, the boat bobbed, warm water lapping at its sides. A tern rested on the bow, sunning itself while, nearby, a turtle surfaced and gulped some air. Several hundred flying fish suddenly burst onto the scene. They flew for a dozen yards as if they had one brain, silver-blue bodies sparkling in the sun, and dove back into the ocean.

For all the life in and above the sea, there was no apparent sign of human activity—no sound from the deck or the small cabin to account for the presence of the lone boat in the middle of nowhere. There were some empty soda bottles in a bucket and a couple of towels tied to a rail. The most hardcore skeptic might become convinced that aliens had made off with whoever had sipped those sodas.

But several yards away were bubbles—two sets of jeweled gases that rose to the surface and popped in the air. The couple who had rented the boat, Henry

and Ana Lindstadt, were forty feet below. Their idea
of a fun honeymoon was to go scuba diving for a couple of weeks, staring at fish. To their delight, the fish
stared back.

In spite of her newly acquired Nordic surname, Ana
Lindstadt was Brazilian. An experienced diver, her keen
brown eyes were able to spot all manner of life that
other divers overlooked. Venomous scorpionfish that
looked like part of the coral, or nurse sharks hiding in
caves. She looked relaxed and in control of every movement—arms folded against her chest to cut down on
drag, kicks strong and easy as she controlled her buoyancy with her breathing. Many years of diving had
taught her that the best way to conserve air was to relax
and take slow, even breaths. Her trim figure and years
of yoga also contributed to her great profile underwater.

Henry, 32, was a couple of years younger than his
bride. Long blond hair, tied in a ponytail, trailed behind his head as he kicked his fins. Usually he took
his underwater cameras along to preserve their
recreation for posterity, but this time he'd left his
gear at home. Ana had asked him why, but at first he
said he didn't really know. Then he'd told her it was
their honeymoon, and he didn't want to bring work
along on the trip; he wanted to give her his full attention. She accepted his explanation, and he came
to believe it himself.

Henry looked back in the direction of his soul
mate. She used her hands to sign "I love you." He
signed "I love you, too." It was a good thing she
couldn't see the expression on his face, though—he

might have been asking for a corned beef sandwich. His attention was definitely elsewhere.

As Ana watched Henry turn away, she thought about their trip. So far they had spent some time looking at wrecks off North Carolina's shore, before heading south to the warmer waters of Florida. Those had been okay, in Ana's opinion, but not top-notch diving experiences. She'd been spoiled by trips to Micronesia and Australia. Hell, even over-crowded Cozumel was spectacular compared to what she'd seen so far. But Henry had insisted on coming to the Bermuda Triangle. Puzzling, because from what she had read, the diving around the Bahamas archipelago was nothing to write home about. A shark show, a dolphin dive, sure, but choreo-graphed encounters with big animals were not her idea of great dives. Still, Henry had gotten it into his head that the southeastern Atlantic coast was where they should go, and since they'd never done the Tri-angle before, she'd let him have his way.

Funny, but he had shown no interest in that desti-nation before he'd seen a clip of some underwater search mission on the Discovery Channel. Ana hadn't thought much of it—sea grass and a few fish common to the Caribbean were all she could see beyond the divers—but Henry commented that the site the divers were exploring seemed very familiar to him, even though he'd never been anywhere near it. The more she thought about it, the more she realized it was that moment when Henry became obsessed with diving in the Triangle. She also had asked to dive North Carolina and Florida for the sake of variety and experience, but he hadn't seemed to enjoy any of that, champing at the bit as he was to get to the Bahamas. Once they arrived on Grand Bahama he had become more excited than he had ever been before about diving, which was saying something. That would have been all right by Ana—she liked seeing him enthusiastic about things—but it was at her expense. He seemed to forget she was there.

So here they were in a pocket of the ocean all by themselves, but in this case that was like being alone in a lousy diner—there were no other people there for a reason. Ana looked around. She caught a flash of fin from a pilot fish and dodged a few thimble–sized jellies. Big deal. But they had never dived here before so . . . you never knew. Maybe a school of hammerheads would pass through, or some giant manta rays. A whale shark would be nice. Conjuring up visions of marine animals she'd like to see helped her keep boredom at bay.

Ana reminded herself that she and Henry were lucky to be diving places that were this warm and clear. Also, the point of the honeymoon was to be together. She didn't need whale sharks to make her happy. She only needed Henry.

Recollections of how they'd met came to mind. Ana was producing a documentary of classic '50s horror films. She had hired Henry to tape her interviews with the aging actors. It turned out they shared the same favorites of the genre, and it soon became apparent that Ana was Henry's favorite of the female gender. He asked her out, she said yes, and the rest was romance. They started their own production company and became quite successful. Working and playing together was so enjoyable, they finally made the time to make it official. They flew with a few friends and family to Niagara Falls and got married on the *Maid of the Mist* as Horseshoe Falls thundered behind them. Everyone wore bright yellow slickers and no one could stop laughing and smiling. Ana grinned at the memory. All the wedding photos had water spots on them, but that just made them better, in her opinion.

So here they were in warm water with not a lot of fish, but no worries. Although, come to think of it, that pea-soup fog that had rolled in just before their dive was disturbing. Nothing to get excited about, though—she had heard that weather in this region was unpredictable. Ana looked around. Visibility was terrific. She looked up. Sunlight glanced off wavelets on the surface—the fog must have burned off. That was fast.

Henry usually let Ana take the lead, she was such a good spotter, but this time he was finning ahead, businesslike, as if he had an appointment to keep. He looked below, searching for something, but Ana didn't know what. She knew he'd love to find a Spanish doubloon or artifacts from Atlantis, but until now, all he'd ever picked up was an odd piece of coral shaped like a man's profile. He found it on a dive in Belize, and immediately bought a leather cord to thread through it so he could wear the coral around his neck. Ana didn't like the ornament, but for reasons she couldn't explain. Divers, she tried to tell him, were on their honor to not pick the ocean floor clean of treasures.

Checking regularly on his dive buddy should have been on Henry's agenda, but eventually, Ana noticed he was ignoring her completely. That wasn't normal for a man on his honeymoon. He just kicked his legs with a strong regular rhythm, scanning the bottom.

Ana spotted some movement on a sandy flat to her left. She kicked hard to catch up to Henry so she could get his attention, tugging on his fin and motioning for him to follow. She swam back to the creatures she'd sighted, her eyes glued to them in her excitement. Skimming along the bottom was a pair of flying gurnards. How lucky was that? They'd only ever seen one before, on a night dive in St. Lucia. Ana hung a couple of feet over the fish, admiring them. She knew not to touch them, as easy as that would have been— their spiny fins were venomous. She cupped her hand and waved it just above the fish, stirring the water. Both fish spread their fins and swam around in graceful S-curves. They looked like flying dragon fish with purple and blue graduating through their long diaphanous ribbed wings. Gorgeous and alien looking. Ana looked around to see if Henry was enjoying them as much as she was, but he hadn't followed her, after all. He was a hundred yards north of where she'd caught up to him, still kicking away as if he were on a mission.

Ana wondered what was up with her Mr. Lindstadt as she headed back over a long finger of coral to try and catch him. She would have to surface sooner than she expected if she sucked her tank dry by chasing him like that. As soon as she caught up with him he disappeared from her sight. She blinked, thinking the optics of her mask had put him in her blind spot. Suddenly, Ana hit a thermocline that gave her the chills. The temperature above and below a thermocline layer can vary by as much as 20 degrees Fahrenheit. This one felt colder than that. Just then, to her right, Ana spotted Henry. Good. Maybe the distortion in the thermal layer was what had made him disappear. She checked her dive computer. They had gone from a balmy 80 degrees to a chilly 52 at 50 feet. Her three-mil wet suit wasn't enough to protect her from that much cold. But as soon as she started wondering if they should go back to the boat, the temperature returned to 80 degrees. That was odd.

Henry was looking at her. She made a shivering gesture, followed by a shrug that clearly said, "What's up with that?" but he turned away from her and continued on his sea hunt.

The water was suddenly thick with life. Many fish were species she'd never seen before. Looking at the ocean floor, the most vibrant and abundant coral formations and sponges Ana had ever seen clustered below her, covered by a moving kaleidoscope of multicolored reef fish. Ana didn't know what to think—the ocean seemed crowded with creatures and plants. They hadn't been in sight just seconds before—where had they come from? What was this site called? A place this lush would surely have been discovered and written up in every dive magazine. They had absolutely hit the underwater jackpot.

Stunned by the variety and multitude of fish, it took Ana a moment to notice how the floor suddenly sloped up. As she moved along she could see, through the thick schools swimming around her, that the slope reached out of the water. They were at the base of an island—but funny, they hadn't seen one when they anchored. Ana pulled her writing slate out of her pocket, scrawled a large ?, and thrust it in Henry's face. Henry looked disinterested and shrugged, "Beats me." Maybe they just hadn't been able to see the island from the surface because of that fog, Ana guessed.

They were starting up the slope when one of Ana's hoses started leaking air. It wasn't a huge amount of loss, but considering the air she'd used to catch up to Henry she didn't want to risk running out. She caught Henry's eye and pointed to herself, then made a V with the flats of her hands to indicate the boat, and gestured toward it. Henry made the okay sign and took the slate from her, wiping out her message to write his own. EXPLORE. MEET ON ISLAND. She didn't like it—he knew they were supposed to stick together when they were on a dive—but with her air streaming out it was no time to argue. Besides, they weren't far from the boat. She gave him the okay sign back, tapped her computer and watch, and pointed, to remind him to be careful. Then she started finning for the boat. When she looked back, she saw Henry swimming up the slope through an ever-changing curtain of glittering fish.

Ana checked her compass, counted her fin strokes, and looked for landmarks on the reef. She was a good navigator. When she spotted a wide coral finger and a mound that looked like an exclamation point, she knew she was near the thermocline. She was relieved that she wouldn't have to pass through it again—she had risen slowly to 25 feet and the layer of bone-freezing chill would be much lower. But she was wrong. She ran into a wall of cold water that set her shivering again. That was more than odd—that was bizarre. It was supposed to be a layer, not a wall. And even though the boat had not been visible before she passed through the thermocline, there she saw it, not far off. Maybe it was because of all the fish that were on the other side of the cold water. But there was something else wrong, too—the anchor line was hanging loose in the water. When they had anchored, the bottom was no more than 100 feet down. Now, 100 feet of line with the anchor still attached was just dangling with no bottom in sight. That was impossible! She had calculated the location of the boat with simple math and common sense and it was right where they had left it—but it couldn't be the same spot. Her heart sank with some indefinable dread.

At 15 feet she checked her dive computer, gambled that she could forgo the safety stop, and swam the last few lengths to the boat. Hanging on to the ladder, Ana threw her weight belt and fins into the boat. Then she climbed aboard. She looked behind her to see what this mysterious formation looked like from topside . . . but there was nothing there. Behind her, a few miles away, was the island from which they'd left that morning, but that wasn't the one she was looking for. She tried not to panic. Maybe the slope they'd seen was just that—a slope. Maybe it rose to just below the surface.

Ana stowed her gear and started up the motor. Piloting the boat to where she and Henry had parted ways, Ana peered into the clear water. There was no reef, no slope, no bubbles.

No Henry.

CHAPTER 2

The Justice League

In space, all is quiet. If an alien spaceship suddenly appeared and passed underneath an astronaut, he would not hear Dolby or Doppler sound effects—he wouldn't hear anything at all. Science fiction film-makers do it all wrong when they send bone-rattling bass tones or Strauss waltzes through the theaters. They may know it's wrong, but they want to convey power or beauty to their audiences. The truth is, the silence can be even more impressive.

Above Earth, even inside the arbitrary boundary of the moon's orbit, there is one hell of a lot of space. It is populated with the occasional satellite, natural or human-made. From some perspectives, these craft look stationary as the Earth rotates above or below—depending on what is designated to be "up"—yet they are actually racing through space at speeds of 25,000 feet per second. Appearances, however, can be deceiving. Everything is relative.

One craft in particular looked rather innocuous. A few lights blinked on its exterior, but one would be hard-pressed to say what might be going on inside, if anything. It could be a hazardous waste dump or a fueling station or any number of utilitarian or military satellites orbiting the Earth. In reality, the craft was much more interesting, being the headquarters for the Justice League of America. Inside were the most advanced systems for fighting crime and keeping peace that had ever been created. Those included teleportation systems, high-tech communication and surveillance equipment, and state-of-the-art defense weaponry. Also inside were some very colorful individuals.

On the same day Henry disappeared in the Bermuda Triangle, one of the craft's occupants sat at her computer station, entering data. That in itself was not that interesting, but what she typed was.

LOG: *August 17*
. . . dogs attacked their owners and neighbors, cats smothered babies and clawed out the eyes of old ladies who had loved them for years. Birds acted like they were in an Alfred Hitchcock film. Dolphins ganged together to upset fishing boats, then drowned all the fishermen and women. Horses and cattle stampeded, trampling their owners to death. Many incidents were caught on videotape, but the people who wielded those cameras usually paid a high price for the footage, many sacrificing their lives.

Initially, reporters and news editors in the media

treated the incidents as a joke, playing down the danger that every pet owner, farmer, or hunter should have taken seriously. Then, scientists theorized the animals were prey to a virus or mind-altering substance. Reporting for the Daily Planet, Clark Kent was the first to realize that the animals were being manipulated by mechanical means.

At the scene of an attack, Superman picked out the signal that triggered the violent behavior: a modified bobby whistle. It created sound waves in a combination of frequencies that caused the animals to become temporarily insane. There were already millions of these whistles in the hands of children, having been distributed through a fast-food promotion.

Authorities around the globe alerted retailers to pull the whistles out of circulation, and cautioned parents to break them or turn them in. The entire roster of the JLA worked around the clock to round up as many whistles as they could.

Batman followed leads from manufacturers and distributors until he narrowed his suspect list to a radical environmentalist group called the Deliverers, who believed that, because humans are destroying the Earth, all humans should be killed so that nature can heal Earth's wounds. The group, of course, would survive to help the world recover, producing only enough people to maintain the species.

Batman traced the group to a lead-lined bunker in South America. The Martian Manhunter was able to incapacitate their leaders by using his telepathic powers. I used my Lasso of Truth to ferret out those mem-

*bers of the Deliverers who were integrated into high
society and government, while Green Lantern and
the Flash—*

Wonder Woman felt a hand pat her shoulder. She
looked up to see Superman smiling warmly at her.

"Good work, Diana."

"You didn't do so bad yourself, Kal," she said, addressing the Man of Steel by his birth name.

There was still some work to do—arresting opera-
tives who were lower down on the food chain and lo-
cating those who had engineered the device. But the
League had broken the back of the operation when
they arrested the leaders. Now they had some time to
take a well-deserved break. Doing the paperwork
didn't appeal to most of the team, especially when
they were feeling the rush of having successfully
completed a job. But duty called, so there she sat in
the Justice League's headquarters, typing the case information about their exploits into the computer. Yes,
it was important for each member to log the details
while they were still fresh, but she didn't feel that
fresh was the operative word. She had been on the
move for three straight days and, frankly, Wonder
Woman wanted nothing more than to take off her
boots, shed her skintight battle costume, and sink
into a warm bath for a week.

Green Lantern, the youngest and most recent addition to the League, joined them. "Did you see the look
on that Deliverer's face when I made the ring create a
giant panther? I've never seen anyone run so fast."

A pointed "Ahem" came from another computer station. Wally West, a.k.a. the Flash, looked at Green Lantern with his eyebrows raised. "Anyone?"

"Oh, well, you know what I mean. Anyone but *you*," conceded Green Lantern.

Wally, in a fine blustery mood, was not willing to let the lad off so easily. He rose to put on a demonstration.

Superman, Wonder Woman, and the other Justice League members who were present—Batman, J'onn J'onzz, and the Atom—turned to watch. "Here's your typical scared-witless wannabe mass-murderer being chased by a giant green panther." He screwed up his face into a comical distortion of the frightened criminal, then pranced around the room waving his arms over his head yelling, "Help! Help! I'm allergic to cats!"

All of his mates, except Batman, laughed at the silly rendition.

Wally stopped and took a bow. Then he said, "And this is how fast I run."

He stood there. Several seconds went by. Finally, Green Lantern said, "Okay, hotshot—run around the room."

"I already did. You must have blinked."

This time everyone laughed, not so much at the routine, which all except Green Lantern had seen before, but just because it felt good. Superman started telling some jokes he'd heard at the *Daily Planet*—reporters always hear the best jokes first—when Diana realized she was on the verge of falling asleep in her chair.

"Come on, guys. We're so tired we're getting punchy." Diana clasped her hands together and mock begged them, "*Please* let me finish up so I can go home." She turned back to face her computer and picked up where she'd left off, her fingers flying across the keyboard.

Her comrades got the message. They rolled their eyes and ribbed and tussled one another before going back to their own stations. Diana smiled. She sometimes felt like she was trying to herd otter pups—they were all so full of juice, especially after winning a battle.

Wonder Woman soon finished her report and headed for the teleportation chamber. Grateful as she was for her many talents, she often wished she could fly in space instead of just over the Earth, so she wouldn't have to have her molecules reassembled. It was definitely disconcerting. But this was going to be her last trip in the chamber for at least a week—J'onn J'onzz and the Atom were taking the station off-line to do a complete systems check. All of the team members would be "working from home," so to speak.

"Goodnight, boys. I'm heading home."

"Hey, you can't call us *boys*," Kyle said. "That's sexist!"

"Sorry, dudes," Diana said, smiling. With her Mediterranean accent she made the word "dude" sound downright delicious.

"Where's home this week, Princess Diana?" asked J'onn J'onzz, the Martian Manhunter. He, like Wonder Woman, came from a foreign land—in his case, Mars. And, like Superman, he was the only surviving member of his entire planet's population, leaving him alone to carry on the legacy of his people. He usually stayed on the space station when he wasn't working. Diana, though, had friends and even relatives with whom she could stay. J'onn J'onzz was happy for her, without thinking of his own loneliness.

"You can find me at my sister Donna Troy's place in Manhattan. She's got the best tub. She also knows a great masseuse in her building."

Before she could leave, Batman spoke up. "Diana, wait." He was monitoring news events. "There's a report of a man who went missing not far from where Paradise Island lies. I know Themyscira is well hidden from our world, but . . . you should see this."

Diana forgot all about bathtubs and back rubs. In an instant she was looking over Batman's shoulder, reading the report for herself.

It was vital that no outsider ever set foot on Themyscira uninvited. Three millennia before, the women on the island, Wonder Woman's Amazon sisters, were charged with guarding a great evil that lay buried beneath their city. If a stranger were to happen on the island, he or she might, by design or accident, open the Pandora's box.

The missing man was a scuba diver. His wife's report made it clear that he hadn't just been caught in a current or met with a shark. He had simply disappeared. Even though Themyscira was camouflaged to protect it from mortal eyes, chance discovery was always a possibility. Once discovered, the island would be vulnerable to trespass by others. Diana agreed with Batman that the situation merited investigation.

"Thanks, Bruce. It looks like I won't be going to New York just yet."

"Want some company?" Green Lantern asked.

"Don't you have a day job, Sparky?" the Flash piped up. "How are you going to win one of those Inkwell Awards if you don't hit the drawing board once in a while?"

"He just wants to get in some sand and surf action. Maybe admire some young ladies on a beach in the interest of brushing up on his anatomy," the Atom teased.

The Green Lantern blushed a little. In civilian life he was known as Kyle Rayner, a freelance artist. In fact, one of the reasons he had come into possession of the Green Lantern ring was because he had the imagination necessary with which to best use its powers. Kyle loved both of his jobs equally, although he sometimes wished there was some way he could show off his actual—and not just virtual—drawing ability while working. At least his teammates had respect for his day job—most people thought illustrating was nothing but fun and wasn't really work at all.

"Yeah, I'd better go finish up some stuff when I'm done with this report. Good luck finding your missing man, Wonder Woman."

Diana's thoughts were with her sisters on Themyscira, so she barely registered his remarks. "I've got to go," she said. "I don't think this is a job for more than me, but keep communications open, just in case—all right?"

"Since HQ will be off-line, Oracle said she can help

us monitor activity from her command post," Batman replied.

Oracle was a computer whiz, one of the best white-hat hackers around. From her high-tech bunker in Gotham City, she siphoned information off satellites—whether she was allowed to or not—and used the data to make sense of senseless situations. Few people knew she existed; fewer still knew who she was. To Batman she was a colleague, one of the many resources at his disposal. But he also considered her a friend.

Wonder Woman thanked Batman warmly and bade him good-bye. The man in black reciprocated with a nod so slight one would need a micrometer to measure it. The others wished her luck in finding her man, and the Flash asked her to stop in Jamaica while she was down there so she could bring them back some hot sauce for the pantry. The request made her smile. She knew he made light not out of disrespect for what she was doing, but for the same reasons pilots ask to borrow gum before a mission—for good luck.

CHAPTER 3

Themyscira

Diana's first stop was Paradise Island, where she had been born. Also known by the Greek name Themyscira, the island that had been occupied by Amazons for more than three thousand years was not noted on any map. Full of contradictions, the island existed in one place, and many, protected from sailors and satellites by a convergence of natural and god-made forces that shielded it from sight. The women never talked about the mechanics of their shield, even among themselves, for fear that word would leak out to Man's World. Even the cleverest disguise can be seen through if one knows where to look.

In ancient times, even before Greece entered its Golden Age, five Olympian goddesses, Hera, Athena, Aphrodite, Demeter, and Hestia, recovered the souls of women whose lives were unjustly cut short. They sent those souls to Earth to live again in strong, immortal bodies. Those women became the Amazons, whose mission was to teach the virtues of peace and compassion throughout Man's World.

The Amazons founded the thriving city of Themyscira. Ares, the God of War and a chief opponent of the Amazons, manipulated events so that Herakles could seduce and then betray their queen, Hippolyta, ultimately enslaving them all. Through strength and cunning, the Amazons overthrew their captors—but a schism developed among the population. Some accused Hippolyta of treachery, holding her responsible for engaging them in an unnecessary war. Those Amazons who understood that Ares had created the situation chose to stay with Hippolyta. They were sent to the remote island, where they became the keepers of a great underground evil, as penance for failing in their mission to promote peace.

They named the island Themyscira after their fallen city. They began new lives, perfecting themselves in all the arts in an effort to present a model of unity and perfection by which Man's World might learn to live in harmony. This goal was in conflict with their roots and interests as warriors, which may have contributed to their lack of success in spreading their utopian ideals throughout the world as they wished. Their goals were also in conflict with their place in the world—the Amazons had to remain aloof from Man's World in order to maintain their purity and dignity, but that removal from the rest of civilization restricted their abilities to demonstrate how their philosophy could enrich their fellow human beings.

The natural island itself was a model of perfection. Its location, in that nether-place the gods created for it, provided a temperate climate ideal for growing all manner of crops. The warm sea brought them varieties of fish and other edibles. Marble beds and clay deposits were plentiful, providing the raw materials for buildings and works of art. A forest gave them lumber, pastures yielded food for beasts and pleasures for the eyes. Snow fell on the lone mountain every year, supplying the island's occupants with fresh water.

The civilized aspects of the island were no less perfect. Classic Greek architecture defined the living portions of Themyscira. Temples built to worship the gods crowded the tops of the hills. Situated below them were government buildings such as the council chamber and library. Those were surrounded by the city's many beautiful residential units. Artisans lived over their shops, so the only formal marketplace was the open area near the council chambers where fruits and vegetables were traded for wine and honey. Everyone worked. Cloth makers and coppersmiths plied their trades as honorably as those who enjoyed the arts of war or science. Labors that were loathsome but necessary—sanitation and waste disposal, for example—were done by everyone in rotation, even the Queen, on an equal basis. Every woman participated in government matters as well, even though most civil disputes were quickly resolved, and the city-state practically ran itself.

On the outskirts of the city lay the athletic fields and the amphitheater. Participation in sport and theater allowed the women to express themselves physically and mentally, keeping their culture vital. Almost every act and labor on the island was also an expression of thanks to the gods, exemplifying their joy of being alive.

The women themselves were marvels. When the goddesses restored their lives, they made sure the Amazons were at their physical and mental peaks. Aphrodite had bestowed upon every woman the beauty of grace and wisdom. Although their bodies never grew old, their minds were able to grow without restriction. Their isolation from Man's World prevented them from learning things that others might consider essential, but their communal search for wisdom and truth led them to many worthwhile and esoteric discoveries.

One of the gifts from the gods that profoundly affected life on the island was the birth of Princess Diana. Almost three thousand years after the founding of Themyscira, Queen Hippolyta realized the isolation imposed on the women was leading slowly to frustration and unhappiness. Polling her sisters, searching for a way to stop the stagnation, she recognized the one thing they, as warriors, had been denied: motherhood. Conceiving and producing a child as mortal women do was no longer in their power, so the Queen fashioned a baby out of clay. Imploring the gods to give the child life, she prayed for all of the women she represented, channeling their unspoken longings to the gods on Mount Olympus. The gods responded, transforming the clay into flesh and bones.

Having bestowed life on the infant, the gods and goddesses presented her with gifts befitting an Amazon Princess. Hera gave the child pride; Aphrodite gave her grace. An assembly of deities granted the newborn beauty, intelligence, strength of body and character, courage, compassion, and humility. Only Ares, the God of War, declined to present the child with a gift.

Growing up, Diana was blessed with having thousands of mothers and sisters to teach her skills and give her love. Every one of the Amazons felt a special connection to the child, and was proud of the part they played in her development. In spite of their attentions, Diana was not spoiled. Her gifts of compassion and humility ensured that she would be loved, as much as she would love others.

Early in her adulthood, a crisis arose that required a representative of the island to fight for the Amazons in Man's World. Almost every woman on Themyscira vied for the honor. Diana thought she was the best candidate, but her mother, the Queen, refused to let the girl compete, trying, as mothers do, to protect her child from harm. Unable to accept Hippolyta's order, Diana disguised herself and joined the competition, besting all. She went on to defend her homeland and represent her people admirably. Since then, she had established herself as Themyscira's cultural and philosophical ambassador.

Now, years later, Diana was returning home again, not to visit, but out of concern for her sisters' safety. She hoped she wasn't too late.

CHAPTER 4

Homecoming

Scanning the ocean in a vast search pattern, Wonder Woman spent hours investigating every object that floated on the surface, from the point where the man had been lost, to any area that could possibly access the sea around Themyscira. Nothing. If the diver were under the water, drowned, the search for his body would have to wait until after she checked in with her sisters.

When Diana arrived on the island she was greeted by everything warm and familiar: her old friends—all of whom were like sisters to her—the sights and smells, the feeling of peace and security. There was no mention of any missing scuba diver, or sign that the man had discovered Themyscira. The Princess felt re-lieved, although not entirely so. She hoped she would be able to stay for a while, but knew that wouldn't be possible if there was someone out there who needed her help—someone who might inadvertently destroy everything she held dear.

"Apolliana, Xanthia, Penelope!" Diana received every woman who ran up to her with a warm hug, kisses on both cheeks, and a kind remark about health or some aspect of dress. "I apologize for my own appearance," she told Chloe, her former tutor who, with her twin, Hermione, had helped educate Diana. "I wasn't able to change out of my battle clothes before my arrival."

The twins smiled. "Your bath will just be that much sweeter, then," Hermione said.

More women poured out of shops or out of council chambers when the news spread that Diana was on the island. "Diana, child!" sang the poet Polyxena as she ran down the stairs that led to the temple of Aphrodite. "Why did you not tell us you were coming?"

"I didn't want anyone to make a fuss over me," she said. It wasn't the main reason, but it was reason enough. "But it seems that my visits are always disruptive whether I warn you or not."

"We'll have a feast!" announced Camilla, the captain of the guards. This elicited cheers and shouts of agreement. Several women ran off to prepare food and set up tables. Musicians hurried to get their instruments. Diana's charming presence coupled with the promise of tales of adventure in Man's World excited everyone. They would have a welcome distraction from routine life on Paradise Island that night.

Diana wasn't surprised by the suggestion—every time she came home they feasted outdoors under the stars. Regaling her sisters with stories and news from the outside world was a real pleasure. And they repaid her efforts with dancing, music, and shows of athletic skill. Everyone took joy and pride in these demonstrations, and everyone would be there to join in.

Diana greeted hundreds more who came up to her with smiles, remarking on each woman's apparent well-being. All the while, she looked around for her mother, Hippolyta, the Queen of the Amazons.

"Hermione," she whispered to her old friend, "where is my mother?" That she couldn't see her disconcerted Diana a little, because the Queen was usually the first to greet any woman who came to the island.

"She had some important work to do," Hermione said. "You will see her soon, dear, don't worry. She is well."

Diana finished greeting each and every one of her sisters, promising to tell them remarkable stories at the feast that evening. She then asked Chloe and Hermione to accompany her to her apartment where she could bathe and refresh herself.

As they climbed the stairs in the palace to Diana's quarters, Hermione asked her what they had all been dying to know: "What brings you to Themyscira, Diana?"

Since Diana had based her decision to visit the island more on intuition than hard facts, she told them only of the positive reasons for her visit. "I needed to see my home again. I miss you all so much sometimes. I miss speaking our beautiful language and praying to our gods from the place where they can hear me most clearly." She kissed Hermione on her forehead, then Chloe. "Seeing you sweet souls again does me a world of good. You recharge my batteries."

The two teachers looked at one another, puzzled. Diana had used a couple of English words with which they were unfamiliar.

"*Recharge*?" asked Chloe.

"*Batteries*?" asked her sister.

"I've been in America too long." Diana grinned. "What I mean is that my spirit gets weary after witnessing the cruelty and injustice that exists in Man's World. My sisters and this place restore me."

The two women were pleased to hear that and flushed a little at the thought of being so helpful to their favorite pupil. As they reached the entrance to Diana's suite, Chloe went to draw her bath while Hermione laid out fresh robes for their former charge.

"When you were born," Hermione said, "it was the best thing to happen on this island in a thousand years. We have to admit that life here can stagnate because of our isolation, and immortality requires us to fight ennui and boredom. A few of our members had gone mad because of the sameness from century to century. Yet no one has lost her mind since Hippolyta brought you to us. You give us hope."

Chloe entered from the other room, having finished drawing the bath. "She's right. We were warriors once and now we tend this island like old maids. You have given us tales of adventures to add to our lore, but sometimes we wish for change, so that we might all live our lives to the fullest instead of limping through the same routines of living from year to year 'til the end of time."

Diana didn't know if Chloe was serious. Sometimes her tutors challenged her with controversial ideas to keep her mind active and looking for solutions outside the norm. Hermione and Chloe had been drafted into service to educate her when she was young. There had been no other children in their lives for three thousand years, so the task was new to them, but they handled it brilliantly. They coaxed her into questioning everything until she arrived at her own conclusions through observation and insight.

If this was an intellectual challenge, which she believed it was, she didn't have the wits for it at the moment. Nevertheless, Diana was surprised to hear the women sounding so discontented. She suddenly realized how lucky she was to be able to go out into Man's World, but she wasn't going to express that thought, especially to those who had already taught her so much.

"In some cultures, the wish 'May you live in interesting times' is considered a curse," the Princess said, taking off her lasso and boots.

"Yes, yes," Chloe said. "But living in Paradise for thousands of years without significant change might also be considered a curse. The ambrosia that gives us immortality also helps to make our immortality bearable by pacifying us to some extent. But awareness of that fact blunts its effectiveness. We can feel something in the air. The tension on Themyscira of late is palpable."

Hermione added, "Have you ever seen horses or sheep before an earthquake? We've never had such an event on this island, but in the days when we lived on Man's World, we saw this a few times. Just before the earth shook, the animals would sense it and group together. That was so they would be able to find each other to procreate after the event, if it turned out to be devastating.

"Many of us sense a coming disruption. We are excited by the prospect, because we are warriors without wars to fight. Yet we fear the unknown, aware that our immortality can be terminated at a god's whim. Danger has excited us, but we don't know in what form it will come."

"You, Diana, are our harbinger," Chloe said. "We know some peril awaits us; your presence here confirms our suspicions."

"Yes," Hermione said, "yours and Artemis's."

"Artemis is here?" Diana asked with surprise. Perhaps she, too, had come in response to the news of the missing scuba diver. "I didn't see her in the square. . . ."

"She was out on the archery field trying out her new crossbow."

"Did she say why she had come?" Diana asked.

"No," Chloe replied. "Like you, Artemis said she just wanted to see her sisters again."

"Funny," Hermione said to her Princess, "that sounded like something you would say, but not her."

Diana laughed, delighted by the woman's candid insight. "Yes, I suppose you're right," she said as she disrobed, "but you know Artemis loves her sisters, even though she may not express it well."

"That you and she arrived unannounced at the same time leads us to believe something else is going on," Chloe said. "But we understand if you're not prepared to sound any alarms yet."

"You see through me as if I were made of glass," Diana said.

"Dirty glass," Hermione countered, having never lost the habit of correcting her former student.

"Come, dear," urged Chloe.

The twins led her into the adjoining room. Fragrant steam wafted over the huge sunken tub.

"How is my mother?" Diana asked as she stepped into the bath. She almost felt too dirty to get in. Perhaps she should have taken a few passes under the island's waterfall before she'd entered the city. That concern evaporated immediately, though, as soon as the warm water swirled around her, coaxing every one of her weary muscles to just give up and relax.

"Hippolyta will see you soon, dear," Hermione said. "She is in the library, reading ancient texts. It must be important because she asked not to be disturbed."

Diana sank under the water to wet her black mane. She had become accustomed to bathing alone, but she remembered the pleasure of letting someone else wash her hair, perfume her body, and help her on with silk robes. There was no self-consciousness about such simple acts here as there was in America. She enjoyed every minute of it, Hermione and Chloe grooming her hair and pampering her, not as servants, but as friends. She had done the same for them and would do so again. It was an act that helped bind them all with love and respect for one another.

When Chloe laced the last jasmine flower into her hair, Diana knew they were done. She walked to the full-length mirror and looked at their work. She was transformed. The lovely rose-colored gown set off the olive tones of her skin with a delicacy worthy of a great portrait painter. Her hair was coiffed in a style that framed her lovely face to best advantage and pleased the eye with clever patterns without distracting. The delicate perfume of the flowers and scents was heavenly. In a way, she was surprised at how she looked. She had worn her warrior's costume of red, blue, and white into so many battles lately that she had forgotten the pleasures of dressing for beauty and comfort. Diana hugged and kissed her tutors again.

"You two are artists," she exclaimed. "I feel like a goddess!"

The twins blushed, an event that occurred often when Diana was home. There was a knock at the door. Chloe opened it to find Artemis standing there.

"Artemis!" Diana cried, as she ran to her old friend and hugged her.

The Amazon in question was a warrior of strength equal to Wonder Woman's. Gifted with the bow and arrow, her goals were the same as Diana's, but her methods were as brutal as Diana's were peaceful. Nevertheless, they had fought many battles against common foes and had forged the strong ties that can only exist between comrades who wage the good fight.

"What a dump!" Artemis said. She tossed her

waist-length golden hair in mock disdain, surveying the apartment.

Of course, the palace rooms were anything but dumpy, having some of the best views on the island, but Artemis used humor to cover up her true feelings. At the moment, she was glad to see her old friend and rival. Artemis dropped onto a divan, sprawling lazily across it like a cat.

"What are you doing here?" Diana asked. "I haven't seen you since we fought together in Gotham City."

"Well, you just can't get good roasted goat in that town, so I thought I'd come home for a bit." Artemis raised one brow as she asked, "And what, pray tell, brings you home?"

Diana wanted to tell her about the missing man, and possibly enlist her help, but she noticed Chloe and Hermione leaning in to listen.

"Speaking of roasted goat," the princess said, changing the subject, "I hear the locals are planning a barbeque."

"That's right—and you're the entertainment. I hope you have some good stories to tell."

"Of course, but what about you?" Diana asked.

"They threw me a party earlier today. Roasted pig with yams and endive salad. Yum."

"You're making me hungry."

"Then let's go," Artemis said. She turned to make sure the twins were included. "Come, beauties. No more fussing over this spoiled girl here. Let's make her sing for her supper!"

The sisters laughed. As they filed out of the room, Hermione and Chloe scooped up Diana's tired battle clothes, apparently not done fussing over their spoiled girl.

The only women not attending the banquet were those on guard duty and Hippolyta, the Queen of Themyscira. On an island where all were treated equally, Diana received more attention than any—not because she was a princess and the best warrior of them all, but because she had been their little girl. Every woman on the island had helped to raise her, and now they gathered to celebrate her visit, forgetting the forebodings they had all felt in recent days.

In the square in front of the government buildings, tables were set up, festooned with garlands and loaded with fruits and breads. Musicians walked among the tables, playing their happiest tunes. Women danced, taking turns so that almost everyone got a chance to express herself with motion and grace. Everyone took turns serving and cooking, eating and clearing. The chatter and laughter was interrupted only when the sun started to set over the ocean.

A call went up for Diana to regale them with her adventures. Some wanted to hear old favorites, many more wanted to hear the latest. Diana grinned as she climbed the steps to the landing in front of the senate building. But when she turned to face her friends, she felt a drop of water fall on her shoulder. She looked up to see if the weather had turned, but the sky was clear of clouds. Above her, though, towered the statue of Athena. Another drop fell, this time hitting her between the eyes. Diana's grin disappeared.

The statue was weeping.

Musicians stopped playing. Dancers stopped moving. Talk and laughter ceased as all eyes turned to the statues that stood around the square. The setting sun sparkled in the blank eyes and in wet stripes that ran down the cheeks of the marble effigies. Demeter, Aphrodite, Hera—they all wept.

A voice cried out, "They weep for us—our doom is at hand!" All around, women jumped up from their seats to run for their weapons and battle gear.

"Stop!" Diana called, but the shouting and banging of bodies against tables drowned her out. Every one of them seemed bent on preparing for battle, but as far as Diana knew, there was nothing yet to fight.

Artemis appeared at her side. "So, Princess. What *really* brings you to town?"

Diana sighed. She started climbing the steps leading to Athena's temple, from which she would be able to scan the darkening sea. Artemis kept pace with her.

"A man went missing in this area—a scuba diver. I had a bad feeling about it so I flew down here." Diana paused as she looked at the last of her sisters rushing off to prepare for battle. "I had almost convinced myself that it was nothing to be concerned about . . . until this, anyway." She gestured up toward the weeping statues.

"I heard the news about him, too—probably sooner than you or you would have beat me down here."

Diana smiled grimly at her old friend. "We were

busy. It was ugly, but it may have been only a minor infraction compared to what we might be up against here, what with—"

Another drop fell, this time landing on Artemis's bare shoulder.

"I was going to ask you to help me look for the man, but with this bad omen, our sisters need a strong leader here. Will you stay, Artemis, and lead them into battle—if that is, indeed, in our future?"

"Of course," Artemis said, standing tall. She, too, searched the ocean and its horizon for any sign of danger, but saw none. "When will you leave to look for this man?"

"As soon as I talk to Mother. I haven't seen her yet." Diana looked down at her robes. "I'll need my battle clothes back soon. I can't leave the island looking like this."

"Nope," Artemis agreed, "too pretty. I'll have the twins get your fighting clothes in order while you talk with the Queen."

Diana thanked her, then set off for the palace library, taking care not to walk underneath any of the statues.

CHAPTER 5

Hippolyta

Hippolyta, the Queen of Themyscira—dark, strong, and lovely—stood under a lamp reading an ancient book. When Diana's eyes met her mother's, they lit up with such joy that tears threatened to spill down her cheeks. Diana ran to her mother and kissed her.

"Dear, it's been too long since your last visit," Hippolyta chided with obvious good nature. She set the book down on a table next to a cushioned bench.

"Mother, did you hear about the—" Diana started. A statue of Hestia looked down at them from the east wall of the library. A wet trail shone on its face where a tear had run.

"Yes. But let's keep our heads. Warnings are just that, and not necessarily predictions of doom." The Queen took her daughter's hand and led her to sit on the bench.

"I know why you're here," Hippolyta said. "A man was lost in the sea nearby. The currents were such that he should have landed here, but I'm sure you've already learned that we haven't seen him. Our best swimmers and sailors have been patrolling the perimeter of the island and they have reported no sign of him. I'm sorry the human was lost, but if he had arrived here . . ." She trailed off.

Diana knew that if any stranger set foot on the island, the Amazons would be endangered. The secret that kept their island hidden from all outside eyes could be found out, or revealed with one careless slip. If the interloper had bad intentions, he could potentially compromise the Amazons' ability to guard the Pandora's box they had protected for so long. If that barrier were breached, the Amazons themselves would be forced to battle the demons of hell to try and save the rest of the world.

If any man—even one with good intentions—happened upon their island paradise, the Amazons would be forced to sacrifice the unlucky trespasser for the good of humankind.

"I'm glad to hear he didn't find us. I wonder, though, what happened to him." Diana looked at the drying teardrops on her gown. "I wish to continue looking for him. I will be uneasy until he's found."

"Of course, Daughter," the Queen said.

Diana changed the subject. "So tell me, Mother, what have you been studying here in the library?"

"Dear, you know that, as Queen, I visit the oracle in the mountain on each new moon. Often, the information she gives me is very indirect. Last night I was told this:

"Beware your opposites;
The other side of the coin
May fall to face you."

"What does that mean?" Diana asked, puzzled.

"When Hermione and Chloe read to you out of the ancient texts when you were small, did they ever read you a story about an island of men?"

Diana struggled for an instant to recall the story. Then, "Yes. I'd forgotten, but now that you mention it . . . I remember now. It was a fable that mirrored our own beginnings. Ares, the God of War, created an army of warriors. Each man was filled with hate for all but his own brothers. He was going to send them out to savage every nation so that he might gain power from their victories over humans. But Zeus got wind of the plan and banished the warriors to an island, much like we were isolated here after your betrayal by Herakles.

"It's not a very good fable," Diana continued. "The ending was not satisfying. It's no wonder I only heard it once."

"I don't think the story is finished," her mother said. "I suspect the island is hidden, as is ours. And from what I've read, if the lost man finds that island, the consequences could be as dire as if he had found this one."

Diana's heart sank. "You really think there is an island of warriors in this ocean?"

Hippolyta nodded. "I think the oracle's message refers to that possibility, and the statues' tears mean the man has found the island." She looked more closely at her daughter. "I wish you to stay on Themyscira until morning."

Diana was already on her feet, pacing. "Rest will come in time. I need to leave."

Her mother continued. "I am not speaking of rest. There's something you need to do first. The oracle, Kretaia, has requested your presence."

The Princess's eyes opened wide. She had never consulted the priestess in the mountain before—as far as Diana knew, only a select few on the island ever had. In fact, most of the women on the island didn't even know of her existence. They consulted the oracle Penelope, who gave advice in the public forum. Any citizen was free to ask advice of her, and many did, asking questions about how one god or another might react to a particular plan or deed. Consulting her was the island equivalent of reading one's horoscope—a lot of advice fit all.

But Kretaia, from what Diana had heard from her mother, and she had heard very little, had impressive and mysterious talents. Sometimes the priestess was very clear, but often, her remarks were confusing or open to interpretation. Diana was uncertain about seeing her. She remembered the story of Croesus, who asked the oracle at Delphi if he should invade a foreign country. "If you do," came the answer, "you will destroy a great empire." Croesus neglected to ask which empire would fall. It turned out to be his own.

"Must I go?" Diana asked. "My understanding is that Kretaia confuses people as often as she enlightens them. I would rather choose my paths without wondering if I'm in conflict with any ambiguous advice she may give."

"Your misgivings are valid, child," Hippolyta responded, "and it is entirely up to you if you choose to see her or not. But keep in mind that she rarely requests the presence of any one person. I would wager that what she has to say will be of value to you."

Hippolyta was not only Diana's Queen, she was also Diana's mother. As much as the Princess wanted to choose her own path, which would have meant her swift departure from the island, she did not want to disregard her mother's advice, or risk displeasing her. Diana's reluctance to sacrifice the time it would take to see the oracle waned.

"I'll go."

Hippolyta and Diana set out immediately to climb up the mountain. The Queen led the way, carrying a torch, sure of every step. Diana was so eager to get on with her mission she wanted to fly her mother to the cave, but that would have been disrespectful. Rituals were followed for a reason. The physical exertion required to climb up the steep grade enabled the supplicant to open her mind to the voices of the gods. Diana soldiered on, continuing up the rocky path without complaint, following her mother's careful steps.

An eagle flew to her right—a good omen, if one believed in such things.

Diana was in the rare position of going to receive an answer to a question she hadn't asked. She thought about rituals from ancient times. Those seeking audience with one ancient oracle were clubbed on the head in an antechamber. Priests then dragged the unconscious petitioner into the chamber containing the priestess. When the person awoke, the oracle poured wine into a shallow bowl and swirled it until a vision appeared. Another oracle held court outdoors so she could hear Zeus speak to her in the rustling leaves of oak trees. Sometimes the leaves formed shapes that told the questioner what he needed to know. Diana wondered how this oracle of the mountain conducted her interviews.

After two hours of climbing, the women came to an opening in the face of the mountain. Hippolyta handed her torch to Diana.

"I'll wait here for you," she said.

Diana took it and walked into the mouth of the cave. Dried guano lay in mounds under crevices where fruit bats slept in the daytime. Other than that, there were no signs of life in the cave. She couldn't even detect footprints in the dust on the floor. Nevertheless, Diana walked on, deeper into the mountain. Finally, she came to a dead end in a passage filled with shadows and jutting rocks. Diana passed her torch close to the walls, looking for a hidden doorway. Startled, she found herself looking into the face of a beautiful woman carved into the wall, the eyes level with her own. The image resembled the goddess Aphrodite. When Diana leaned in closer to examine it, a sweet gas poured out of its lips. Within seconds she fell to the floor.

When Diana came to, she was seated on a plush rug, leaning up against the rock wall. It was pitch black. There were no ill effects from the gas, but the Princess thought that some kind of warning about what went on in here would have been nice. She would have a talk with her mother later.

"Hello?" she called out. "Priestess Kretaia?"

"It is good that you came."

Diana couldn't tell the age of the woman speaking. She could be sixteen or sixty. Her voice was soft and silky—the kind one might hear introducing soft jazz on a radio station in the States.

"What have you to tell me?" the Amazon asked.

"Just this:

"What is written comes to pass.
What is passed becomes the past."

Diana didn't understand what she meant. But before she could open her mouth to ask for elaboration, she smelled the sweet gas again, slipping from one blackness into yet another.

Diana walked back down the mountain, grateful to be back in the clean, cool night air. Hippolyta led the way again, holding the torch. To Diana, the night was as bright as day after the blackness of that cave. She felt oddly refreshed after the encounter, and wondered if it might have to do with that sweet-smelling gas.

"Why didn't you tell me about the face in the wall with the gas?" she asked her mother.

Hippolyta's smile had a guilty edge to it. "I didn't know. Every time I go there it's something new. Nothing I could have said would have prepared you for whatever she had planned, so I thought it best to say nothing at all. Besides, no one ever shares anything about their experiences with anyone who hasn't already gone there. I'm sorry, darling—it's part of the ritual."

They walked further, paying attention to each step.

"That woman has quite an imagination for getting one in and out of there," Hippolyta continued. "She certainly does keep you on your toes. If you should see her again, though, you'll know not to be frightened—she means no harm. Frankly, I think she's a frustrated performer. I've seen her in hundreds of guises."

"I didn't see her at all. She was just a voice in the darkness."

Hippolyta frowned at that. "What did she tell you?"

Diana quoted the oracle's prophecy to her mother.

"What do you think she meant?"

"I have no idea," Diana replied. "I was afraid of getting a cryptic answer like that. Maybe she was referring to the Fates. But the Fates weave, they don't write. Besides, you've always taught me that it's best not to think about them too much for they can baffle us with uncertainty about our choices."

"As if choice is even ours," Hippolyta added. "Some say that our choices are predetermined by who and what we are, reinforcing the notion that the Fates rule us. Even though I believe in the Fates, I prefer to think that we are able to make choices that lead to different paths. The Fates' advocates deny that any choice is freely made—that our paths are set in stone. Either way, as long as we ourselves don't know the outcome of our journeys, we can choose to believe that we have choice. Happiness is more attainable that way."

Diana thought for a moment. "I don't want to know what's in store for me—that would spoil the fun of living. Life would not be as sweet. It would be like watching a rerun on television."

Hippolyta stopped walking and turned to face her daughter. "I'd rather you not use vulgarities, dear. You know I don't like that word, television."

"Sorry, Mother," Diana said as they continued down the mountainside.

"Diana, dear, you need to sleep at least a few hours before you carry on," the Queen insisted. "You would be no good to any of us in the shape you're in at present. I know you are eager to leave, but your search can wait until morning."

Diana didn't have the energy to argue with her, so she knew her mother was right. Too many battles had almost been lost because of bad judgment owing to lack of sleep.

"All right, Mother," she said. "I'll leave at dawn."

As the Queen and Diana made their way down the mountain, each became lost in her own thoughts. The hour was past midnight when they finally reached the bottom. In spite of that, Hermione and Chloe were waiting for them with warm tea. The twins ushered Diana to her rooms and helped her prepare for sleep. She would only be able to rest for a short time, but her sleep would be deep—her safety assured for the next few hours, at least.

Diana rose before dawn and put on her battle uniform. The twins had laid it out for her after restoring its brilliance while she slept. Her tiara sparkled, and the strong cloth of her costume, woven by the best artisans on the island, was as clean as if it were new. The uniform fit her like a second skin, allowing her to fly through the air with little resistance. It also afforded her flexibility when she was forced to engage in hand-to-hand combat.

Some cultures found her attire obscene, but those were the same cultures that insisted women hide their bodies in part or in whole to satisfy notions of purity and decency. Diana felt those cultures to be oppressive toward women, but she respected their mores and outwardly complied with the rules by donning more conservative clothing. But now she was going to a part of the world where thong bikinis were sometimes acceptable dinner wear. Her uniform would not be a problem. Diana smoothed her small suit over her form and hooked her golden lasso to her right hip.

It served her well, the lasso. A useful tool, it compelled anyone she caught in it to tell her the truth or do what she wanted. The lasso could, however, be used against her. Wonder Woman didn't go around advertising that fact, but if she were bound in it herself, she would become powerless and would be likewise compelled to do as her captor wished. As much as she tried not to get in those situations, Fate sometimes had other ideas.

Diana looked at the silver bracelets on her arms. Every Amazon wore a pair. They were conferred upon the women not as ornaments, but as shackles when Herakles enslaved them. The Amazons continued to wear the metal bands as a reminder of what could happen if they let their guard down against those who would dominate them. When she looked at her bracelets, Diana also thought of how many bullets and missiles she had deflected with them. They were useful defensive weapons.

She checked herself in the mirror. As pleased as she had been with the beautiful image she had presented the previous day, Diana was prouder still of this one—strong, capable, intelligent, and good.

The Amazon Princess went to the balcony and opened her heart to the gods, praying for strength to do service. She prayed for peace for her people and for the world. When Diana was finished she felt strong and centered. The sounds of people starting their day drifted up to her, but she decided not to bid them goodbye. Too much time had been wasted already; she needed to track down the missing man, and locate the opposite island that seemed to threaten these noble women she called sister.

Charged with purpose and full of hope, Wonder Woman leaped off the balcony, into the still-dark sky.

CHAPTER 6

Ana

Ana couldn't believe her eyes. She had certainly
heard of super heroes, but the last thing she expected
to see was a figure in a bright red and blue costume,
silver bracelets and golden tiara flashing in the sun,
flying straight toward her. Ana briefly considered that
her stress over losing Henry was making her see
things, but whoever that was in the sky kept getting
closer and more defined. It was Wonder Woman—and
she landed on the deck of the small boat. This amaz-
ing creature walked right up to her, smiled cautiously
with her brilliant set of perfect teeth, and extended
her hand in greeting. Well, what could she do? She
turned off the motor and took the tall woman's hand.

"Are you Ana Lindstadt?" Wonder Woman asked.

"Yes. What can I do for you?" Ana congratulated
herself on her outward composure. She thought it
might have been aided by the calmness her new ac-
quaintance projected.

"I'd like to help you find your husband."

Ana dared to find some hope in her words. The Coast Guard had told her they would "look for" Henry. This Amazon just said they would *find* him. Wonder Woman didn't say they would find him alive, but Ana knew instinctively that she could trust anything this woman said. *Even if we find Henry*, Ana thought, *well . . . not as I would want to find him—at least I would know.*

"Thank you. I appreciate your offer and welcome your help." Ana cleared a space on the built-in bench that lined the starboard side so Wonder Woman might sit down. "If you don't mind my asking, why are you so interested in one man lost in the ocean?"

"For several reasons. One is that I read about your loss and my heart went out to you. I am familiar with this ocean—it is full of tricks and puzzles. I'm sure you know how the magnetic field is skewed here."

"Yes. I had to learn how to compensate for the variance between true north and magnetic north. But, also, the weather around here changes from minute to minute."

Wonder Woman's eyebrows went up. "Did anything unusual happen the day your husband disappeared?"

"When Henry and I started out in the morning the sky was clear with a wind of two knots, blowing south-southwest. When we surfaced from our first dive, we were in the middle of a thick fog. We did our surface interval—do you know anything about diving?"

"I free-dive, myself, but I know the basics of your

discipline and why you take a surface interval," she said. "At depth, nitrogen from the compressed air is dissolved into the body's tissues. If one is down too deep for too long, or rises to the surface too quickly, the nitrogen will form bubbles in the blood vessels, causing decompression sickness."

"That's right. Neither Henry nor I ever want to see the inside of a hyperbaric chamber so we dive conservative profiles. Anyway, we rested for an hour on the boat to off-gas nitrogen, then we motored around until we found what looked like a good reef. We dropped anchor, it hooked onto something solid at about 100 feet, and we got back in the water. It was somewhat dark underneath because of the fog cutting the light, so I considered going back to the boat to get my dive light. I carry a small one in my pocket for emergencies, but I wanted the large one. As soon as I thought about it, though, everything lightened up. The fog was gone. Poof. *Adios*."

Wonder Woman's eyes settled on the horizon as her mind sought reasons for the sudden change in weather conditions. Violent storms often sprang out of nowhere in these waters, but the mysterious fog sounded like the work of a god. Could Poseidon have done it? Zeus? She didn't think Ares could control weather, especially over an ocean—that was Poseidon's realm. But anything was possible; the gods sometimes trespassed into the domains of others.

Ana went on with her story, detailing Henry's odd behavior, how they passed through the wall of cold water, how they found the sloping walls of what looked like an island, and how she had to turn back to the boat when her hose sprang a leak. Wonder Woman listened and asked questions.

"You are very good at relating facts and details without coloring the story with suppositions," Diana told Ana. "I can almost picture the events as clearly as if I had been there myself. Thank you."

"Thank you for coming to help," Ana said as she picked up a waterproof neoprene bag, riffling through it. She pulled out her wallet, taking from it a picture of Henry, and showed it to Wonder Woman.

"He looks like a good man," she said. "I see kindness in his eyes."

"He's the best!" Ana agreed. "He would never hurt a fly. He's smart and funny and he's a careful diver. I know he's been lost for more than a day, but I know in my heart he's still alive."

Wonder Woman didn't say anything to that.

"Well, what do you think?" Ana asked, putting away the picture. "The Coast Guard didn't believe me. They asked more than once if we'd been drinking or using drugs. I realize they have to rescue a lot of drunken boaters, but neither Henry nor I drink anything stronger than root beer."

"I believe everything you said, for starters," Wonder Woman began. "I, too, have a story to tell. Unlike yours, it is not told from facts, but found in ancient texts. Still, I believe there is much truth in it."

"Lay it on me."

Wonder Woman then told Ana the fable of the Island of Warriors.

When she was done, Ana said, "I've heard talk of
your own island, populated by immortal women.
Given that, the existence of an island of warrior men
wouldn't surprise me. If you suspect that's where
Henry is, then I'm with you. Let's go find it."

Not having far to go, Ana started the motor and
opened up the throttle. Three dolphins rode in the
boat's wake, leaping out of the water and swimming
alongside the boat for a few minutes, until they suddenly veered off and disappeared. Diana looked at
the sky. The sun was at its peak and the few clouds
about were small and light. Except for the island from
which Ana had started an hour earlier, there was no
other landform in sight. Ana slowed the boat.

"We're getting close," she said. "What do you have
in mind?"

"I'd like to dive down and find that thermocline. It
may be the portal into the dimension that holds this
island of men."

Ana shut off the motor. The boat slowed until it
rocked easily on the dark blue sea. Puffs of exhaust
from the motor caught up to them and fouled the air
for a moment before dissipating into the ether.

"I want to go with you," Ana said, "but we have a
problem. There's nothing to anchor to here. This is the
same area Henry and I found in the fog, only then there
was a reef underneath. Here," she checked her depth
finder, "the bottom lies at 480 feet. I can't anchor, so one
of us has to stay on the boat. I nominate you."

Ana saw Wonder Woman react with mild surprise.
She didn't blame her—the super hero was probably

used to everyone deferring to her. But Henry was Ana's husband, therefore, she should be the one to look for him. As Ana explained her position, a wind started up. Suddenly, waterspouts appeared on the horizon, descending from black clouds.

"Where did those come from?" Ana demanded.

"It's a trick!" Wonder Woman had to raise her voice to be heard over the noise of the towering funnels. "Some god is forcing us to leave the area! It is too dangerous to stay! I will fly you and the boat to safety!"

"No!" Ana shouted. "If it's a trick we must stay to fight or Henry will be lost to me forever!"

For a second, Wonder Woman said nothing, but then she nodded her head and called over the wind, "I was thinking the same thing. You have courage, my friend."

Ana started up the motor and turned the boat away from the paths of the advancing waterspouts. Any one of them could suck up the boat and pulverize it into splinters and scraps.

The wind stirred the water, producing heavy chop that slowed the boat's progress. Ana was scared, but determined. Wonder Woman pointed out that maneuvering the boat would not save it from destruction—the spouts would catch up in a few minutes if they didn't blow out. Unfortunately, there were no signs that they would.

"Ana, you keep moving! I'm going to see what I can do about this!"

Before Ana could say a word, Wonder Woman leaped into the air and flew directly toward the three giant waterspouts, praying she would have the strength to defeat them.

In moments she crashed into the first spout. She had seen the Flash dissipate cyclones by flying through them in the opposite direction, thereby canceling out the wind's force. Wonder Woman didn't know if she would be able to do the same with this waterspout—she wasn't as fast as the Flash, and this wind was reinforced by tons of water. Nevertheless, she had to try.

The spout thundered around her in a clockwise direction, so she flew in the opposite path, the water thundering against her. She had to keep her eyes shut. Objects she guessed to be fish slammed into her at 100 miles an hour. She held her silver bracelets in front of her head to block the blows.

After a couple of minutes that felt like hours, she managed to break whatever invisible thread held the thing together. The construction of wind and water dropped to the ocean like so much rain and dizzy fish. In a moment it was as if the spout had never been there.

Wonder Woman didn't pause to reflect before she plunged into the second twister. This one had sucked up a school of electric rays, most of them the size of dinner plates, but unintentionally wicked, nonetheless. As Wonder Woman raced through the torrent, several of the fish stung her with their spiked tails. Each sting caused her to jerk and spasm, but she

willed herself to ignore the pain and felt the spout
snap, broken. As the cyclone of water dropped to the
surface of the sea she felt like dropping with it, her
energy spent. There was a mighty force behind these
creations.

Looking down, Wonder Woman saw Ana's boat.
The third spout was huge—much larger than the two
she had unwound—as if it had simply absorbed the
strength of its brothers. She didn't know if she had the
strength to defeat this one, but it was speeding right
toward Ana. Wonder Woman could see that if she
didn't do something, the boat would be sucked up
into the spout in just a few minutes and Ana would
be battered and drowned. The Amazon Princess dove
into the spout.

The ferocity of the water and wind stunned her. She
fought to fly against the force, to cut it in half so it would
fall like the others. But the walls of water and debris beat
at her without letting her breathe. The thundering fury
made her feel tiny and insignificant. The roaring in her
ears combined with the pulsing blood in her head to
produce aural hallucinations. Low, rumbling voices bellowed at her to quit, to give up—to die. Losing con-
sciousness became a real possibility.

An endless barrage of fish slammed into her. Some
were small, but most felt as large and blunt as sand-
bags. Wonder Woman prayed to Hera to give her
strength. Just when she thought her hold on her mind
and body was going to fail, the wind stopped, and the
water and fish fell to the ocean below, taking her with it.

Wonder Woman knew she hadn't done that—the

waterspout had been about to defeat her. As she fell, too stunned to pull out of it, she opened her eyes to see the blue ocean rushing toward her. But there was no boat. Had the waterspout swallowed it? Or had she been swept to another part of the sea? She prayed to Hera for Ana's safety.

Diana could see an island below. The warm air revived her as she fell, until she transformed her free fall into a smooth glide that took her over the solitary land mass.

This must be it, she thought. Henry was there; she could feel it in her battered bones.

CHAPTER 7

Gotham's Oracle

The woman known by some as Ms. Gordon, and to others as Oracle, puzzled over the information she read on one of her many monitors in the room. She had noticed the waterspouts, but hadn't thought much of them at first. There wasn't enough activity in the area to merit JLA attention, and local authorities would be able to handle any evacuations necessary on nearby islands.

Then she remembered that the Triangle was where Wonder Woman had gone to look for the missing diver. Oracle tried to contact the Amazon Princess, but her signal went unanswered.

Oracle was a key member of the Justice League, even though she was confined to a wheelchair and rarely left her computer center. She had been born Barbara Gordon, daughter of Police Commissioner James Gordon of Gotham City. Growing up, her quick mind and agile body got her interested in both reading and gymnastics. Her parents often joked that they couldn't tell if their daughter would become a bespectacled librarian or run off to join the circus. The young Barbara Gordon ended up mastering both disciplines, achieving a balance of mind and body that impressed a friend of her father's, Batman.

Under the Dark Knight's tutelage, Barbara Gordon pursued a career as Batgirl. She proved herself a worthy member of Gotham City's crime-fighting team until her career was cut short when she was crippled by Batman's nemesis, the Joker.

As a bumper sticker on the back of her wheelchair read, though, YOU CAN'T KEEP A GOOD MIND DOWN. With her degree in library science, Barbara had mastered the fundamentals of information gathering, but now she set out to learn computers inside out, from silicon to software. She learned the finer points of networking, security, and even started dabbling in artificial intelligence. Information flowed into her network and was interpreted, sorted, and logged for use by the JLA. Barbara, wishing to conceal her identity from those criminals who would do more than merely cripple her, went underground in her Gotham City tower, and became known as Oracle.

Oracle also worked with the team as a sort of cosmic switchboard operator. Members could keep in touch through her, find information, and listen to her counsel, which was based not on the whispers of gods, as were the words of Greek seers, but on the hard data in her computer banks.

At the moment, systems were cross-indexing information about the Bermuda Triangle's atmospheric and geologic activity with data relating to other disturbances, looking for patterns or precedents, and making predictions, when appropriate.

When she couldn't locate Wonder Woman, Oracle considered buzzing Batman to let him know what was going on. But Wonder Woman was often out of touch. She was unreachable when she visited the well-hidden island of Themyscira, and the Bermuda Triangle, where she said she was going, was notorious for fouling up signals.

Oracle made a note of the inability to contact Wonder Woman on an e-mail memo that would go out to the rest of the JLA, then looked at her watch. It was the middle of the day, but she had been running on empty for a week. She wished she had time to catch a few Z's.

Instead, she pulled up maps and data for the Bermuda Triangle so she could brush up on the history of the place.

CHAPTER 8

Looking Glass Island

Wonder Woman's flight took her around the perimeter of the island. It was shaped just like Themyscira, except in mirror image. This island was just as large, just as abundant with natural resources, and would be able to sustain just as large a population. The places where there would be pastures and cultivated fields, though, were overgrown with native vegetation.

Diana flew over the middle of the island. There was a mountain that was the twin of Themyscira's own Mount Aeolus, and there were hills like those on her home island, but these were naked of buildings. She felt odd and alone, as if she had gone back to a time when her sisters did not exist.

Wonder Woman had expected to find a bustling population of men living in conditions similar to those on Themyscira. However, because she didn't see anyone, she began to wonder if this was the right mysterious island—there could be many such hideaways created by gods and forgotten in time. But then she spotted huts and shelters made of bamboo and thatch. They were constructed not unlike the men's houses she had seen on the island of Yap in Micronesia. In one sense they were primitive, made without hard tools such as hammers and nails, but they were also very sophisticated in their use of natural materials. Strips of palm leaves were braided into strong rope and woven around supports. The thatch roof was crisscrossed in such a complex manner that rain could not penetrate from above. The openness of the framework and flexibility of the materials would enable them to stand against all but the strongest hurricanes. *The people who live here*, thought Wonder Woman, *must be strong and resourceful.*

Then she spied an armada of perhaps forty boats arrayed in a couple of coves on the leeward side of the island. The inhabitants probably relied on fish for food, in addition to whatever grew on the island. Flying lower, she could see the boats were strong, agile crafts that would be maneuverable in battle. She wondered if they did, indeed, care so much for fish.

Diana still hadn't seen a single human. She finished her survey of the island and touched down on a sandy beach. At home, this stretch of sea would be dotted with Amazons swimming with dolphins. Here, the topography of the land was reversed . . . backward. She felt slightly off balance, the mirror image quality of the place making her uneasy.

Something thudded behind her. She whirled around and saw a coconut rolling away from the tree from which it had dropped. Sunlight glinted off a pair of eyes. If it hadn't been for those tiny reflections, Diana doubted she would have found out she was being watched. The figure blended in so well with the island flora that she had to look hard to make out the outline. It was, indeed, a man. She walked over to him slowly. He didn't move a muscle, except to close his eyes. If she blinked she would have lost him.

As Diana neared, the outline resolved into a three-dimensional human form crouching in the brush. She stopped five feet in front of the man and cleared her throat. Suntanned eyelids opened, revealing soft hazel eyes that looked directly into hers. Diana did not see malice or fear in the eyes, just mild curiosity, as the man stood and faced her.

He was tall and lean, with the muscles of one who works. Clothing consisted of a single piece of woven bark cloth tied around his waist. His skin tone was similar to Diana's, his hair black. He could have been a long lost cousin.

"Hello," Diana said. Although she had meant to speak in English, it rolled off her tongue in Ancient Greek. "I come in peace." She hated using clichés, but it was doubtful that these men would have heard the phrase before. Besides, it was the truth.

"Who are you?" he asked in the same language.

Her instincts had been right: These men were creations of the gods.

"I am Diana. I am also known as Wonder Woman," she replied. "I have come in search of a man who was lost at sea almost two days ago."

"Come, I'll take you to him," the man said. "My name is Pelias."

That was easy, Diana thought. She looked into the scrubby jungle of palms, pines, and twisted oaks and saw movement. Men arose out of hiding places and approached. They were all of similar proportion and appearance to Pelias, dark, handsome men with short-cropped hair. Not one grew facial hair, and she doubted any of them could—a symptom of their immortality, perhaps. They moved quietly, never taking their empty eyes off her. Some were carrying spears or were armed with bows and arrows, but she didn't feel that she was in danger from any of them. They seemed like simple, peaceful hunters.

"Pelias," she said, "may I ask you about your island and your people?"

"What would you like to know?"

"How long have you lived here?"

"We have always lived here."

Immortals often lose the concept of time, Diana thought, especially if, like the people on this island, they were cut off from the rest of the world and had no reference to historical markers. This fellow's answer didn't prove the island men were immortal, but if they were, they were a danger to Themyscira, in spite of their outwardly peaceful manners. She tried a different tack.

"Do you have wives and children?"

"I don't understand those words," came the reply.

"Children are people who look like us, but smaller. Wives, or women, produce children in order to replace us when we die. Women are like me," she said, indicating her breasts and general shape.

"What does it mean, die?" he asked.

"When you spear a fish and it stops breathing, it dies."

"We have never seen a warrior die," Pelias said. "We have never seen another like you. We are the warriors. We are the only people. Our god told us that."

If there were no women or children on the island, then these men were the fabled exiles of whom she'd heard. Their placid demeanor didn't fit the story, though. The warriors in the old tale were filled with hatred for all but their own kind, and this man didn't seem to hate her. Still, she decided to proceed with caution. The less they knew about her and her island, the better.

"Are you a god?" Pelias asked.

Diana thought quickly. She didn't like to misrepresent herself—doing so might complicate or doom a righteous mission. But to these people she could be a god. They had seen her fly, she wore clothing unlike any they would have seen before, and her form was unlike theirs. She had no way of knowing if being perceived as immortal and powerful would be to her advantage or not, so she gave an ambiguous response as a precaution.

"The word for a woman god is goddess. Please—call me Diana."

As they walked along, trailed by a growing number of men, she half expected Pelias to ask from where she had come, how had she found them, or any number of questions. But the man didn't want to know anything about her. He didn't look intimidated by her presence, as most men did. Neither did he seem attracted to her, which she might have thought a natural reaction of someone who had been stuck on an island with only men as companions for what may have been thousands of years. Instead, he exhibited no sign of excitement at someone new, or dread of someone different. Outside of his initial curiosity about her form, the man seemed oddly devoid of feeling, and his brothers seemed to share that quality. They moved as if by rote.

"Who is your leader?" Diana asked.

"I do not know what you mean."

"Is there any one man who advises the others on what to do? Are you the leader? You were the first to talk to me—the only man to talk to me so far—so I think you might be the man to whom all the others look for guidance."

"I talk to you because you found me first. That was not a good thing. A good warrior does not give himself away so easily."

Was that response purposefully misdirected or did he just not understand the concept of leadership? Diana mulled that one over a bit before asking another question.

"How did you find the man who came to you two days ago?"

"He rose out of the sea, just as the god showed us he would."

That got her attention.

"How does your god show you what will happen?" she asked. She was wondering if there was a priest here who mirrored the priestess in the cave on her own island.

"We visit a hole in the mountain. It tells us what will happen."

So, they have an oracle, or something like one, Diana thought. Although she didn't relish the idea of getting gassed or conked on the head to find out what was in store for her—or the world back home for that matter—a hike up the mountain seemed like a good idea.

"May I visit that place?" she asked. "What is the name of your mountain?"

"It is called God Mountain. I will take you there now, if you wish."

Diana wanted to see Henry Lindstadt first. "Please, may I see the man you found? I'd like to be able to tell his wife that he's all right."

Pelias stopped. "There is another like you here?" he asked. "Another with those?" He pointed at her breasts.

In spite of herself, Diana blushed. "She's not here, exactly, no."

Pelias looked at her for a moment with his head slightly cocked, as if he was trying to make out what she meant. Then he resumed walking. The beach narrowed where the jungle grew closer to the edge of the island. It disappeared, forcing them to climb through brush and over fallen palms. Finally, through the foliage, Diana could make out a few of the thatched structures she had seen from the sky. As they approached the living center, which was located between the foot of the mountain and the ocean, more warriors came out to watch as Pelias led her into the open space in the middle of the structures.

Diana looked around. *This is an island of bachelors, all right*, she thought. It could have been quite beautiful, as was her own island, but the place was littered with broken pottery, banana peels, mango seeds, and other food remains. Several stakes jutted out of the sand upon which were skewered the catch of the day: loads of yellowtail jacks, grouper, and even a small reef shark. Fallen trees lay where the wind left them, and not necessarily to be used for firewood. *If these men had beer*, she thought, *there would be cans all over the place.* The scene was so unlike anything on Themyscira that she lost that off-center feeling she had before. Now she felt like Snow White coming upon a bunch of messy dwarfs.

Diana spotted a field of yellow out of the corner of her eye and turned to look at it. A scuba tank was propped up against a stump. It was strapped to a vestlike apparatus known as a buoyancy control device that functions as it is named. Nearby lay more dive gear: a regulator, wet suit, fins, and a mask. Henry's things . . . but where was Henry? She looked behind again at the long line of men who were staring at her. One of them had long blond hair. He wore a piece of coral around his neck on a leather cord, although none of the other men wore any adornments at all. Instead of a loincloth he was wearing swim trunks. It was Henry, as she had seen him in the picture Ana had shown her. Diana walked up to him.

"Henry Lindstadt, I presume," she said in English, smiling. She held out a hand for him to shake.

The man did not shake her hand, nor did he return her smile. Instead he looked at her much like the other men did, without curiosity or emotion.

Diana hooked an arm through his as if she were chatting up a guest in her home, then led him away from the others toward the ocean. It was unlikely that any of the men understood English, but she didn't want to take any chances.

"I am Wonder Woman, although my friends call me Diana," she said. "Are you all right, Henry? You seem a little out of it."

"I'm fine."

Diana was glad that Henry still understood English. She continued: "Ana will be overjoyed to see you again. She loves you very much, you know."

"Ana?"

Diana studied the man. He didn't seem to remember his own wife with whom he had been honeymooning just two days earlier. She would not tell him that the last time she saw Ana a deadly waterspout had been racing toward her boat. Diana tried to maintain every confidence that Ana had survived the event. Hopefully the spout had been there just to transport Wonder Woman to this dimension, and Ana was safe on her boat, back in her own world.

"Do you know who you are?" she asked him. "Do you remember what happened to you?"

Henry looked at her blankly. "You called me Henry Lindstadt. All I know is this island. This is where I live. This is where I've always lived."

That wasn't good. Diana knew it was too soon for

Henry to be suffering from Stockholm syndrome—
he'd only been on the island for two days. Besides,
hostages don't lose their memories of the past, they
just gain empathy for their captors. Perhaps Henry
was under the influence of some drug. Diana decided
she would take him off the island that night, whether
he wanted to go or not.

In the meantime, she wanted to find out more
about the island. The Amazon led Henry back to the
men. Glancing at the scuba gear, she made a note to
herself to check the air supply in the tank when no
one was looking. It would be easy to pick up Henry
and fly him off the island, but finding a way back to
her own dimension might be a problem. The waterspout had held the portal through which she had
gained entry to this dimension, but the sky was currently cloud-free. Henry, however, had accessed the
dimension through the thermocline on what Ana had
described as the leeward side of the island. There was
a chance that the portal was still active. Unless she
learned of other possible escape routes, underwater
might be their best bet. Maybe the cave in the mountain held information that would be useful to her.
Diana let go of Henry's arm, letting him rejoin his
brothers as she picked out Pelias from the crowd.

"Pelias," the Princess ventured, "will you take me
to the hole in your mountain where your god shows
you the Fates?"

"Follow me," he said.

Without ceremony, Pelias left his comrades and
started walking toward the base of the mountain.

That he was so willing to show Diana everything about his island was puzzling. Defensively, it was a bad idea, since she could very well be seeking their downfall. Why was he so compliant? Did the island men have no secrets because they had nothing to fear?

The sun shone high overhead, so Diana knew that, even allowing for an hour inside the cave, they would be back down well before sunset. Seeing inside the cave might be difficult, though, so she grabbed a torch that was leaning against the side of a hut. Diana also scooped up some sticks and sisal with which to light it. She then followed Pelias up the narrow trail.

CHAPTER 9

God Mountain

Not a word passed between Diana and Pelias on their way up the side of the mountain. At one point, she looked to her left and saw a crow glide past, cawing loudly. *A bad omen,* she thought. About to chide herself for believing in such things, she remembered the good-luck eagle she had sighted when she had climbed Mount Aeolus with her mother. The Amazon had to admit she was more eager to dismiss superstitions when they were not in her favor.

What the oracle had told her mother came back to her:

> *Beware your opposites:*
> *The other side of the coin*
> *May fall to face you.*

It would be unfortunate if this mountain held an oracle who dispensed contradictory prognostications, Diana thought. What she really wanted to find in the cave was a map of the island, complete with the AAA logo, pinpointing dimensional portals and booby traps. She knew she wouldn't be so lucky—gods and their messengers liked to have fun with facts by shrouding them in mystery and ambiguity.

The name of the mountain was disturbing—God Mountain. If the ancient texts were right, that god would be Ares. Ares, the God of War, was not the most powerful god, but he was an accomplished troublemaker. As an example of his low character, his animal mascot was the vulture, the ugly fowl that fed on the misfortunes of others. Ares was hated by his own mother and father, Zeus and Hera, for his unwholesome appetites, and was therefore an outcast of Olympus. Hades, God of the Underworld, favored the God of War because the conflicts Ares instigated helped populate his domain. Ares was capable of making trouble for humans, but he was never worshiped. He craved adoration, but the most he succeeded in getting was reluctant attention. From time to time he made efforts to expand on that.

If this is his mountain, Diana thought, *I must tread carefully*.

Diana and Ares had tangled before, and she did not relish the prospect of doing so again. He was quite powerful and capable of killing her, since she was no longer immortal, having left Themyscira to be the island's ambassador to Man's World.

Diana recalled the story, which took place before she was born, of Ares's attempt to start wars in every country throughout the world. Millions died before the other gods intervened, convincing him to stop. After all, they argued, if all of the humans died, there will be no one left to praise the gods. Hades, the Lord of the Dead and ruler of the Netherworld, would have exclusive domain over all potential worshippers. Therefore, there would be nothing for the gods to do but make mischief among themselves, and they'd already been doing that for many millennia. Ares saw the logic of their arguments and stopped the wars. His memory, though, was notoriously short. When the human population seemed to recover enough, Ares always started something up again. It was his nature to do so.

Diana wondered if there could ever be such a thing as a therapist for gods. It couldn't hurt—there was a staggering amount of dysfunction in that Olympian family. Hera, for instance—the grande dame and Queen of the deities. She was the Goddess of Marriage and Birth, yet she was the most jealous and insecure woman to be found. It didn't help that her husband—and brother—Zeus liked to play the field. Could therapy get her over the urge to punish young women just because her husband fancied them? There was a lot of anger behind her actions.

And what of Zeus? He was the Rain God, the Cloud-Gatherer. Mightier than all the other gods with his ability to throw lightning bolts and rule the skies, Zeus still had a bit of an inferiority complex. The youngest child of the Titan Cronus, his father had wanted him dead. Indeed, Cronus had eaten all of

Zeus's siblings. His mother, Rhea, hid him, and fed her husband a stone instead of her only remaining child. When Zeus was grown he slipped his father an emetic that caused him to cough up Zeus's brothers and sisters. Together they battled their father, and Zeus eventually won control of the universe.

But that, apparently, wasn't enough for Zeus—he chased after any pretty thing in a tunic. Maybe it was just the primitive instinct to want all children to be of his seed. The disharmony it sowed in his marriage was passed along to others, usually unhappy humans. And—given his ego—Zeus would never consent to let someone counsel him anyway.

Then there was Aphrodite, Goddess of Love, Beauty, and Sexual Rapture. Diana loved her dearly, but wondered why the loveliest of women would be Ares's paramour. She'd even born him several children, including Fear and Terror. There was good grist for a super shrink's mill—why good goddesses fall for bad gods.

Diana continued to amuse herself with thoughts of psychological help for the Olympians, but almost every imaginary session ended up with the therapist turned into an animal or a statue. Eventually, though, she recognized that they were near the entrance to the cave, and her focus shifted to the business at hand.

Diana pulled out the sticks and sisal she had taken along with her. Looking around, she was glad she had done so—there wasn't a stick or twig to be seen. Once they approached the entrance of the cave, Diana sat on her haunches and started rubbing the sticks together. Her hands moved so fast they seemed to blur, and the sisal immediately caught fire. She touched the head of the torch to it and stood. Pelias showed no sign of admiration for her resourcefulness. He just led the way into the cave.

Inside, the cave was similar to the one she had so recently visited on Themyscira, but different, as if it had been pulled inside out. The sides of the cave seemed to have been formed naturally. There was enough room so Diana didn't have to crouch, and there were several bends in the tunnel that mirrored those she'd walked through just the previous night. There were a few shafts leading up to the outside, which allowed light in from above. Ancient dust motes danced in the rays, almost threatening to cheer the place up. Still, the interior was dim enough that Diana was glad she had the torch with her.

About 30 feet in, Pelias stopped and faced the wall, gesturing toward it. Diana looked. The location was analogous to the spot where she had breathed in the gas from the carved face. But this wall was high and broad and fairly smooth. On it were cave drawings, primitive yet detailed. They were laid out left to right, with those in the beginning of the sequence situated closest to the entrance. The lines were carved into the rock, and solid areas were filled in with paint. Diana held the torch close to the wall so she could examine the drawings closely.

The pictographs illustrated the history of the island. The first image showed Ares creating the island out of a volcano. Diana realized they were inside that very volcano, which appeared to have been dormant since its inception. Then the unknown artist carved into the wall thousands of warriors, probably one figure for every man on the island. This part of the wall had apparently been used to teach the men, for it showed how to make nets, haul in fish, and how to clean and cook them. More drawings showed how to make bows and arrows, spears, and other weapons such as catapults and slings. The mechanics of boat building and a primer on navigation were carved into a spot on the wall that received natural illumination from a hole in the cave ceiling. Diana sensed that its placement was not arbitrary—from what she could tell, setting to sea in boats was an important aspect of these men's lives. Diana wondered, were they supposed to invade another land—her own perhaps?

She turned to Pelias. "Who made these drawings?"

"They have always been here," he stated flatly.

Diana was not surprised by his answer. To him, what was had always been. And, according to the lines and erosion of the paint and chisel marks, the story told here had been carved long ago, presumably when these men and the island had been created.

As Diana looked further, what she saw made her heart sink. First there was a figure that looked like a man wearing scuba gear rising out of the ocean. Then a figure shaped like a woman with flowing black hair flew down onto the beach. Next, the two figures went into the water. The following pictograph showed the man rising from the sea again, holding a round object. From there, the story told by the carved images got worse:

The sphere exploded with a burst of energy and all the men became quite huge in appearance. Her own figure was tied up and made to lead the men in boats to an island that resembled Themyscira. The men battled woman warriors and defeated them, killing all including Diana and the Queen. Diana's severed head led them to the underground chamber that housed Pandora's box. They released the evil that the Amazons had guarded with their lives and set out to conquer the world with the hordes of demons that issued forth from the underground crypt. A battle scene depicted hell's demons and the island's warriors putting the Earth to flame and ruin, enslaving or killing all. The last drawing showed Ares rising out of the terrible conflagration, ready to assume the throne of Olympus.

Diana felt sick. If the Fates were real, then this future history laid out how she would betray her own people and lead the island men to slaughter them all. From there, wiping out the world with the pestilence contained on Themyscira would be relatively easy. Diana would rather kill herself than commit such treachery, but she couldn't do that, either. Was her fate carved in this stone? Was the course of events presented here a plan or a certainty?

She had often debated her twin tutors about the existence of the Fates. The Fates—Moire in Greek—were three sisters. Clotho, the spinner, spun the thread of life. Lachesis, the Disposer of Lots, assigned everyone their destiny. Atropos, she who could not be turned, carried the shears that cut the thread of life. If the fables were to be taken literally, one's destiny was set from the moment one first drew breath. That an individual might exercise freedom of choice was an illusion—the Fates had already spun the story of that person, and his or her fate was not to be denied or altered.

Diana stared at the pictographs and wondered if they had been carved by the Fates or by one of their minions. No one had ever seen the Fates—there was a lot of debate on Themyscira over whether they were real or philosophical constructs.

To her friends in the Justice League, the Fates were pure fiction—characters invented by the Ancient Greeks to support and embellish their religious beliefs. The Flash, for one, had once told Diana that he didn't believe in the Fates because he couldn't accept the notion that his choices may be predetermined. At the same time he had scoffed at the idea that Hippolyta was real. To him, she was just a player in the myths he had studied in school, not the leader of women—and mother—that Diana knew. When he was faced with physical proof of her existence, the Flash was forced to reassess his beliefs about many other figures from Greece's past and present.

Diana understood her friend's strong desire to disbelieve in the Fates. No one wanted to admit powerlessness over their future, which was what the Fates represented. Of course they could be the fancies of long-dead philosophers, but Diana knew better than to dismiss as unreal figures from her culture's past just because no one had ever laid eyes on them. No, she didn't know if the Fates were real, but she believed their existence possible. What she could not believe was that she would betray her own people and the rest of the living world.

So far, Diana had been figured accurately in the account—she had flown onto the island after Henry had risen from the sea. And, yes, she planned to take Henry away by going back into the ocean, but she could not imagine any reason why they should be forced to return. And what, she wondered, was that round thing?

Pelias was still standing mutely off to the side. As guides went, Diana had seen worse, but still, he left a lot to be desired. If her mother were with her, or Hermione and Chloe, Diana would argue the validity of the images, or plan some way to fool the Fates. But Pelias offered her nothing. Still, standing by helplessly as this scenario unfolded—if it was, indeed, fixed in her future—was not going to happen.

Diana scanned the images again to fix them in her memory. There was a danger in doing so, she knew, because the act might subconsciously reinforce the notion that the images of her future were absolute. Ignoring the pictographs would be folly, though. Surely there was a clue in the images that would help her avoid a horrible fate.

At last, turning to Pelias, Diana signaled that it was time to go back down the mountain. Putting out the flame of her torch, she set it against the entrance to the cave. She also deposited more sticks and sisal, just in case she might need them on a return trip, if there was to be one. There was no picture indicating such, but that didn't mean it couldn't happen.

CHAPTER 10

Island Life

Back in the living center, several hours later, Diana made a point of ignoring Henry. She didn't want to tip her hand that she would be taking him off the island that night, even though the drawing in the cave showed that she would. Settling down and shutting her eyes, she mentally reviewed the drawings: she and Henry going into the water, he rising from it again with a round object in his hands, she shackled and made to lead the men to—

Diana cut off that thought. There was no point in reviewing the images that detailed her betrayal and downfall—they simply were not going to come true. She believed in mind over matter—if a thought is reinforced it can become real simply because the one who thinks it believes it will. She had seen it happen many times before. Diana, therefore, painted in her head her own version of how things would play out on the island. After helping Henry into his gear, she would get him to swim down to where Ana had indicated the thermocline would be. They would then pass through it and arrive on the other side, back in their own dimension. From there she would drop Henry's weights and gear and fly him to the closest island, the one from which Henry and Ana had set off the morning he disappeared. Diana played the thoughts in her head many times to imprint them over the horrid scenario the carvings in the cave represented. Eventually, she came to believe she would succeed.

When no one was looking, the Amazon Princess made her way over to the scuba gear. Henry's dive computer was relatively easy to turn on and operate. The first stage of the breathing apparatus was still attached to the tank and had never been closed off. Holding the computer near the receiver on the tank, Diana saw that it held over 2300 pounds of compressed air. That was more than enough for a dive to 50 feet with a duration of twenty or so minutes. Henry would have time for a safety stop at the end of the dive to off-gas nitrogen. As a result, Diana's confidence in her plan increased with this bit of good fortune.

A few of the island men came in from fishing and saw her fiddling with Henry's gear. But to Diana's relief, they didn't seem to care. Just to be safe and to cover her interest in the equipment, she took the mask and fins to the shore and put them on. She then dove into the low surf, marveling at how the split fin design sped her along. As well as she could swim underwater, these were well-engineered propellers. Diving down, she delighted in the mask, never having used one before. In her youth she used to dive with her sisters to fetch oysters or spear fish. Even in the clear sea that surrounded her island, the going was very blurry underwater. Now, for the first time, Diana could see everything clearly. She looked at her hand. It looked big to her, but then she remembered that the optics were such that the water magnified objects by twenty per-cent.

The fish, though—they were incredible. Pollutants and over-fishing had depleted the world's supply of fish to a small fraction of what the sea used to support. But because these waters were in a different dimension—a cleaner, older place—there existed species that had long since been wiped out by human greed and arrogance. Turtles as big as tables came close enough to touch. Some fish were familiar, huge versions of grouper, yellowtail, and mackerel; but many were unlike any species of fish she'd ever seen. She was swimming in an ichthyologist's wet dream.

Diana was able to hold her breath quite a long time, but not forever. After several long minutes she surfaced and filled her lungs with fresh sweet air. Looking back on shore she could see some of the men watching her. Well, what else was there for them to do?

Suddenly, off to her right, a dark form swam, barreling down on her, as huge and as fast as a speeding truck. Diana didn't need to look to know it was a shark—the biggest she'd ever seen. It happened to be a bull shark, of the man-eating family. Diana didn't wait to find out if it was hungry or not. Using Henry's powerful fins to propel herself out of the water, she burst into the air and flew. The shark leaped up after her, apparently quite hungry, and snapped shut its powerful jaws on the sparkling spray of water drops left in her wake.

At that moment, Diana decided that swimming in the tropics for relaxation was highly overrated.

When she got out of the water, the sun was close to setting, but the air was still warm and dry. The cold soon left Diana's body, and she sped the process by standing next to the cook fire. Gutted fish were skewered on spits, roasting over the open flame. There were also palm leaves wrapped around tubers and roots. Dried seaweed and a variety of colorful fruits filled out the menu. When the sun dipped below the horizon, she sat down to eat with the men. How many of them there were exactly was hard to tell, as they kept coming and going.

Diana knew in some more primitive cultures women would never be allowed to sit with men during a meal. These men, though, still hadn't grasped the idea that she was a female, nor could they harbor any of the attendant prejudices against—or for—her sex.

Pelias sat to her right, but he was as outgoing as usual, which is to say he would have been welcome in any library. The man on her right was no different. She was able to pry his name out of him, Crotholis, but not much more. He had speared many fish that day and had cleaned even more. Diana hadn't needed to be told that—the aromas that came from his direction told a compelling story worthy of Hemingway. Crotholis handed her a piece of fish. When she looked at the hand that offered it, her appetite disappeared. She contented herself with watching the men and trying to memorize as many faces as possible, but it was difficult because they all seemed to have been cast from the same mold.

As the colors deepened in the sky, Diana glanced at Henry once in a while to see if there was any change in his demeanor, but he seemed to be no more or less out of it than he had been when they met. Trying to start conversations with more of the men as they came up to the fire to get food was next to impossible. Diana didn't take it personally—they seemed to be a naturally taciturn race.

After the meal, the men faced the mountain and started to pray. Diana thought they would choose to pray facing the sea, since that was where the heavens were widest. But the men did as they had apparently always done, chanting in unison, sending their supplications up the side of the mountain and into the sky.

Diana prayed, but faced the sea. She implored Poseidon to give her safe passage through his realm. She prayed for strength from her matron goddesses. She thanked Zeus for his wisdom in keeping Ares in check. Mostly, though, she reveled in the universe—what she knew of it, anyway. Letting her mind open to the cosmos, Diana tried to touch it with her thoughts. In that way she felt she could connect to all things, which she did with humble respect.

As Diana stood praying, the earth beneath her started to rumble. The tremor quickly escalated to sharp jolts, knocking Diana off her feet. Coconuts flew off trees. The surface of the sea rippled as if some gigantic monster was stomping on the island. Diana looked up at the mountain. Was the volcano waking up? Was it going to erupt?

Then, just as suddenly as it had started, the tremor stopped.

Diana looked around to see how the men were reacting, but they were gone—every single one of them.

CHAPTER 11

Night Shift

The Flash was doing his shift in a back room of the Watchtower. He was alone, keeping an eye on various monitors and the global situation map. It was routine work most of the time, and he frequently walked over to the coffee station to refill his cup. J'onn J'onzz made the best coffee in the solar system and he'd teleported Flash a fresh pot of it right before he took the HQ off line. The Fastest Man Alive poured a cup and sipped. *What is it about Martians and coffee?* he wondered. Too bad J'onn was the last of his kind.

The Flash heard a blip come from one of the monitors. He zipped over to it without spilling a drop of the hot liquid. Seismic activity in the Bermuda Triangle. That was where Wonder Woman had gone to look for the missing scuba diver. He dashed over to the panel that told him the rating of the quake on the Richter scale. 4.9. A baby. Still, he sent her a signal and waited. No response. He found himself tapping his foot maniacally. That was some strong coffee.

The man who was also known as Wally West didn't worry too much because signals were always getting lost in that area. Diana would pick it up eventually and phone home, so to speak. Still, he made a note of the quake and the coincidence of Wonder Woman's location in case she didn't report in soon.

Flash considered calling Oracle but, having read her e-mail about the smaller quake that preceded this one, he figured she would know about it already. That woman was *wired*. The Flash looked at his tapping foot again, and realized he was, too.

Keeping both eyes glued to the monitor that displayed activity in the Bermuda Triangle, the Flash barely blinked, but there were no more blips. Batman wouldn't be taking over the shift for a couple of hours yet, and Wally West had the feeling it was going to be a dull watch—possibly as uneventful as a night on a tropical island in the middle of nowhere.

CHAPTER 12

Escape

Diana had been thrown by that tremor, but she didn't understand why the men had disappeared so quickly. Were they afraid of the earthquake? That would be a natural reaction, but she hadn't heard a word of exclamation or wonder when they left. They had just vanished, not even stopping to put out the remains of the evening's cook fire. Considering their deadpan reactions to every other oddity they'd witnessed lately, maybe they'd just gone to sleep.

The Amazon had planned to stay on Henry's heels so she wouldn't have to figure out which of the men's houses he slept in, but now it was clear she would have to do just that. But first, since she was finally alone, it was time to set up Henry's gear. Pulling apart the Velcro on the pockets of his buoyancy control device, she found a couple of useful items: a small watertight flashlight and a writing slate. The light was probably a backup item used for emergencies in case

his main light failed on a night dive. Her thumb
flipped the switch, and the light went on. That was
good—they would need it. She turned it off again and
put it back in the pocket with the writing slate.

Scanning the jungle for the roofs of the men's
houses perched on the sides of the mountain, Diana
realized she wasn't sure how many there were. Trees
obscured some of the buildings so she hadn't tried to
count them when she'd made her flight over the island. Each building, she figured, would hold a certain
number of men. It was time she got an accurate head
count. She would do that while she looked for Henry.
There were enough stars that she wouldn't really
need the flashlight yet, so she walked quietly toward
the nearest hut.

The men could number in the hundreds or thousands—she had no way of knowing. They had been
coming in and out of the living center so frequently
with their hunting and gathering routines that she
hadn't been able to hazard a good guess. Also, they
all wore their hair the same and wore similar loin-
cloths. Except for Henry, they seemed interchange-
able. Diana might have been able to get a precise
number had she counted all the figures on the wall in
the cave, but that hadn't occurred to her at the time.
And, now that she thought about it, those drawings
might do more than accurately account for every man
on the island—they might give each man power. Just
as a pharaoh's name carved in a cartouche supposedly gave him the power of a god, the engraved figures might imbue the men with life and whatever

purpose their creator wished them to have. Diana wondered what would happen to a man if his corresponding figure on the wall were obliterated. She would never do such a thing, of course. Still, she wondered how strongly the representations influenced reality. Were they magic? Or fate?

Her thoughts went back to numbers when she arrived at the first hut. As disorderly as they were in their outdoor housekeeping, they were orderly in their manner of sleeping. The spacious hut was open to the night air. Overhead was the thatched roof common to every structure on the island. On the floor was a woven mat that covered the entire surface. On top of the mat were one hundred pallets, lined up in five rows of twenty. All of the men were already fast asleep. Diana could not see a guard on duty—they had no reason to post one.

One hundred men per building made a head count easy enough. She flew low over the area and counted fifty huts. Five thousand men was a small army by some standards, but it would be a formidable number to deal with if they invaded Themyscira.

Passing lower, Diana flew through the first hut. Her passage was quick and silent. She saw that Henry was not among the sleeping men, so she proceeded to the next, with the same result. She continued, glancing at every man and reconfirming her count, until she found Henry. She slowed and touched down in the low jungle outside his hut. Her internal clock told her it was about ten o'clock. They would have plenty of time to sneak out, get Henry geared up, and swim away. These men would be asleep until sun up, many hours away. The problem was Henry. He didn't want to leave the island. So how was she going to get him away from the other men without waking them? His pallet was smack dab in the middle of the floor. If she woke even one of the ninety-nine others, she'd have a bit of explaining to do. Diana looked more closely at the men's house. The supports under the roof were like an elaborate set of monkey bars.

Quiet as a ghost, Diana climbed up a support beam in the corner of the building and into the rafters. Crawling through the cross beams, she made her way to a spot directly over the sleeping Henry. She unhooked her lasso from her side and knotted the end, passing a small loop through the end of the golden rope. Then she lowered the loop down to Henry's arm that was resting on his hip. The loop of the lasso touched his hand, tickling it, and he lifted his arm as if to swat away a fly. When he did so, she deftly caught his hand in the loop and pulled the rope gently so it tightened around his wrist.

That woke him up. He looked straight up at her and was about to shout when she put her finger to her lips. Since he was compelled by her golden lasso to do what she wished, Henry stifled his protest. Then she motioned for him to stand and he did. She pointed toward the beach where his scuba gear was and pantomimed sneaking out slowly. The trick was to move through the rafters at the same pace he moved through the men's house so that she could hang on to the golden lasso. Luckily, he stepped over the other men without waking them. Diana shimmied through the rafters directly over his head. Finally, when they arrived at the side of the hut, Diana signaled Henry to wait while she climbed down the side. In a moment, they were outside in the low jungle.

Diana put her hand on Henry's shoulder in an effort to reassure him that all was well and he was going to be all right. Her touch, however, had no effect on him. He just stared straight ahead.

There were still a couple of dozen huts filled with sleeping men that lay between them and the beach, so Diana decided to cut to the chase. She picked up Henry and flew into the air, over the other huts, landing a few feet from the gear.

"Henry," she said, "we need to get out of here. I know you don't want to go, but it is important that you do. If you stay here, thousands—if not millions—of people may die."

Henry looked at her as if she were telling him the traffic conditions for a city he'd never heard of.

"I need to keep this golden lasso around some part of you so that you'll do as I want. I realize how disrespectful that is—you've never done anything against me or my people. But it's evident from the drawings in the cave what is intended for you, and I must do what I can to prevent it."

Still no reaction from Henry. In fact, he stifled a yawn.

Diana didn't know if anything she could say might get through to him, so she gave up and started helping him on with his gear. Henry stood like a mannequin, making it next to impossible to maneuver him into his wet suit. Instead of ordering him to put it on, she decided the water was warm enough that he would be able to do without it. She strapped his dive computer and watch onto his left wrist, then asked him to put on his boots and mask. The rest of the gear was heavy or awkward, so Diana carried it into the water, leading Henry on the end of the golden lasso.

When they were waist deep, she helped him on with the vestlike buoyancy control device, to which the tank was strapped, so it rode comfortably on his back. Then she strapped the fins on over his dive boots. Opening the valve on the tank, she put the regulator in her mouth to check the air flow. She gave the regulator back to Henry, activated his dive computer, and made sure his mask fit snugly over his face. He was all set, the golden lasso still looped around his right wrist. As long as he could see or hear her he would have to do as she wanted. Then the Amazon Princess said, "Let's go," and they swam into the dark, warm water.

Diving at a human's pace was not Diana's idea of a good escape, but grabbing up Henry and speeding him through the sea to the thermocline would have endangered his life. Doing so without the scuba gear would put him at risk of drowning, and speeding through with it could blow out his eardrums if he didn't equalize the pressure in his sinuses and inner ear quickly enough. Although the island men would be asleep for many hours, there was no turning back. The prudent thing to do was to follow through as they had started.

The inky darkness of the water reminded her of the oracle's cave. Diana remembered the dive light, so she reached into the pocket of Henry's BC and fished it out. With it came a writing slate on which she read the last message Henry had written to Ana. Diana erased the words from the slate and held onto it, to use in case she needed to communicate with her reluctant dive buddy.

The flashlight's beam penetrated only about 15 feet of water, but Diana wanted to have some idea of what was around her. The little light proved to be quite a comfort, but also a necessity because Henry kept trying to swim back to the island. Besides tugging at him, which she disliked doing, the only way to let him know her wishes underwater was to use hand signals or the writing slate. She shone the light on her hand, and pointed to deeper water. Henry saw it and obeyed.

For a while Diana could make out stands of coral and creatures that came out in the night—octopus, squid, and giant red crabs—as they swam over. She wished she had a mask to see through, like Henry had. In the artificial light the coral's colors popped out as if under a black light. Intense oranges, yellows, reds and purples—it was gorgeous. Diana couldn't help but think of that overgrown bull shark, and hoped he was sleeping peacefully somewhere else. But soon the bottom dropped away and they swam through water with no discernible landmarks. There were just flickering sea worms flocking to the narrow beam of light she held in front of her.

Diana aimed the light at Henry's wrist to check his computer. It indicated they were at a depth of 30 feet, about 100 yards off shore. They had to descend 20 feet and go out another 150 yards or so to be at the same

depth and place where Ana had said they would find
the thermocline. Diana pointed the light at her hand
and caught Henry's eye, gesturing that they descend.
He nodded and continued on. Diana felt she could
use a breath of air so she caught Henry's eye again
and pointed to his backup regulator, then to her
mouth. He unhooked it and handed it to her. She took
a couple of long breaths and hooked it back in place.
At the same time as she did that, Henry saw a glow
beneath them. He started swimming down toward it
as fast as he could. Diana was unprepared for the sudden move and lost her grip on the lasso. Henry kicked
with powerful strokes, propelled by the split fins so
he stayed just out of her reach. Diana tried to grab the
rope, but she couldn't see well enough to get it in her
grasp. How deep were they? What was down there?
She kicked fiercely, but Henry still kept out of reach.

   Finally, he stopped. He was on the floor of the ocean,
tugging at the glowing thing. Just then, another earthquake started. The rumble filled the water. Diana could
see coral shaking violently, and swimming in it was disorienting. They didn't seem to be in any danger, but
she wanted to grab Henry and get him out of there.
She swam as well as she could through the booming,
surging water. Her vision was blurry, but when she
reached Henry she could see he had hold of a round,
coral-encrusted object about two feet across. It was the
thing pictured on the wall of the cave. But it glowed
and pulsed, as if it had a heartbeat.

   Even though the water temperature was a balmy
82 degrees, Diana shivered.

CHAPTER 13

Team JLA

Batman was up again, as usual.

He didn't require as much sleep as most people, nor could he sleep well when he did, because his dreams had been shot through with nightmares ever since he had witnessed the murder of his parents when he was a child.

Some survivors of such an event might withdraw into a safe, private world. The young Bruce Wayne had certainly inherited enough wealth that he could have afforded to do that. But *his* reaction at seeing his mother and father die so uselessly was rage. Rage and a desire for justice. And so he became a crime fighter.

Wealth enabled him to benefit Gotham City, his home, with public works projects that provided jobs and community to the crime-torn city. That was his day job, which he performed under his own name, Bruce Wayne. Wayne ran charitable foundations, schmoozed with politicos, and flirted with society women. The job had its perks.

At night he was the Batman. Instead of wearing Italian-made black tie and tails, the costume he preferred for his more hands-on job was inspired by his patron creature of the darkness. The black cowl and cape, the protective body armor, even the specially designed boots and gloves, inspired fear in even the most hardened criminals. His old friend and trusted accomplice, Alfred Pennyworth, was an inspired tailor.

Batman didn't mind that the JLA headquarters were off-line for a week—he preferred to do his routine monitoring shift for the League at his own place, anyway. For one thing, he was better able to keep an eye on his own city on top of scanning the world for hot spots of activity. The Batcave was as well equipped as the orbiting station—in some ways it was better. And he could get his fill of Alfred's coffee more easily. Flash kept insisting that J'onn J'onzz's java was the best in any world, but Batman was prejudiced in Alfred's favor. The man was a master of many things.

Just as he was thinking how good another cup would be, he noticed a blip on one of his screens. The Bermuda Triangle—right where the scuba diver had disappeared. The Flash had relayed a message—he had done the shift previous to Batman's—that there had been a small quake there and that Wonder Woman was incommunicado. This blip looked like a substantial earthquake, possibly the kind that precedes a volcanic eruption. 5.8. Batman checked a map. There were no known volcanoes in the immediate area. Wonder Woman had been there for a day or more, looking for the missing man. He checked the display that kept track of the members' locations. All were accounted for but Wonder Woman.

Batman did a more detailed search. Sometimes signals were lost due to magnetic interference, which was known to happen in the Triangle. He tried various filters and configurations, but still he couldn't find her.

Oracle contacted him before he could call her.

"Did you see that?" she asked.

"I got 5.8. Have you notified the Coast Guard and public health officials on nearby islands?"

"Done."

"Have you heard from Wonder Woman?" There were a dozen reasons she might not have checked in, some of them bad.

"No. Let me see what I can find out," Oracle said.

"Get in touch if you learn anything, will you? You know how to reach me."

"Will do," Oracle said, signing off.

Superman woke to a signal that was imperceptible to his sleeping wife, Lois Lane. He got out of bed and picked up the call from another room.

"Kal—have you heard from Wonder Woman since she left for the Triangle?" Batman asked, without preamble.

Superman blinked—even super-powered alien beings needed a moment to wake up. "No," he answered. "What's wrong?"

"A seismic disturbance just occurred right where that scuba diver went missing. It looks like it measured 5.8 on the Richter scale. It could be a precursor to an eruption, but there are no known volcanoes in the area."

"Maybe it's a new one."

"Possible," Batman agreed.

"And you can't find Wonder Woman?" Superman asked. "Let's go see what's up."

He said it casually, like they might want to drop in on a neighbor. Inwardly, though, Superman was concerned. Diana was not the type to just drop out of sight like that.

"I have a boat down in Florida," Batman said. "I'll take the Batwing down and go from there. Meet me at these coordinates."

With that, he gave Superman the longitude and latitude of the place where Wonder Woman was last known to be.

Then he added, "I'll get Atom to cover my shift and I'll see if Flash can meet us down there. You want to get hold of Green Lantern? That ought to be enough manpower."

Superman agreed before they disconnected.

Kyle Rayner was burning the midnight oil and then some. Illustration work took longer than one might imagine. The drawing part went pretty quickly; he found he could be freer with a pencil because he could easily erase any mistakes. Inking, though, took longer, the lines tougher to remove once they were laid down. Some artists didn't care about mistakes because they could scan the images into their computers and Photoshop the daylights out of them. But Kyle preferred to have a clean original—it was a matter of pride. Therefore, his meticulous hand-crafted work would just have to take a little longer.

He was concentrating on some intricate hatching when the jangling phone jolted him back to the world of three dimensions. The beauty of working this late at night was that the phone never rang.

"This better be good—you almost made me mess up a line."

"Kyle—Wonder Woman has disappeared. Meet us at these coordinates," Superman said, giving Kyle the same information that Batman had given him. "Flash is running down there and I'm taking off now. Can you make it?"

"No sweat," Kyle said, rinsing the ink out of his brush. "I'll get there as soon as I can."

Kyle hung up the phone and put his tools and work away. Then he went to the charger that held his ring. He didn't use the ring when he did his art—that would be cheating. Besides, it made it hard to hold the brush right. He picked up the ring and got the same thrill he'd gotten every time he'd done that. He then slipped it onto the middle finger of his right hand and the power surged into him—the power to make anything he could imagine become a big green reality. Kyle's clothing suddenly disappeared. Instead he wore his black and green body suit and mask. As he stepped out onto the terrace, he asked himself what might be the best way to transport himself to the Bermuda Triangle. He was capable of flying down just by thinking of himself flying, but for long trips he preferred the comfort of a vehicle. Something sleek and wild.

As the answer popped into his mind, Kyle sat in a shiny green sportster rocket. Flipping a switch, the Green Lantern entered the desired coordinates and blasted off. If his friends from art school could see him they would turn green with envy. He smiled at that because until a small blue alien gave him the ring in an alley behind a dance club one night, Kyle's favorite color had been red. But things change, as his life had when he first put on the ring.

The young man had been chosen by the Guardians of the Universe because his spirit was such that he would not be tempted to use the ring for anything other than noble purposes. Also, he had the imagination necessary to take full advantage of the ring's capacity. Using his powers to fight for justice made him proud and left him humbled. But it hadn't all resulted in adulation . . . while momentarily distracted in battle, he had lost the first woman he had ever loved, the remarkable Alexandra DeWitt. Would he trade the power the ring gave him if he could have her back? Absolutely.

Sometimes Kyle wondered what would have happened to the world if the ring had been given to someone who abused its power. His active imagination came up with plenty of foul scenarios. The ring could create monsters, plagues, a doomsday machine. In the wrong hands it could—

The idea made him so uncomfortable he made himself think about puppies. Black and white Border collie puppies. *And they should be cute*, he thought, *because that is a really good feature to have in puppies.*

That got his mind off the unpleasantness, but as he flew over the cityscape, his mind went back to more serious matters. Wonder Woman was missing in action. Kyle, the youngest member of the JLA, had tremendous respect for the Amazon Princess—he loved her as much as he loved anyone. But he would not let himself go to worst-case scenarios. She was a woman with extraordinary talents. Instead, Kyle used his fertile imagination to explore positive explanations for her disappearance as he sped south.

Wally West paused to look at a picture of his uncle, Barry Allen. Barry, a previous incarnation of the Flash, had died fighting crime several years earlier. When Wally was a kid, he had worshiped the Flash, not knowing he was the love of his Aunt Iris's life.

Thinking back on that time was a mixture of pain and pleasure. Wally had been kind of a sad, lonely kid, the product of a dysfunctional home. But one summer while he was staying with his Aunt Iris, whom he loved more than his own mother, Wally met the Flash and got to hang out with him. Oddly, the same accidental convergence of chemicals, clumsiness, and lightning occurred for a second time, and shot Wally through with the same freakish ability that the Flash had. After a little training he was able to run faster than the speed of sound. Years later, he would learn to run faster than the speed of light.

His abilities included the power to vibrate his molecules so quickly that he could pass through solid walls.

The synthetic costume he wore protected his body from friction burn. The soles of his boots were made of a durable substance Barry Allen had invented. Wally was certain they struck fear into the hearts of running-shoe company executives; if the formula were ever leaked, shoes could be replaced far less frequently. The colors Wally wore made him feel fast even when he wasn't moving—hot red with electric yellow lightning bolts. Mercury's wings on his earpieces actually produced a bit of drag, but not so much that it would ever make a difference. Even though he didn't regard the Greek gods as highly as Diana did, he respected their abilities and legacies. He would never discard those wings.

As he locked up and mentally plotted his route, Wally knew he would reach the Triangle first. With HQ off-line, everyone was on their own as far as transportation was concerned—no instant teleporting. Flash was a given to win, and if Lois didn't slow Superman down with too many questions or kisses, the Man of Steel was a sure bet to show, followed by Green Lantern to place, and Batman to finish. No one disparaged Batman for his relative lack of speed. He was the only member of the group who had no superhuman powers. Batman couldn't fly without aid of machinery or gadgets, nor could he read minds or outrace a speeding bullet. But he was an ordinary man with extraordinary abilities and an uncanny mind for detection. *And often*, Flash thought, *his well-*

considered entrance to a situation gives our team a distinct advantage.

Wally relished the prospect of running through the night. The evening air would cool his passage—there'd be fewer vehicles to dodge, fewer distractions in general. The last part of his trek would be over miles of water. He'd be sure to get a good running start in Georgia.

Just as he fixed his trajectory in his mind, Oracle contacted him with a minor emergency:

"A train derailment on a mountain pass—do you have time to transport some of the injured to hospitals?"

As the Flash adjusted his plans, he realized Superman would probably beat him to the island, after all. *Can't win 'em all*, he thought, as he streaked away into the night.

CHAPTER 14

The Orb

The Amazon Princess felt the earthquake subsiding. The water still seemed to shimmer a little, but she could finally see well enough to find the end of the golden lasso. She picked it up. Then she used the flashlight to try to catch Henry's eye, in order to signal him to drop the orb and swim away with her. But Henry wouldn't look at her; his eyes were glued to the pulsing orb. Diana looked at his computer—they were at 88 feet. Too much time at this depth would eat up Henry's air and put him in danger of decompression sickness if he surfaced too quickly. Diana tugged at the lasso to make him break his grip on the orb and follow her. Instead, her strong pull helped Henry dislodge the orb from the surrounding coral. Remembering the slate, Diana transferred the flashlight to her mouth so she could illuminate the writing surface. She wrote: DROP ORB COME WITH ME. Diana thrust the slate in front of Henry's face, where he would have to see it. Henry, however, didn't drop the orb, nor did he follow her. His eyes were closed.

Dropping the slate, Diana reached for Henry's hands and tried to pry the orb from his clutch, but when she scraped a knuckle on it she was suddenly overwhelmed with dread. It was a spherical entity, crusted over with corals and barnacles, possibly a meteoroid, she thought, lodged in the reef for thousands of years. But space debris didn't pulse and glow with angry red light like this thing did. Curiosity overcame her. She touched it again, and a terrible silent scream shot into her body, stabbing with snaky fingers into every nerve. Diana shook like an epileptic until she was able to pull her hand away. The scream's tendrils congregated in her head, strangling her brain, until she recoiled in fear.

The shock exhausted Diana's air supply. She had to take a few seconds to recover before she could reach over to grab Henry's backup regulator. Thankfully, he didn't resist, seeming not to care that she was there. He just continued to crouch on the ocean floor, his eyes shut, hugging the orb to his chest as if protecting it from her. *But that's backward*, Diana thought. *As long as he holds onto it, it is protecting him from me.*

The Amazon had to weigh their chances for escape. She could tug at Henry with her lasso, signaling that she wanted him to go with her, but it was clear that he would not let go of the heavy sphere under any circumstances. Diana knew he would require a fair amount of air in his buoyancy control device if he refused to drop the orb, and even more for the number of yards he would have to swim to get through the thermocline. The computer on his wrist indicated his air supply was down to 1100 pounds. At this depth, and at his present rate of consumption, Henry would run out of oxygen or get the bends. Since there was no decompression chamber in this dimension, he could die a painful death or be crippled for life. Moving forward, toward the thermocline, was no longer an option. But safety was within reach—they had to go back to the island of men.

When Diana pulled at the lasso in the direction of the island, Henry finally opened his eyes. He pumped air into his BC so he could have more lift to compensate for the weight of the orb. Then he started swimming calmly back. Rising faster than a foot per second would be dangerous, so Diana kept an eye on him as she helped propel him forward. If he ran out of air, she could give him mouth-to-mouth underwater.

After what seemed like a month of slow ascent, they were fifteen feet below the surface. Diana looked at Henry's computer and saw that he would not have enough air to take a full three-minute safety stop, but she signaled him to hang at that depth as long as he could to force more nitrogen out of his tissues. While he did, she took the fins off his feet and put them on her own. Henry was spent, and she would need the extra boost to haul him to shore.

After only a minute, though, Henry ran out of air and surfaced. Diana followed suit. She breathed in the sweet night air and looked around. They were about twenty yards from the shore and would be able to swim the rest of the way. The orb weighed him down so his head kept ducking under the water; Henry looked half dead. Diana prayed he wouldn't swallow too much seawater or, worse, inhale any. Using all her might, she grabbed him by a strap on his equipment and hauled him toward the beach.

Five thousand men lined the shore. No one said a word, they just watched. The effect was eerie. Diana wouldn't have minded some help in getting Henry clear of the surf—the orb weighed him down so much. But not one of the men on shore moved a muscle. The fins came off as soon as her feet found sand. Her lasso threatened to tangle in Henry's air hoses so Diana dropped it, needing both hands to manage his dead weight. Incoming waves helped push him toward shore, but then he'd lose ground as they washed back. Tugging at Henry, hefting him forward inch by inch, she finally got him out of reach of the relentless waves. Diana plopped down onto the sand and panted. When she glanced at the glowing orb, the memory of the terrible feeling that had overcome her when she touched it filled her with dread once again. A spasm of shivering overtook her body, but it wasn't from the cool breeze.

Henry, on the other hand, seemed to gain strength from the orb as soon as it came in contact with the air. He shrugged off his dive gear and the lasso that now hung loosely around his wrist, coiling it up and throwing it at the feet of one of the men. A second later, while Diana was still struggling to get her breath, Henry rolled onto his knees, then stood, never letting go of the pulsing thing. He hefted the orb to chest level, then, like Atlas hoisting the world, he heaved it over his head and onto his shoulders. As he turned to show it to all those who lined the dark beach, the men burst into a blood-curdling cheer. The globe's coral shell cracked audibly, then shattered and flew in all directions. When a jagged piece shot toward Diana, her forearm instinctively flew up in front of her face. The chunk hit her silver bracelet and bounced off harmlessly.

Diana filled with horror when she looked at the throbbing orb. It was smooth now, a perfectly spherical mass that sent a sick red wash of light over the men. Ten thousand eyes shone red with its reflected rays. Still disoriented, her hand shot automatically to her side, fumbling for her lasso. It wasn't there. Without further thought, she got up and flew over Henry, intent on knocking the glowing orb out of his hands. Instead, as soon as she touched it, the same screaming feelings of loss, pain, and suffering filled her, but this time the intensity was unbearable, and Diana fell to the sand. Her lasso was lying nearby, but out of reach. Unable to get up, she crawled toward it, but pain and shock slowed her movements. Before she could get within reach, an island man scooped up her Golden Lasso of Truth. Groaning with frustration and dread, Diana looked back over toward Henry.

She watched as the blond man held the orb up over his head, like an athlete showing off a captured trophy. His muscles gleamed and stood out bigger and thicker than she thought possible. This was not the

man that Ana knew and loved, nor even the same
man Diana had kidnapped from the men's house earlier that night. Henry was a man transformed by the
powerful object he now held. He looked dangerous,
as if he were fueled by hate. The sight made Diana
want to weep, but she wouldn't, for any display of
weakness might inflame the men to violence. She
shrank back as the men cheered and howled at the
glowing thing like wolves baying at the moon. The
noise filled her with despair.

Looking on, the drawings from the cave wall
formed in her mind. One image had shown Henry
emerging from the sea with the orb. Now, that event
had transpired. Further on, the drawings showed the
men forcing her to take them to Themyscira. Their
leader held her captive with her golden lasso. That
now seemed entirely possible. The thought compounded her feelings of horror, revulsion, and helplessness.

Diana also remembered when she had asked Pelias
who their leader was. He hadn't understood the concept, and now she knew why—Henry just hadn't
taken his position yet. The man was obviously channeling some kind of energy from the orb and, from
what she could see, he was acting like a man possessed. Diana felt relief that Henry's bride wasn't
there to see him like this, then immediately sent a
small prayer to the gods asking for Ana to be alive
and well.

Henry, still holding the orb above his head, turned
toward the living center and started walking. The

howling from the chorus of men died down as they
fell in behind him. The one who held the golden
lasso—Diana recognized him as Crotholis, the man
who had offered her fish at dinner—came up to Diana
as if to tie her with it. Diana tried to fly out of reach,
but Crotholis caught her with one hand by her ankle,
dragging her down with his weight until the combination of fatigue and shock forced Diana to drop to
the sand. She kicked and beat her fists on the man's
head and shoulders, but to no effect—he slipped the
looped end of her golden lasso around her neck and
yanked it tight.

As soon as the lasso bound her Diana was powerless, and was compelled to do whatever the man
wished her to do. The pictographs in the cave seemed
more likely than ever to become reality. If she didn't
escape from her own lasso, she could be compelled to
ruin her own people, triggering the downfall of civilization. She felt as bad as one could feel without
going mad.

Crotholis stood, and jerked the lasso so that Diana
was forced to stand, lest she be strangled. She saw
Henry holding the orb high, leading the men toward
the living center, where smoke rose over the trees
from the cook fire. Crotholis joined the mass of men
following Henry, pulling Diana along as if she were a
dog on a leash. Even though her will and strength
screamed inside her to revolt, she was powerless to
resist.

The red orb glowed and pulsed in the dark blanket
of night, attracting all eyes to it. Whenever she even

glimpsed the sphere, Diana's mood grew black with certainty that she would fail. Her knees buckled. Crotholis yanked the rope, causing Diana to lose her footing and fall onto the sand. The loutish man ignored her plight and started to drag her. Half of Diana didn't want to resist—if she were strangled she wouldn't be able to help the men find Themyscira. But her indomitable spirit wouldn't let her give up, so she grabbed at a fallen tree, lifting herself so she could walk.

The men marched silently, moving like automatons, every step in synch. But whenever one came upon a broken branch or length of driftwood, he would pick it up. Eventually, each man carried a piece of what looked to Diana like firewood. Were they going to start a fire and burn her alive? No, that wasn't what the pictographs indicated. Diana looked ahead at Henry in the lead with the orb still held high over his head. What was that thing, magic? Was it from space, or had it been created by the same hand that had made this island? Diana tried to concentrate on the problem—she needed to do anything she could to force out the dark thoughts that were overwhelming her. She knew that if the orb existed in this dimension, it was most certainly a creation of the god Ares. And by focusing her thoughts on her enemy, she would find some resolve.

When Crotholis came to some dead scrub pines in his path, he stooped over and picked up an armful of wood. When he foisted the load on Diana, she had to wonder if she was carrying the fuel of her own destruction. Looking past Crotholis's shoulder, over the tops of trees, she saw smoke and a glow coming from where the cook pit would be.

The time was well past midnight. Normally all of these men would be sleeping peacefully in their huts. Tonight, though, when they arrived at the living center where they prepared their meals and ate, there was a fire going. Henry, the first to arrive, stopped in front of the pit, holding up the orb so that he faced the mountain on the other side. The long line of men filed by the pit, each tossing in his piece of wood before taking a place behind Henry. As more men filed past, the flames grew into a bonfire.

The men stood shoulder to shoulder in staggered rows behind Henry. Diana again wondered if she would be tossed onto the fire like some desiccated branch. Crotholis led her to a spot on the far side of the pit so that she faced Henry and the phalanx of warriors. He then stepped back behind her, holding onto the end of the golden lasso that bound her.

All the men had thrown their wooden sacrifices into the fire and had taken their places behind Henry. The air was filled with the heat and crackling of burning wood and the smell of the smoke. Henry, who still held the heavy orb high over his head with no apparent effort, finally spoke.

It took a moment for Diana to realize, to her horror, that Henry was speaking in Ancient Greek.

CHAPTER 15

Batman and Oracle

Cruising on autopilot, the Batwing flew over the southern United States, heading for Florida. Batman spoke to the computer.

"Calling Oracle."

A few seconds later, it sounded like his young friend was sitting beside him.

"Yes?"

"Any more activity in the region in question?"

"Yes, another quake. This one registered 5.2. Smaller than the last, but too big to be merely an aftershock. From the pattern of seismic activity, it looks like a volcano is forming."

Batman peered out into the night sky, but saw nothing out of the ordinary. "What about aid?" he asked.

"The Coast Guard and the Red Cross are heading to any islands that might take hits from tidal waves, but so far no one is heading to the hot spot except for a few field geologists and volcano experts."

"Do what you can to keep them away from the area. Have their governments restrict their access."

"How?" Oracle asked.

"However you can."

The last thing they needed was civilians getting in the way of what could turn out to be a sizable operation. Batman didn't believe in hunches, per se, but too many indicators were pointing to trouble.

"Understood."

Batman knew Oracle had her own secret ways of getting things done. Some things were not necessarily legal—hackers, as a rule, did not respect rules—but her devices were never unethical; no one was ever harmed by her subterfuge. She was the daughter of a big-city police commissioner, after all.

"Any other news?" Batman asked.

"Gotham City Ghouls over the Keystone City Kops, seven to five, bottom of the eighth."

The names were changed to protect the innocent and provoke a laugh. As usual, Batman kept his poker face.

"Go team," he said in his most deadpan voice, just to vex her. That, to him, was funny.

The task Batman had asked Oracle to carry out was relatively easy to accomplish. A suggestion in the right quarters that there was hazardous waste contaminating the area would be enough to keep out stray Richter readers and reporters. It would also act as a good cover story as to why four members of the JLA were heading down there to take a look.

Oracle had a sudden pang of envy for those brave people who were going out on an adventure. They got to fly, rappel, turn invisible, or create big green super tools while she sat in her wheelchair all day, talking to people behind disguised voices while digging for data.

Indulging in self-pity was not her style, though, so she turned her thoughts back to the business at hand, punching a few combinations into her keyboard.

Her voice filter menu popped up. She chose British>Male>Older>Authoritarian. This was one of her favorite oral disguises, a cross between James Mason and John Cleese. That voice was rarely refused anything, and had one of the highest trust ratings. If her contact turned out to be female, she could always slip a little Sean Connery into the mix.

Oracle knew how to get things done. And after that was finished, she would take a power nap.

The thought made her remember that working at home had its perks.

CHAPTER 16

Big Bang

Henry stood facing the island men with his back to the fire, addressing them in Ancient Greek. Maybe he had studied the language in college, Diana speculated, but there was no way he could be so fluent with the oral version unless he had lived among native speakers. Besides, he'd only been on the island a couple of days. The orb must be speaking through him.

Over the crackle and pop of the burning driftwood, Diana listened.

"Brothers, we are here to praise Ares, the God of War. Ares is might. Ares is right. Ares is all. Without him we are weak. With him, we have the power to enslave mankind so that they may serve us and our glorious master.

"Ares created you so that you may serve him. He led me to the Sphere of Power so that I may lead you. I bring you this sphere, a gift from Ares. He foretold

that this day would come, when I would retrieve the
power and unleash it.

"Step forward, brothers, and receive your gift.
What strengthens us weakens others. As weak as you
are now, you will soon be strong."

The men cheered in unison. Henry turned to face
the fire, braced himself, then heaved the orb into the
middle of the pyre.

Diana was unprepared for what happened next.
When the orb crashed into the flames, it sent out an
explosive fireworks display of lasers and guided light.
Missiles of brilliant energy shot out toward the men,
striking them with red and yellow rays that seemed to
infuse them with power and . . . something else. But
what was it?

Before Diana could determine what it might be,
several missiles flew at her. She fended them off with
her silver bracelets, ricocheting them back into the
fire. Crotholis, her watchdog, was still behind her,
holding on to the end of her lasso. *That is who these
missiles are seeking*, Diana realized. She was not the intended target—she was just standing between a man
and his orb.

The Amazon Princess could not see her captor, she
was so busy deflecting the rays, but each time she
heard one hit him he let out a cry of rapture and
jerked sharply on the golden lasso. One such action
caused Diana to lose her balance, so that one bullet of
light got past her defenses, piercing her leg. The pain
eclipsed all other sensations, causing her to collapse.
Another wave of helplessness and despair washed

over her. What was good for the gander was definitely not good for the goose.

The bulk of the light missiles went toward the men, transforming them. They became bigger, stronger. Faces that had echoed the glory days of Greece became ugly. When one man howled his thanks to Ares, Diana could see that his canine teeth were almost as long as a wolf's. They all now had thick bony ridges over their brows instead of smooth foreheads. Their nostrils were enlarged and distended; they looked feral and dangerous. Fingernails grew into claws. Hair sprouted on their torsos and faces. They became huge, animal-like; vicious. Thousands of eyes glowed bright red. And in those eyes she recognized the worst quality the orb had given them. It was hatred.

Just when it seemed the orb had shot out all of its energy, the earth trembled again. The movement started with a low rumbling sound, but quickly escalated to violent jolts. Diana gasped, just as a gush of light burst straight up out of the fire and into the heavens, lighting the sky as if it were day. The column of light burned and cut the night like a red-hot poker slicing through butter. Stars disappeared, the sky turned absolutely white, and a deafening sonic boom shook every atom in the air.

Diana felt as if she'd been punched from all angles on every square inch of her body. Then, just as suddenly as it had flared up, the column of light fell back into the orb that lay pulsing in the fire. When she looked up, the positions of the stars looked different.

The earth stopped shaking. Diana got to her feet,

and looked around her. Everything seemed to be normal—as normal as a freak island filled with immortal warriors who wanted to enslave the world could be, anyway.

The fire burned on, popping out a small cinder every now and then. The trees and huts were all where they had been, no worse for wear after the shake up. But the sky had changed. The stars were not the ones she had gazed upon earlier when she had prayed to the gods on the beach. They were the stars of her own dimension.

Diana looked out to sea. There, where Ana had been when Henry had disappeared, was a boat—Ana and Henry's boat. Somehow, Diana realized, the explosion of light had transported the entire island into the dimension where the men could do the most harm.

Ana was sleeping on the boat when she felt the vibration. Her sleep was not deep—that would not be possible until she had Henry back. So when the air tickled the hairs on her skin, her eyes opened wide. Ana got goose bumps, even though the air was comfortably warm. She stood up and looked around. The stars provided only enough light to separate the dark sea from the sparkling sky. The vibration made her uneasy—another in a series of unnatural events in the Bermuda Triangle.

Her experience from the day before flashed into Ana's mind. She had watched Wonder Woman head straight into the waterspouts. One by one the Amazon Warrior had made them disappear. Ana guessed that she had flown counter to the motion of the spouts, canceling out their energy. The woman had super-powers, but still, that took a lot of guts. Ana remembered how the last one looked like it was going to catch her boat and pulverize it. Wonder Woman had flown into that one, too. Just when Ana was wishing she had written a will, the tornado of water had vanished, taking Wonder Woman with it. But the last one hadn't unwound and dropped like rain to the sea as the first two had. It had just flat-out disappeared.

Ana had spent the rest of the day and night alone, bewildered. The sea and sky seemed to be full of smoke and mirrors; she didn't believe that people and things could just vanish like that. Some big-time magician must have been at work here. Ana would not give up hope that Henry and Wonder Woman were still alive. Perhaps they were just hidden behind a secret panel somewhere. The magician would let them out when he was good and ready. Ana wasn't about to give up and go back to Grand Bahama. Her intuition—her faith—told her to stay.

So when the vibration started, Ana was less surprised than others might have been. As curious events go, it seemed kind of harmless. Still, she scanned the surface of the water for abnormalities. The Bermuda Triangle was tricky.

She was unprepared, though, for the blast of light that filled the sky. Everything became white as some unseen force blew her over the side of the boat and into the ocean. A giant sonic boom bludgeoned all her senses. She looked around to find the source, but it was everywhere. Then, just as suddenly, it was gone.

All that was left was the ghost effect in her eyelids and a ringing in her ears.

Waves buffeted the boat and slapped at her face. She was blinded for a moment. Ana knew she hadn't burned out her rods and cones, so she remained calm and waited for the ghost in her head to take a walk while she treaded water. When she opened her eyes, though, she saw something she hadn't expected to see.

The magician had pulled an island out of his hat, situated right where it should have been when Henry disappeared. This wasn't some tiny key, either—it was big, obscuring stars and horizon that she had been looking at just a few minutes before. Ana was horrified by its sudden emergence, but also glad. Henry was on that island—she knew it. And so, too, was Wonder Woman.

Ana swam to the boat and pulled herself up over its side. From her slightly higher vantage point, she could see a column of smoke rising from a glow that could only mean a fire. She picked up her dive light so she could signal to people on the island that she was there, but then stopped herself. It might not be a good idea to let anyone know she was there just yet. Ana put the light down and thought about how sound would carry. If there was enough surf on the shore and roar in the fire, it might be enough to cover up the sound of the motor. Why she was suddenly so wary was a mystery to her, so she stopped to consider. With all that had gone on, Ana didn't just expect to walk onto the island, say "What ho," and take off with her man to resume their honeymoon. Something weird was going on, and she needed to proceed with caution.

The light blast had caused the boat to drift into a current, which had taken it further from the place where the fire was burning. *Good*, Ana thought. Quietly, she lowered the anchor. Minutes before, she hadn't had enough line to hit bottom. Now she knew it would catch at about 60 feet. Ana didn't have to check the depth locator—she was right. The anchor touched bottom and hooked on a reef. Hopefully, the boat would not be going anywhere.

Clad only in her swim suit, Ana put on her dive skin. It didn't supply the thermal protection of a wet suit, but it allowed for easy movement and covered her limbs with dark material. That and her black hair provided good camouflage. Rather than risk detection by starting the motor, she would quietly swim to shore for a closer look around. As it was, Ana couldn't see through the trees to the place where the fire burned. That meant that any bogeyman dancing around a bonfire wouldn't be aware of her boat. For added protection, she strapped a knife onto her ankle. Normally, Ana didn't use one unless she was diving around kelp or fishing lines, but now she was glad she had it. Booties and fins went on next, then she looped the corded handle of her dive light around her wrist. She wedged a bottle of water under a nylon belt and tugged on her mask.

Praying that all the local sharks were fast asleep, Ana slipped over the side of the boat, into the inky water.

Oracle woke to the sound of a computer voice.
"Emergency. Wake up. Emergency. Wake up."

The hacker wanted to throw a brick at it, but she was fresh out.

She shook her head to get some blood circulating. More alert now, she pulled her wheelchair close to the cot and maneuvered herself into its seat. Her fingers pressed the proper controls to make the vehicle move where she wanted, which was directly to the bank of computers. No time to brush her teeth and hit the john; that was for regular folks. Oracle prided herself on being quite irregular.

She made it to her bank of computers in record time. When she got a load of what the computer was squawking about, her eyes opened wide in disbelief. It wasn't another flare-up in the Middle East, nor floods wiping out farms in the Midwest. This was something even bigger.

A brand-new shiny island had popped up out of nowhere, following another sizable earthquake.

Oracle jacked into her geographical and seismic data centers to see if a tsunami was in the works. Often, when an earthquake hits or a volcano erupts, forces send water surging across the ocean to wreak havoc on whatever shore has the bad luck to be in its path. Something this big must have sent shock waves around the Atlantic.

But, on checking, there seemed to have been relatively little fallout from the island's sudden appearance. There were no lava flows, clouds of poisonous gas and debris, or even tidal disruptions that are common when an island emerges from the sea. The absence of those occurrences seemed to rule out natural causes. By indexing wind direction readings from the surrounding landmasses and monitors in the area, Oracle could see that air had been displaced by the island's appearance. Therefore, she concluded, it must have popped in from another dimension.

"Batman, come in," Oracle said into her head mike. A computer connected her to the Batboat.

"Batman here," said the Dark Knight. He had jumped from his plane into his boat in Palm Beach. The fully loaded craft skipped over the water so fast it would have became airborne, if it had wings. Two sheets of foamy white water arced away from each other at the stern.

"An island just came out of nowhere and plopped down exactly where you guys are headed."

"That fits with what is happening down here."

"What's going on?" Oracle asked.

"I felt a shock wave—not much, but from my position, just the right amount of force to indicate a dimensional breach or transfer."

"Okay. I'll keep you posted on anything else I find out, but it sounds like you'll know better than I will, soon enough."

"I ought to be there in two hours. Over and out."

Oracle wheeled her chair to her window and gazed into the lights of the city. With the right equipment, she could find out what was going on behind every one of those windows out there.

Tonight, though, Batman would be her eyes and ears for the more interesting story. She just hoped he would be all right.

* * *

Superman had just passed over the southeast coast of the United States. It was outlined with clumps of city lights. Then he was over the sea, spots of light blinking from oil rigs far below. The moon was barely a sliver in the sky, so the brightest lights were the stars. The dark sea and the clear view of the Milky Way had a calming effect on him.

Then the sky turned white. The flash seemed to originate from the area where he was headed to search for Wonder Woman. As he braced himself for the coming shock wave, he speculated on what it might be. Atomic bomb? Meteor impact? Alien interference? Nothing good. But when the shock wave hit him seconds later, he could barely feel it. That surprised him because the visuals implied a stronger impact. But at least it ruled out a nuclear blast or meteor. If either of those had hit the earth, there would have been all kinds of detritus in the air. Alien interference was harder to rule out because it could take a variety of forms, including many that existed beyond imagination.

Calculating the distance between himself and the event and the seconds it took to reach him, Superman noted that the mild shock wave implied the introduction of a physical body into a defined space, much like the way a body that materializes in a room displaces air.

So, what happened? Superman wondered. It was a much larger displacement than that which occurs when a space vehicle appears out of a different dimension.

Could it be a city or a landmass? The Man of Steel figured that a mass about the size of Manhattan appearing out of nowhere would cause the same effect. If he was right, he now had an easy target to locate.

Superman continued to fly toward the source of the light blast, even though the aftereffects of whatever it had been were no longer visible. Soon, based on his speed, time of travel, and position of the stars, he knew he was where he wanted to be.

To his surprise, he looked down upon an island that had not been noted on any map he'd ever seen.

Looking toward the southeast, over the black silhouettes of mountains, the Flash saw the sky blank out. The brightest point seemed directly in line with where he would go next, the Bermuda Triangle.

Gasps and shouts of "What's that?" came from all around him as emergency medical personnel and the last victim of the train derailment all looked to the sky.

By reflex, the Flash shut his eyes tight and braced himself for a shock. If he hadn't been waiting for one, he wouldn't have felt it—the effect was miniscule. Perhaps it was more potent closer to the source of light. Initially, that made him glad because it ruled out several extremely bad possibilities.

When he opened his eyes again, the scene had returned to normal—a star-strewn sky domed over the dark mountain pass. The cars of the freight train still lay broken and twisted in a zigzag of costly disorder. The Flash returned to strapping an injured man to a gurney, his movements a blur. A medic quickly inspected his work before giving the thumbs-up for the Flash to race to the hospital. Helicopters churned the air overhead, but none had been able to land because of the rocky terrain. The Flash was grateful he was able to help—every one of the train's crew was going to be fine, thanks to his speed.

As his feet flew over the mountains, he wondered what the bright light meant. He came up with possibilities, but no firm conclusions. The desire to finish this job urged him to run faster, but he had to hold himself back—he was carrying an injured man.

Soon, he deposited his passenger at the hospital where he had taken the rest of the train's crew. This man was the last one. A crowd of people cheered him on his speedy delivery of their loved ones to safety, so he had to resist the temptation to leave long enough to shake some hands and hug some happy, tear-streaked wives.

A photographer arrived at the hospital, running toward the crowd, eager to get a good picture of the super hero for her paper. She shoved through the relatives and hospital workers, snapping the shutter—but too late. All that showed up on the film were happy people and a red streak.

The Flash was on his way to the Bermuda Triangle, itching to find out what had caused the sky to turn white.

From inside his sleek green rocket, Green Lantern saw the sky blanch and prepared himself for a tumble. But nothing happened. Well, almost nothing—he just felt a little bump. Relief flooded his mind—it wasn't a nuclear blast or anything of that magnitude. Still, it was not a natural phenomenon, and it probably had something to do with Diana's disappearance. Wanting to discuss the event with someone, he knew only Batman was wired at the moment. Kyle imagined up a squawk box—sometimes he added details to his constructions as he went along—and contacted the Dark Knight.

"Batman, this is Lantern. Come in. Did you see that?"

"Affirmative."

"Well?" Green Lantern pressed. "What do you think it was?"

"Oracle's data indicates an island has materialized, precisely where we are headed."

"Where do you think it came from?"

"There's no way of knowing right now. We'll find out more when we get there."

Kyle mentally kicked himself for trying to engage Batman in speculation. The man was a detective, a scientist, and didn't like to make conclusions without evidence. Kyle still felt a little intimidated by the older man. Batman had that scary, angry edge to him, but that wasn't what threw him. Neither was it the man's ferocious intelligence and determination—Kyle was comfortable with his own gifts.

"Kyle," Batman said over the box, his voice softened a bit, "you'll probably arrive ahead of me. Let me know what you see when you get there."

That's it, Kyle realized, *the man has class*. He instantly resolved to watch the older man and learn

anything he could about behaving like a gentleman in
this often uncivilized world.

"What's your current location?" asked Green Lantern.

"About 25 kilometers out of Palm Beach, heading
straight for the given coordinates. I'll be there in less
than an hour."

"See you there, then," Kyle said. "Over and out."

After Batman signed off, Kyle thought about Batman, Superman, and his other teammates. He liked to
draw them when he was noodling around. Sometimes
he drew events that they had been involved in, sometimes his friends figured in scenarios that were pure
fantasy. Once he drew a picture of himself kissing
Wonder Woman just to see how it might look, but the
drawing made him feel like he had violated her privacy so he erased her and drew in a lingerie model instead. What was a good imagination for if he didn't
exercise it once in a while?

In spite of Batman's reluctance to speculate on the
origin of the mysterious island, Kyle's imagination went
to work on it—he couldn't help himself. His favorite
line of thought led him to Atlantis, Aquaman's home. If
one such underwater city could exist, there might well
be another waiting to rise up again, with brilliant light
heralding its emergence from the sea. Kyle wondered if
any of the other fellows had thought of that. He briefly
considered calling Batman to tell him his theory, but
prudently stowed the impulse.

He would find out about the island soon enough.

CHAPTER 17

Bound

Five thousand men were ecstatic. They faced the mountain to praise Ares in booming voices that echoed and layered over and under one another, weaving an aural tapestry of hate and devotion. Diana's eyes widened with dread as she thought of how these men might plunge the world into chaos and horror.

The island now inhabited *her* world. These men—*these warriors,* she corrected herself—wanted to invade her home and kill everyone in it as a first step in conquering the world. Ares was behind this, running the show, but how could she hope to engage him in battle when he wouldn't show himself?

Diana pictured Ares as the warriors chanted his name. Tall and broad-shouldered—often appearing gigantic—he rarely revealed his face to anyone. He wore his crested battle helmet with the visor drawn down so that he could see out, but no one could see him. There was speculation that Aphrodite had clawed his eyes during a violent session of lovemaking, but that wouldn't explain his reluctance to show himself. Diana figured it was part of his act—the rigid impenetrable mask frightened mortals and even some gods. That, combined with his full battle dress and armor, inspired thoughts of resignation and surrender in even the strongest generals in the field.

A mask could hide a person from others, but it influenced the wearer at the same time. A person almost always took on the characteristics of the mask and behaved accordingly. Batman, she imagined, was probably a sweetheart once he took off that cowl. Diana imagined herself sneaking up on Ares in his sleep and pasting a big yellow happy face on his mug. Would that make him a nice guy? *No*, she realized, *because it would not have been his choice.*

Wonder Woman felt a tug of the lasso on her neck. She had forgotten for a moment that she was still bound, but the fact was unavoidable and her heart sank anew. Crotholis, on the other end of the rope, jerked her over to the palm tree that was nearest to the fire. Diana looked at her captor. He was *huge*. He seemed to have almost doubled in size since the moment she'd met him. His muscles bulged and rippled. He looked like a dumb, overgrown body builder crossed with a horned toad. And he wasn't the only one—they all looked like that.

Diana could offer no resistance when he tied her to the tree. She was still weak from having been struck by the light missile, the wound in her leg throbbing and sending searing shivers of pain throughout her body. Her helplessness made her sick with humiliation and regret as Crotholis made sure the lasso was knotted tight. Then he walked away, seeming to forget instantly that she was there. Diana considered that the men didn't operate well as individuals—they were more like ants or bees. The masses of drones did all the work, in this case warring, while one leader called the shots. Henry was their apparent leader, but Diana knew he was not the bad guy here. He was the merely a puppet operated by Ares's unseen hand.

Wonder Woman stared into the fire, as humans do. The dancing flames evoked memories, indefinable at first, but enchanting, nonetheless. Gaming in the coliseum, diving in the lagoon—postcards from home wrapped in flickering light. It was easy to keep her eyes fixed on the fire; it helped her forget what was going on about her.

While Wonder Woman stood tied to the tree, hypnotized, Henry called on his warriors to take action.

"Soldiers—retrieve your weapons and bring them to be blessed by Ares."

The warriors filed away from the camp to fetch crude instruments from their arsenal—spears, sets of bows and arrows, and primitive axes made of wood and stone that had previously been used to bring them food or build their shelters. They weren't much compared to modern instruments of war, but these tools could easily kill. Diana saw the men returning with their clubs and spears, and shuddered at the thought of what they might be used for.

When each soldier returned to the camp, he advanced to the fire and raised his weapon over his head. The roasting orb shot accurately at each object, hundreds at a time, transforming stone-tipped spears into sleek steel javelins, and clumsy clubs into studded iron maces. Each man hefted and admired his new piece of equipment, throwing or swinging his weapon to learn its power.

Henry looked on, his long blond hair dancing on the hot currents of air generated by the fire at his back. When all of the men were reassembled with their new toys of war, he addressed them once again.

"Tonight we set sail for Themyscira, where our weapons will taste blood. With each woman you destroy, Ares will grow stronger. As he grows stronger, so, in turn, will we. Feel our strength. Know that more awaits us. Understand that the more power we have, the harder it will be for any to take it away. Ares will rule the world through each and every one of us. Ares will rule the heavens through our deeds. We will not be stopped—we are invincible!"

The men cheered in unison, a blood-curdling animal cry of adrenaline and lust.

Overhead, however, something streaked by. If anyone had noticed, they would have seen it fly to the mountain and stop.

Superman had arrived.

The Man of Steel had spotted the island as soon as he started looking for it, exactly where the scuba diver had gone missing and where Diana had headed to search for him. It was the right size to account for the displacement of air, which told him that this island had existed in another dimension until just a few moments before. *What had caused that?* he wondered. Explanations presented themselves automatically, a checklist of phenomena he often had to deal with: natural causes, alien interference, divine intervention, magic. He could not rule out any of those possibilities without further investigation.

As he dropped closer to the island, Superman made out a small white dive boat off the leeward shore. He circled the island, spotting an armada of primitive battle ships. And someone was up late—there was a huge bonfire burning. When he was closer still, he saw people—thousands of them. They were grouped around the fire as if in ceremony. Then he picked out Diana, tied to a tree near the fire. Using his telescopic vision, he saw that she was bound by her own lasso.

Superman didn't want to barge into the situation without knowing more about it. One wrong move and Diana could be hurt. Instead, he flew to a spot on the mountain so he could survey the scene.

Seeing Diana tied up like that pained him. He loved her like a sister or a best friend. His wife, Lois, had at first been somewhat uneasy with their closeness. Who wouldn't be?—Diana was a knockout. Over time, though, the two women had become friends, and Lois's envy-green eyes went back to their original lovely shade of blue. Lois had sent her true love off on this mission with deep concern for Diana's well-being. Superman was not going to break his wife's heart or let down his friend.

But what to do? He used his unique vision to see through smoke and jungle. Diana appeared to be drugged or otherwise incapacitated. Several thousand men milled around the bonfire, some chanting and praying, others holding their spears or clubs up to it. Small fireballs shot out from the fire, illuminating the weapons and seeming to turn them from wood or stone to metal. It seemed there was magic at work here. The chants, primitive and hostile, carried up the side of the mountain to where he was perched. Superman could make out none of what they said, but he recognized, from having heard Diana speak, that the words were Ancient Greek.

The fire emitted an odd glow. Something in the flames pulsated, so the Man of Steel focused on it: a spherical object cooking in the flames. It glowed red, seeming to expand and contract with each angry pulse. That was his enemy, he knew—not the men.

Superman considered his options. He could swoop down and carry off the orb. Okay, but where would he take it? Fire seemed to catalyze it, so maybe he should carry it to one of the poles. Taking it to an asteroid would be even better, but that would require a working teleporter or space vehicle, neither of which were available at the moment. And what if it contained kryptonite? He didn't know the orb's origins—if it had come from space it could very well hold a piece of the one element that could destroy him.

Superman peered into the orb. There were chunks of lead in it, as well as almost every other element in the spectrum. The lead could shield kryptonite from his vision, but he didn't think that was likely—there would have been telltale bits of green radiation.

So far so good, but he had to consider more contingencies. What if he was right and the thing was magical? Magic was the only other thing that could harm him, and that covered a lot of territory. Supernatural beings dealt in magic, as did gods from Asgard and Olympus. Even some aliens possessed magical powers. Superman hated magic because it was never logical. It had reasons behind it, but no mind.

The men finished transforming their weapons, Superman noticed. He wondered why, if the orb was magical, it didn't turn the weapons into assault rifles and laser launchers. *Even magic has limitations*, he thought.

The Man of Steel watched as the men listened to a speech by their leader and cheered. The speaker, paler than the others with long blond hair, wore swim trunks instead of woven bark. This was the diver Diana had sought, Henry Lindstadt. His were the actions of someone possessed, adding strength to Superman's guess that the orb was magical.

Superman focused on the orb. Now that it was done transforming clubs and arrows, it appeared to rest calmly in the fire, shooting off rays of light at irregular intervals. Then, as if it sensed it was being watched, one hell of a beam shot up the mountain, directly at Superman. He dodged to his right. The missile ricocheted off the rock wall behind him and disappeared in the sky like a burned-out meteorite. Was it magical? *Almost certainly*, he thought. Now what? If he zoomed in to pick up the orb, he risked being put out of commission. If he did nothing, Wonder Woman might be killed. For the moment she seemed relatively unharmed. Good.

Superman could wait until his teammates showed up—the Flash and Green Lantern wouldn't be long, if they weren't there already. Concern for Diana deepened, though, when he saw Henry go to one of the men's huts. Superman watched, his gaze penetrating the thatched roof of the building. Henry put on a robe made of finely woven plant fibers that covered him from his shoulders to his toes, then donned a mask. The mask was similar to those he had seen in museums, ones that were used in Greek tragedies. A caricature of hatred, it was carved with deep lines and painted with the rusty brown of dried blood. Once the mask was in place, Henry picked up what appeared to be a dive knife. He tested the sharpness of the blade by running it over his finger. Drops of red ran out of the cut. Superman saw Henry lick the blood and, looking through the mask with his X-ray vision, he saw him smile.

The man was going to do something. *Human sacrifice?* With that thought Superman put away conjectures and considerations and leaped into the air, intent on flying down to untie Wonder Woman and speed her away. But as soon as he was airborne, the orb shot a barrage of light missiles at him. The Man of Steel dodged, narrowly escaping the savage darts. More missiles followed, an array of fireworks that became a blitzkrieg of searing light. Superman was able to evade the projectiles by flying erratically, but soon there were too many of them. The closer he got to the fire, the faster came the assault. Finally, one of the missiles hit its target, striking Superman in the neck.

Because the Man of Steel rarely suffered pain, the sensation was all the more shocking when he felt it. The color drained from his face, and his body lurched, unable to connect purpose to his flight through the air. His hesitation allowed more of the lightning darts to strike him, each one jerking him as if he were a string puppet operated by a spastic madman. His velocity interrupted, Superman should have just dropped, but the bolts of light shot up at him with enough force to keep him suspended.

Finally, the orb stopped its onslaught. Superman, only a dozen yards away from Wonder Woman, fell to the ground.

Diana didn't see a thing outside of the fire; it was hypnotic. The flames flickered and leaped, licking the sky, dancing on the wood they ate. The fire started to paint a picture. Peering into the heat, she saw her home. The flames formed images that were familiar to her—Themyscira, her friends, her mother. The images seduced her into staring deeply into the fire, where the orb pulsed and throbbed like a sleeping beast. Diana saw her mother hail her, and felt joy. Then she saw her mother playing a game with friends, which morphed into women splashing in the waterfall. That illusion flickered away and came back as animals racing or flowers blooming . . . Henry's pep talk to the men was only so much buzzing in her ear . . . the images in the fire were much more interesting.

Suddenly she heard a hard *thud* as something fell nearby. Turning her head to see what it was seemed like a bother, but she finally did so. There she saw a man dressed in red and blue lying in a heap near the fire, not 30 feet away from her. A slow thought came to her mind: *I remember him . . . he's Superman.*

Warriors started swarming around the fallen super hero, looking at him as if he were a game animal. Diana saw Henry enter the crowd dressed in a robe and mask. Before she could see what he would do, the fire flared out to catch her eye, as if extending a long arm, and snapped its fingers. Straining to see Superman suddenly felt like too much trouble so Diana followed the fingers of flame back to the comfort of the fire. The flames soothed her and made her feel warm inside.

The orb pulsed, rewarding Diana's obedience with memories of happier times on her island home. Lasting only long enough to make her forget about Superman, the pleasant diversions in the fire turned into laser horror shows of her sisters dying, old and withered. Diana's head filled with grief and despair; whatever strength she had draining out. One small part of her brain realized that her proximity to the glowing orb was the cause, but that knowledge failed to help her replace the negative thoughts and images with positive ones. Using all her will, she turned her head away from the fire and its hellish visions. What she saw then was Superman lying still as men kicked him savagely and poked at him with spears and arrows.

Henry turned to look at her. His mask reminded Diana of Ares—not what the god looked like, but what his presence felt like. The leader of the warriors advanced to the fire. Taking out his knife from a fold in his robe, he held it up for the blessing. A fire bolt jetted out from the orb and hit the blade, transforming it into a double-edged sword. Turning to face his men, Henry raised it above his head with both arms in order that all his men recognize its authority. They fell silent at the sight of the gleaming steel weapon, and prostrated themselves to honor it. Henry then turned and walked over to Diana. Through the holes in the mask his eyes bored directly into hers. But she didn't see Henry. She saw madness.

Using his sword as a teacher would a pointer, Henry touched it lightly on various parts of her body—her head, her hip, her shoulder—as he informed her of his plans. He whispered them into her ear, coating each word with malice and mockery.

"You are bound by your golden rope. I know what it did to me—it made me helpless to resist your commands. But now that it binds you, you will obey me," he said.

"You will lead us to your homeland. With your help, our boats will pass through the veil that protects your island from all eyes. When we set foot on your land, your sisters, too, will be helpless . . ."

The voice in her ear faded as Diana stared into the fire.

The golden lasso around her neck tightens when the boats land on Themyscira. Henry looms over her, his mask a part of him now. He puts his sword in her hand. The day is bright and sunny. The sea is turquoise, but it will soon turn red.

Warriors storm the beach. The Amazons charge at them with strength and speed, able to take down the first to attack, but the massive males are driven by pure brutality. Their hearts are small, and hard to target. Their muscles are thick, as if they are armor. Arrows sing, spears connect with meat and bone; screams of pain and rage tear the air. Diana can only watch as Artemis, fighting hand-to-hand with a warrior, is stabbed in the back. Her eyes connect with Diana's, admonishing her for leading the warriors to the island paradise. Blood trickles from her mouth as she dies.

Henry orders Diana to advance to the palace, right through the middle of the battle. Sprays of blood dapple her shoulders and limbs with bright red. On her left, a warrior is raping Chloe. Tears run down her face as she claws for her knife, but it is out of reach. She sees Diana and screams for help. Diana is unable to do anything but walk past her. Another warrior is finished savaging Hermione and cuts her throat. Diana makes no sound because Henry has forbidden her to speak. Screams fill her head, though; only death will be able to silence them.

Polyxena, the poet who sings of love and beauty, fights as fiercely as her sisters, but is brought down by a mace that takes off half her face. The poet is still alive. Jerks and twitches animate her body as she tries to gurgle out a scream. Diana turns her head away from the horrid sight. Henry notices and commands her to look. A warrior approaches the wounded woman, kneeling to mount her. Diana's internal screams of rage and despair grow louder.

The sword she carries mocks her. She wants to swing it around and cut off Henry's head, but she's powerless to do so. He holds her golden lasso.

On they walk, stepping over the bodies and torn limbs of Amazons. Blood stains the ground. Vultures circle over- head in the bright afternoon sky—these are Ares's birds, biding their time. Tears flow down Diana's face as she and Henry climb the palace steps. The heads of statues turn, fol- lowing her progress.

Hippolyta waits for them at the top, wearing full battle armor, wielding a sword that equals Henry's. Warriors rush at her from all sides. The Queen cuts them down, moving efficiently, coldly. Singly or in groups, the men cannot touch the mercurial woman. The bleeding bodies of warriors paint the steps with long red fingers. As the last of this group falls, Hippolyta pauses to regard her daughter. Her face is a mosaic of conflicting emotions: love, hate, pride, shame, regret, hope. Diana feels only despair, know- ing what she will be forced to do.

Hippolyta faces her beloved daughter, sword raised, and beckons her to come forward.

"Come, Diana, puppet of Ares. One of us must die now."

Diana doesn't respond; she merely advances on her mother, her sword at ready. Henry keeps his distance be- hind Diana, gripping the lasso so tightly that his knuckles are white.

"Kill her!" he commands.

Diana lunges at her mother, tears streaming down her face. Hippolyta blocks the thrust and pushes away the of- fending sword. The older woman has the advantage, being positioned above her daughter. Diana swings her blade at her mother's midsection. Hippolyta springs back lightly, and the blade only scratches her armor.

"Kill her!" Henry screams.

Diana does her best to resist his commands, but the lasso's power overwhelms her. She knows she is evenly matched with Hippolyta and the duel might end with her own death. That becomes her hope, for she doesn't want her last moments to be filled with the horror of killing her own mother.

"Kill her!" Henry screams again and again.

Diana cannot resist his will. She lunges at her mother. Hippolyta sidesteps the attack and smashes her sword down on Diana's, knocking it out of her hands. All it will take is one swift swing, and Diana's head will bounce down the steps. But she can't do it. Her arms hold the sword, poised to swing, but she is unable to kill the one she loves the most.

Hippolyta lowers her arms to her sides and drops her sword. It clatters on the marble steps.

"Kill her!" Henry commands, one last time.

The Amazon Princess picks up the sword and climbs the steps to be level with her mother. She hefts the sword over her shoulders and swings. Her mother's face registers only grief for her daughter as she waits for the blade to connect. Then the Queen's eyes widen with apparent disbelief as the blade separates her head from her body. Her head falls, as if in slow motion, to the steps and starts its journey down. Lips form words, but no sound comes forth. The queen's body crumples and falls, rolling a few steps to stop with her neck pointing down, pumping a torrent of blood that tries to catch up to its missing head.

Henry laughs maniacally.
Diana's unleashed screams threaten to rip her in two.
The statues look down on them, crying rivers of tears.

". . . our men are strong and grow stronger with each hour. When we find your sisters, we will be able to defeat them easily. With each woman we defile and destroy, our lord Ares will grow stronger. And as he grows stronger, so in turn will we. The blood of your sisters will taste sweet. And when we have drawn the lifeblood of every woman on the island, we will claim it for our own. Then the swarms of hell that you guard will be ours to use. Armies will cower and nations will crumble. The world will bow to us. We bow only to Ares."

With that, Henry touched his sword between Diana's feet and scraped it up between her legs, then over her torso, as if he were drawing a line to cut her in half. Diana wished he would, so her screams could escape. Continuing, Henry stopped the blade under her chin, pointing up to her skull. He dug the blade in just deep enough to release a drop of blood. It rolled down her neck, and disappeared between her breasts.

Satisfied, Henry lowered his sword, turned, and walked off toward Superman so that he might examine him more closely.

Diana's gorge rose. She didn't want to think about the monstrous images she had just seen, but it was impossible to block them out, just as it was impossible to turn her gaze away from the fire that burned in front of her.

Hippolyta's face formed in the flames. Hope shimmered briefly as Diana realized that she hadn't killed her mother—yet—but it vanished when she saw the red wound dripping blood from her mother's neck. The Queen's lips formed the words that she had tried to speak when her head rolled down the palace steps. This time, Diana heard her.

"Now the world will burn."

Diana threw up as a vision of what was to come formed in the fire—cities in rubble, their inhabitants vaporized. There wasn't much inside her to rise with her bile, so she retched up fear and panic.

The images in the cave—they were all coming true.

The dry heaves hadn't stopped when Diana heard someone come up behind her. It didn't matter who it was. It could be someone about to slit her throat and she might only feel gratitude for sparing her the hell that was waiting for her.

"Diana," came a whisper. "It's me—Ana."

CHAPTER 18

Figments

Wonder Woman didn't believe it. Ana wasn't there. The fire was playing a trick on her. It wanted to give her hope so when it crushed her with despair it would be all the more satisfying. The voice was probably made by the hiss and crackle of the fire. Diana ignored it. She could be tricked by only so many ghosts.

"Wonder Woman—don't make a sound or move until I tell you to."

Ingenious devil. The orb's fire imitated the sound of Ana's voice without having heard it, just as it mimicked her mother's voice so Diana could hear her last admonition. She wished she could block out the sound with her hands, but they were tied. The Amazon tried anyway. Miraculously, her hands were free. Was that a trick, too? Surprise made her turn her head to look.

There was Ana crouching in the brush, coiling the golden lasso and signaling her to be quiet. She was almost lost in the shadows, wearing a black dive skin, her face and hands smeared with mud. Was this a figment created by the fire? It must be. Ana was dead. She had been killed by the waterspout.

"They aren't watching you. They're all looking at whatever that is on the ground—let's go," Ana whispered with urgency.

Diana didn't feel like moving. This Ana was a lie. Why should she do what it told her to do? Diana put her hands back behind her because they were probably still tied. Her gaze returned to the fire. The flames lulled her with images of her friends. This time nothing bad happened to them so Diana decided to just stay there and watch. There was Chloe, braiding Hermione's long hair. Next to them stood Polyxena, reciting her latest poem. That made Diana feel better. Ana's voice upset her, though. It kept urging her to move.

"Come on!" the figment insisted.

No. Diana stood against the tree, watching the fire. She felt something move her hands. Then she felt the loop of her lasso being slipped over one wrist. A tug, as it tightened. Another tug as it signaled her to move away into the brush. Diana did so, not because she wanted to, but because she couldn't help herself. There was nothing left in her, mentally and physically, with which to resist. She looked dully at the warriors chanting to the glowing orb. The lasso, though, compelled her to move. Her eyes stayed locked on the fire as she stumbled into the brush, the flames reaching out to her as if they were lovers. The lasso pulled her further and further from the beautiful fire until, finally, it was blocked from her line of sight by trees. Diana blinked and turned her head. She saw the figment. It held the other end of her golden lasso. Maybe the figment would give it back so she could return to the fire.

Ana didn't like what she saw. Wonder Woman looked like she'd been drugged and brainwashed. It was a good thing she had thought to use the lasso. Ana's purpose was to use it as a tool of nonverbal communication—she could tug one way or the other without tipping off the warrior chorus line. It turned out to be the only thing to which the Amazon responded.

And Ana was very glad to get clear of the fire with the creepy glow thing in it. That orb gave her a very bad feeling, in more ways than one. It made her feel sad and defeated, as if all of her best friends had died at once. Maybe those native men were burning some toxin, she wondered. The men, however, seemed to be getting off on it. What kind of substance could make some people crazy with strength and vitality while causing the opposite in others? Surely there was no such thing as a gender-biased drug; men and women just weren't that different. Having been schooled in the arts and business, Ana wouldn't have bet a drug could affect the sexes differently, but she knew it would be best to stay the hell away from that thing, whatever it was.

Ana looked around. No one had followed them, but that didn't mean the warriors wouldn't start looking for Wonder Woman as soon as they noticed her

absence. Time to move again. Ana wrapped the end of
the lasso around her wrist and knotted it, just in case.

"Come with me," she said.

Diana looked at her blankly and followed. She
didn't move very quickly—she shuffled like a zombie
in a George Romero film. If the tautness of the lasso
slackened, so did her pace.

Ana looked behind and around them constantly.
Still, no one was after them. That was puzzling, but
stranger things had happened lately.

She led her friend deeper into jungle so they were
completely cut off from the light of the fire, even from
the stars in the sky. Ana hoped the island's spiders and
snakes would keep to themselves. She was a brave
woman, but everyone is entitled to their phobias.

Suddenly, an angry cry rose from the direction of
the fire, followed by a bellowing chorus. "I guess they
miss your company, girl," Ana said. "They know this
jungle better than we do, so let's get us out of here!"

Without a word of warning, Wonder Woman
leaped into the air, jerking Ana up along with her.

Henry screamed in rage and disbelief. The woman
had been tied to the tree with her own golden lasso.
There was no way she could have slipped out of the
binds. One of his men must have let her go. Maybe
one of them stole her so he could usurp Henry's
power.

His scream activated the men. They didn't know
what the cause of their leader's distress was, but his
pain was theirs, so they screamed along with Henry,

echoing his frustration and anger. It wasn't until their leader walked to the tree and pointed to where the woman had been that they understood what had happened. Their howls and screams became louder as understanding passed among them, but the sounds died quickly when their leader began to speak.

"Who let her go?" Henry looked at the thousands of men, as if expecting one of them to step forward and admit responsibility. "We need this woman. She is the key to finding the island of Amazons, they who stand between us and victory over those who deny Ares as the one true god. Those women keep the armies of hell—our armies—under their control through seduction and treason. We have to kill them, but we won't be able to find them without that woman."

Henry walked up to the man closest to him, who happened to be Pelias. He poked his sword under Pelias's chin, clearly ready to drive it up into the man's puny brain if he heard anything that he didn't like. "Where is she?"

"I do not know," he answered.

The blade thanked him for his honesty by cutting off his life quickly.

Henry waved the bloodied sword in front of his men, letting the red drops fly off to hiss in the fire and stain the sand. He was sure none of the warriors had ever seen a man die by another's hand before. If any one of them reacted negatively, though, there was no visible sign. Henry considered that Pelias's fate was of no concern to them because there were so many more just like him. And he knew not one of them would dishonor their god by begging for his life—they would be too stupid to know when they were in danger.

Henry himself had a slightly different take on the situation, having a vestigial memory of a moral code. In cutting off the man's life, he had cut the last link to that memory. Henry looked at the blood and liked what he saw. His first kill, righteous and clean. Ares would approve. Ignorance had been no excuse for Pelias not telling Henry what he wanted to know. Maybe he should kill every one of these stupid men and deal with the problem himself. If the spilling of blood made his god stronger, it would surely do the same for him. Henry swung his sword around, intending to take another man's life, when a thought occurred to him:

If I kill all the men, Ares will think I am his rival. What makes me stronger might anger him. I still need him—I don't even know yet the extent of how he can help me—so I will play this game his way for now.

Henry lowered the sword to his side. The man he spared barely noticed that he was still alive.

Stupid animals, Henry thought. *Perhaps Ares will let me kill them once we release the armies of hell from captivity. These idiots are only good for rowing and—*

He stopped himself. Ares had given him these men for a reason, just as he had made Henry their leader. These men just needed someone to tell them what to do.

"Warriors!" he bellowed in their tongue. "I want a dozen men to guard the war fleet. The wench might try to sabotage our vessels."

When no one moved, Henry picked out twelve

men and shoved them in the direction of the fleet,
cursing under his breath their utter lack of initiative.

"You men," he said, indicating two dozen nearest
him, "stay with me. You will be my personal guards."

Then, addressing the rest of the warriors, raising
his voice so that the many thousands might hear him,
Henry bellowed over the fire, "Everyone else—find
the Amazon and bring her to me. Use the golden rope
she carries on her hip to bind her—she will be powerless once you do that. Whoever brings her to me will
be the first to learn what women are for before we invade their miserable island!"

The men cheered, even though they didn't fully understand what Henry meant. Then they descended on
the tree from which the captive had escaped, trying to
track her footprints. So many men milling about the
scene nearly obliterated the tracks, but one of the first
men there picked up the scent and began to follow it.
The others filed into the jungle behind him.

Henry looked around until Superman, lying on the
ground, caught his attention. He walked over to the
Man of Steel and, to release frustration, kicked him in
his side, good and hard. Pain shot from Henry's foot
to his brain, angering him so that he swung his blade
down, hoping to teach the fallen man a lesson for
hurting him. The sword clanged. Henry looked at it
and saw a huge dent where the blade had struck the
man. That gave him pause. Possibilities occurred to
him, ones in which this being could help him. But first
he needed to consult his god. He eyed Pelias's body.

"You!" Henry shouted at one of the men. "And

you!" to another. "Throw that body on the fire. It is a gift for Ares!"

The two warriors took hold of Pelias's hands and feet and heaved him like a sack of grain into the fire. Burning branches broke and flared, sending up sparks and ash as if celebrating the new addition. The man didn't have much fat on him, but he would burn brightly.

Satisfied with his one and only act of housekeeping, Henry gave the two men a new order. "Stay here and watch this man," he said, indicating Superman.

"The rest of you," he said, gesturing to his remaining guards. "Come with me!"

Henry started toward the mountain, followed by his dull companions. It was time again to consult the pictures in the cave.

A hot cinder popped out of the crackling fire and landed on Superman's face. He opened one eye and saw several pairs of feet leaving the area, plodding away from the fire, toward the mountain.

The fire.

Superman felt its warmth invite him to look into it. Racked with pain and overwhelmed by fatigue, he had barely enough strength to lift his head so that he might see the flames.

They were beautiful.

As Superman stared into the dancing fire, he started to remember a world he'd never known. It was a beautiful world filled with people who loved him. He looked deeper into the fire and saw his parents, Jor-El and Lara, who smiled at him.

A thought leaped to his mind: *Don't look! It's a trick!*
But Kal-El didn't have the energy to shut his eyes, let
alone turn his head away. Besides, the story the fire
told him was a good one, a story about what might
have been . . . or maybe it was an actual memory, he
could no longer tell.

The Man of Steel lay still, his eyes fixed on the fire,
as it wove for him a lifetime of memories . . .

*Kal-El runs to the tree and scrambles expertly up the
trunk, as six-year-olds who specialize in having fun will do.
He sees his father run after him, crouching over with arms
flung forward as if he is a terrible Pariwite from Kan-zass,
Krypton's sister planet. Jor-El snarls and paws the air,
holding back laughter as Kal-El shouts melodramatic curses
that he learned from his fairytale books.*

*"You will never catch me, vile beast of Kan-zass! My
faithful servants will bring me weapons with which to slay
thee! Your flesh will feed my family for months, if only I
can ever get out of this tree!"*

*With that, Jor-El falls to his knees, laughing. Kal-El is
delighted to bring his father such joy, so he plays his part to
the hilt.*

*"Laugh, you treacherous Pariwite! The harder you
laugh, the more of our purple air you will absorb into your
six lungs! Our air is specially designed by scientists like
my dad to make you shrivel to the size of a plachee nut! I'd
rather slay you with my weapons, but I don't see any servants around, so shrinking will have to do! Laugh, monster, laugh! HA HA!"*

Jor-El is helpless with laughter. He makes a few weak

attempts to mimic a Pariwite, but that just sends him into
fresh convulsions. Kal-El jumps down from the tree and
lands on top of his father as if he is tackling a dangerous
beast. His father howls, they mock-fight, and both start giggling, until Jor-El lets his son wrestle him to the ground,
triumphant.

From afar, they hear Lara call them to supper. Kal-El
looks up the hill at his lovely mother and wonders why her
hair is bright red. He blinks and looks again. Her hair is its
normal dark color.

"C'mon, champ—race you to the house!"

They run like thieves. Another glorious day in a never-
ending series of glorious days.

CHAPTER 19

Love

Had Ana not tied the lasso around her wrist, she would have been left behind when Wonder Woman leaped into the air. "Let's get us out of here!" was general enough that Wonder Woman might have flown back to the comfort of the fire, once the lasso escaped Ana's grip. But it hadn't. For a moment Ana almost wished it had because, from her position trailing below the flying woman, she was being ripped across a few ragged branches. Ana regained her wits enough to climb up the rope, hand over hand, so that her body stayed clear of the rough jungle canopy. A few scabs and bruises were a given in her immediate future, and her dive skin looked like it had been run through a Cuisinart. Still, Ana considered herself lucky.

Monkeys disturbed from their slumber screeched at the two women as they flew through the night—a most unnatural sight. Owls hooted and insects buzzed, but the sound of the angry warriors faded as they flew on.

Finally, Ana sensed that if this remarkable woman didn't rest, she might fall and take her passenger down with her. There was a promontory below. From there they could keep an eye on the men's camp.

"Diana—try to land us on that flat area," Ana shouted, pointing to the top of the rocky formation.

Wonder Woman looked and dropped, clumsily. Clearly, she'd lost a lot of strength. Ana held on tightly while she wriggled the knotted lasso off her wrist. She kept her eyes open, ready to jump if it looked like a bad end was coming.

The Amazon lost altitude rapidly—too quickly to make the top of the promontory. Ana cringed when it looked like they would slam into a jagged ledge. Her movement steered Wonder Woman away from the sharp rocks so they were able to glide free of further obstacles and down to the base of the formation. They landed on the ocean side, where the steep cliffs cradled a small sandy beach, tumbling like conjoined parachuters who'd misjudged their drop. Ana couldn't be disappointed that they'd landed below, rather than on top of the mound—it was a well-protected location. They were lucky Wonder Woman had been able to get them as far as she had. How they'd get off the patch of beach, exactly, they would have to figure out later.

Slightly dented and bruised, Ana got up and, brushing off sand, walked over to help Diana to her feet. But the Amazon didn't make an effort to rise. Instead she lay on the sand, a tumble of long limbs and black hair, staring ahead with a blank look in her eyes.

Ana dropped to her knees and wrapped her arms around the woman.

"What did they do to you? Talk to me," she begged.

Wonder Woman raised her head and looked into Ana's eyes with such a look of horror and sadness that Ana felt like crying. She had seen that look before. Years before, she was in Ireland shooting a documentary when a bomb went off outside a shopping center, killing a dozen people. One woman had lost her two daughters, aged two and three. Ana, trying to help the wounded, came upon the young mother. When she looked in the poor woman's eyes, she saw the same mixture of grief and pain that she now saw in Wonder Woman's. The look in those eyes brought up every memory of heartbreak she'd ever known. There was a world of hurt in there.

So maybe it wasn't such a good idea to talk about what the men had done to her. Ana didn't know what to do right away, but she took the lasso off the Amazon's wrist, sensing that it was humiliating for her to be held by her own rope. Diana looked at her again, but there was no sign of recognition in her eyes.

In the States, Ana would have rushed the woman to a hospital for whatever drug or psychiatric treatment was available. Thinking about hospitals brought back memories of when her brother had been in a coma. His doctors urged her to talk to him because, even though one part of his mind was shut down, other parts were still active. So Ana talked to him, hoping he heard her. She told him about all the cheer-

ful and mundane things going on in her life. It made
her feel better, after she got used to his lack of response. And then one day he came out of his coma.
He hadn't heard everything she'd said, but he knew
that she had been there for him, pulling him back to
life.

So Ana started talking to Wonder Woman. There
was no telling if it would do any good, but the effort
would keep Ana's mind away from thoughts of bugs
and snakes, until the sun rose, at least.

First she told Wonder Woman how she and Henry
had met and fallen in love, going into detail about
how they, as the world's happiest lovebirds, had
spread joy and looniness as they spun about in their
first year together. She talked about all of her wonderful family and friends, how they supported her in her
decision to start her own business, and how they all
welcomed Henry with open arms. Her dogs and cats
were funny creatures who, when Ana described them,
became real as she related stories of their adventures
and odd habits.

At one point Ana wondered why she was talking
so much about the wonderful people in her life. She
realized she was afraid. If something happened to her
she'd never see her loved ones again. That thought
made her press on with her tales—she didn't want to
leave anyone out of her oral scrapbook.

Ana was in the middle of telling a seriously silly
story about her crazy aunt who raised ferrets when
Diana smiled.

Ana noticed, relieved, and cracked wise. "Hey,

lady, quit smiling. I haven't gotten to the punch line yet."

Diana looked at her. This time her eyes opened up to her soul. She was back.

Ana gushed. "Oh, honey, I thought you were broken." She threw her arms around Diana and hugged her, rocking the Princess as she would a frightened kid.

Diana's eyes filled with tears, spilling down her cheeks. She started crying, mostly out of relief, but also to release some of the horrors she'd been fed at the men's camp. She didn't try to stop herself—she knew she had to let those poisons out of her system.

Diana felt Ana's arms around her, holding her tightly while she sobbed. She felt no embarrassment in pouring out her grief and despair—it was a step up from where she'd been. Ana cooed and comforted her until the sobs stopped, at which point she pulled the water bottle from her belt and handed it to her friend.

Between sips, Wonder Woman spoke aloud of things she had seen in the men's camp, listing horrors as they occurred to her: "Men turning into savages . . . their leader intent on conquering the world . . . forcing me to take them to Themyscira . . ."

Ana spoke up. "Remember what you told me about the oracle? She said, 'Beware of your opposites.' What is the opposite of the thing that made you this way?"

Diana knew the answer without having to think about it. "Love."

"And what did I just tell you all about?" Ana asked. "*Loooooove*," she joked, drawing the word out like she was a kid rubbing it in to a pal she was teasing. "Wow," she said with a smile, "just saying the word makes me feel better. Being near that fire really creeped me out." Ana shook her head as if she were getting rid of a pesky insect. Then she asked Diana, "How do you feel now?"

"Much better, thank you. I was hallucinating, I know, but the dreams were so real they convinced me that everything was hopeless. I thought I would be leading the world to destruction. I saw myself killing my own—"

"In that case," Ana said, cutting off a walk down Bad Memory Lane, "tell me about people you love."

Diana saw what Ana had done and approved. She needed to think about positive things to counter the evil that she'd been exposed to . . . her recent nightmare was still too fresh. So she talked about her friends. She told a funny story about Flash and a sweet one about Batman. She told Ana about her friend Julia Kapetellis and her daughter Vanessa who lived in Boston. And with each friend she remembered, Diana felt stronger. She could feel herself being healed by the power of love.

Diana knew, too, that by talking about love they were praising Aphrodite. She told this to Ana and said, "If you don't mind, I would like to thank the goddess."

"Of course I don't mind," Ana said. "I'll give you some privacy." With that, Ana got up and walked to a mango tree growing on a rocky ledge, searching the branches for ripe fruit.

Diana stood facing the ocean with her bracelets crossed over her chest. She opened her heart to Aphrodite, she who stood for goodness and beauty, grace and love.

Praying felt good. Her head cleared. The images of death and violation faded and were replaced by the warmth she felt when she was with her friends and family. Strength returned to her body and resolve regained its place in her heart and mind.

Finally, Diana smiled and lowered her arms. Finding her friend, she said, "Ana, you are a wonder. Thank Hera you made it through that storm safely. And thank you for getting me away from those men. I feel good now—you did just the right thing. I don't know how you knew what to do, but I'm grateful."

"*No problemo*. Talking about love is easy for a gal on her honeymoon," Ana said. "And, speaking of Henry, have you seen him?"

Ana had asked the question lightly, but Diana knew that she was covering grave concern. There was much to admire in this woman who had kept that question to herself for as long as she had. The Amazon also knew she would have to tell her the whole story, and not try to protect her from the truth. Ana could take it.

And so she did. Diana told how she had found Henry, about the pictographs in the cave, and how their escape attempt had turned into disaster. She told Ana about the orb and how it seemed to be possessing Henry's body, using him to lead the island men to war against her own people. She made it clear that once the orb was destroyed, it was possible that Henry would return to being the man that Ana loved.

"How will we destroy the wretched orb?" Ana asked.

Wonder Woman liked the way Ana said "we" instead of "you." She was a woman worthy of living with the Amazons.

"I don't know yet," Diana admitted. "It is powerful. It may be Ares himself. Whenever I touched it, it sapped my energy. Just being near it—" She cut herself off, shivering.

"Tell me about Ares," Ana said. She used her knife to peel the skin off a mango she'd plucked from the tree. "I read about your gods in high school, but I never thought they were real." Ana's hand flew to her mouth, as if she regretted her last words. "I'm so sorry—that must have sounded awfully rude."

"*No problemo*," Diana said, smiling. "The gods usually keep to themselves on Mount Olympus, content to relive their glory days. When they meddle in modern affairs they disguise themselves well. Only when they mix with beings of their own time do they make themselves known."

"Then do you know why Ares is causing so much trouble?" Ana asked, offering Diana a chunk of fruit on the end of her knife.

"Ares was born to Zeus and Hera, who despised him," Diana said. "Mortals fear and hate him, as well. He's murderous, bloodthirsty, and a coward. If he is wounded—and even though he is a god he *can* be wounded—he has been known to bellow in pain and even run away. Yet as unloved as he is, he has his supporters. His sister Eris, which means discord, helps him; as does his son, Strife."

"Oh, my goodness," Ana said. "Can you imagine naming your child that and sending him to school?"

"In America, he'd end up in a rock band."

Ana laughed, which lightened Diana's heart even more.

"Usually, though," Diana continued, "Ares crafts his terrors alone. He has been known to possess people, even things. He is sneaky about it, because of his cowardice. He lies, brags, and thinks he is more powerful than he is. It is because Ares was hated and ignored that he seeks attention now. In the end, he sorely wants to overthrow his father and rule Olympus.

"When countries war with one another, Ares gains power. One time, two such countries were in their third century of conflict. Their resources were exhausted from the continual back-and-forth of retaliation and retribution. The king of one country made overtures to the king of the other to stop the war and turn to peaceful activities that would help their states grow. They were at the table discussing their peace agreement when a slave came up behind the first king and fatally stabbed him. The king's generals blamed the other king and the countries fell back into their war. Hundreds of thousands more died before the fighting finally stopped for lack of men to fight it. And no one ever guessed that the slave had been possessed by Ares."

"And I bet he left the slave's body before he was slain," Ana guessed.

"That's right. Ares loves to manipulate situations, then watch while humans go after one another." Diana looked up, to the top of the promontory. "Speaking of which, I suggest we fly to a higher point. That looks like a good defensive position. From there we'll be able to keep an eye on what's going on in the men's camp."

"You feel strong enough?"

"Yes, thank you."

With that, Wonder Woman lifted Ana off the beach and flew her to the top of the promontory. There they found a flat area the size of a volleyball court from which they could survey the sky, the sea, and the men's camp. Diana peered in that direction and started visibly.

"What is it?" Ana asked.

"When I was tied to the tree, something happened. After you helped me escape I chose to remember it as an hallucination."

"What?"

"Superman," Diana said. "Superman fell from the sky."

"Kal-El—what would you say is the most important social responsibility of the people of Krypton?"

The student looks up from his history book to see his teacher, Lo-Ess. She's so pretty, he thinks, as he tries to focus on her question. Her hair is brown and wavy. Soft.

Krypton. Planetary responsibility.

"Conservation," he mumbles.

"I beg your pardon?" Lo-Ess asks. "Speak up, please, so everyone can hear." She says this with kind encouragement.

Kal-El recovers himself. He feels as if he has been dreaming, or maybe he is dreaming still. His duty, though, is to give his teacher a thoughtful answer. "Conservation," he says clearly, "with an emphasis on population control and antimaterialism. It's the only way to keep Krypton's population in harmony with the planet's natural resources and other life forms."

"Well done," Lo-Ess says.

As she moves on to detail the economics of reproduction licensing, Kal-El's eyes wander outside where the purple sky domes the beautiful landscape. No brother or sister waits for him there. He is the only child that Jor-El and Lara would have. In fact, he had been created in a lab from their genetic contributions. That they had fallen in love was a happy circumstance because they are the perfect mother and father.

The children in his school are also without siblings so they band together and pretend to be of one tribe. They make up songs and play games that reinforce their bonds, yet they never forget their singularities. Their parents are responsible breeders, as were their parents before them, as they will be when they come of age. There's a peculiar loneliness in being responsible.

Kal-El's eyes wander back into the classroom again and settle on Lo-Ess. She's so lovely, he thinks, losing himself in her features.

CHAPTER 20

Welcome to the Jungle

The Flash touched sand and immediately slowed down. He found himself on an island that was not supposed to be there. The last time he'd spoken with Batman, they'd discussed the possibility of a volcanic eruption. But from the looks of the vegetation and topography, this island had obviously existed for quite some time.

The Flash stopped, looked, and listened. An owl hooted in a pine tree. Rats scrambled around in dried leaves, looking for edible treasures. Wavelets tumbled on the beach, washing up hermit crabs that scuttled for the security of rocks. Palm fronds rustled in the warm breeze. Flash neither saw nor heard anything that indicated there was human life on this piece of earth, yet he knew in his bones that this place was where the action was—he would just have to look around some more. The top of the mountain would provide a good vantage point. Maybe Superman was there, waiting for him with a plan of attack, or at least an update on the situation.

Zipping into the jungle, the Flash ran right by a few warriors who were crouching in the brush. In spite of their new bulk, the men were still masters of camouflage. Only if they'd moved would he have been able to spot them. Sometimes speed can be a disadvantage.

He ran straight up the side of the God Mountain, ignoring the trails and switchbacks used by those less fleet of foot. At the peak, he stopped and surveyed the situation. Boats, huts, a bonfire with a few figures hovering nearby. Okay, the place was populated, but not very civilized. He spotted something red and blue near the fire. Was it—?

Flash's eyesight, though good, was not superhuman, so he ran down the mountain to get a closer look. As he ran, bolts of light flew at him. He thought they looked like fireworks—nothing to be too concerned about.

Pulling up to a stop behind the trunk of a large tree, he soon realized that the shots of lightning were very much cause for concern. Several of the laser streaks flew directly at him—only his instinct and speed kept him from being hit. Flash looked behind him to see what happened when the bolts struck inert objects. Nothing. As soon as the darts passed him they faded like tired Roman candles.

Magic, thought Flash. He hated magic as much as any other member of the team. But magic always had a master or mistress behind it, so it could be defeated if one attacked the source.

The Flash darted from tree to tree, narrowly avoiding contact with the light rays, until he was in a position to see what it was lying near the fire: Superman.

Flash's first impulse was to run over, pick up his fallen comrade, and take him to safety. But he knew it would be a fool's errand. In the split second it would take for him to lift Superman, he would be open to attack. Looking closer into the fire, Flash could see a pulsing red orb, which seemed to be the source of the bolts. Obviously, the magician's magic wand.

He scanned the island—what he could see of it from his position—and spotted a jagged point from which he would be able to watch the orb while he waited for reinforcements. Zipping over to the promontory and straight to the top, he almost ran into a couple of women.

"Hi, Wonder Woman," he said, trying to sound nonchalant. "What are you doing here?"

Diana threw her arms around Flash and kissed him on both cheeks.

"I'm glad you're here, Wally," she said. "This is big—much bigger than I thought at first." Then, remembering Ana, she introduced the two. "Wally, this is Ana Lindstadt. It is her husband I came to find."

Wally took Ana's hand to press it with his warm ones. "I'm pleased to meet you. I'm sorry to hear of your husband's disappearance."

"Oh, we found Henry Lindstadt," Diana interrupted, "but he's now an agent of Ares."

Ana's face paled behind her mask of mud and she slumped a little. Diana realized her mistake in offering the facts up so coldly. She went to her friend, putting her arms on the woman's shoulders, and led her away from the Flash.

"Dear, I'm so sorry. In trying to get information across quickly, I was thoughtless. Please, forgive me and try to ignore us—I need to fill Flash in on what's been happening."

Ana blinked, straightened her shoulders, and took a deep breath, composing herself. "There's no need to apologize. I don't want you to have to pussyfoot around me—I know what the facts are."

Diana gave Ana a quick hug. Then they both walked back to Flash to resume their exchange.

Flash's brows were creased with concern. "Ares has caused trouble before. He's a formidable foe," he said. "Tell me what happened."

"Tell me, too," Green Lantern said, walking up behind them all as if he'd just stepped out for some fresh air.

Thousands of warriors streamed through the jungle. Since they had lived there for several millennia, they knew every square foot of the island. Moving through it at night, however, was new for them. Regardless, the men applied themselves to their task with determination. Their leader had told them to find the woman—and that was what they would do.

Even the island's worst tracker would have found traces of the woman without difficulty because she left a distinctive mark: a boot print. The men had never seen such an impression before. Furthermore,

the tracks that led away from the tree where she had
been bound were accompanied by another set of
prints, also with unusual markings, also a lightweight
biped. The two were easy to follow—they left plenty
of bent twigs in their wake—so all of the men
searched along the trail. Close to five thousand filed
through the jungle like a gargantuan line of ants.

The warrior who led the way eventually stopped,
right where the line of footprints ended. He looked
around, dropping to his hands and knees so he could
investigate the ground. The tracks disappeared as
surely as if those who had made them had been lifted
into the sky. The warrior laid out the mystery to his
brothers, who stood dumbly, not knowing what to do.
None of the men wanted to assume a leadership
role—that was clearly not intended or it would have
been carved on the cave wall. But someone had to let
the rest of the warriors know that the beings were
gone. The first warrior explained to all the men within
hearing distance, who relayed the news to warriors
waiting further behind. Word passed from warrior to
warrior until everyone knew the woman they sought,
and the one who accompanied her, were lost to them.

No one moved, because there was no leader to tell
them what to do. Brows thick enough to set teacups
on furrowed with worry. After a time, though, the
men forgot why they were there. The sun was not in
the sky—they should be sleeping. One by one they
turned back toward the living center and started fil-
ing back to their houses.

They would have continued, had not one of the

men used the opportunity to gaze at the sky. The stars fascinated him, as they had fascinated humans from the genesis of the species. He even stepped out of the procession so he could stop and take it all in. The Milky Way was rich with light that night, girdling the sky with its brilliant spatter of stars. Other warriors, seeing this man looking up, stopped and joined him in stargazing. Eventually, the thousands of men were all motionless, staring up at the twinkling lights.

One of the men detected movement—not a shooting star, but a moving space devoid of stars. A black hole traveling across their sky. The shape was almost that of a human. The warrior pointed it out to his comrades, and soon, several thousand pairs of eyes followed the path of the back void. It crossed in front of other stars, bisected the Milky Way, and headed straight toward the rocky promontory on the south side of the island, near their favorite fishing spot. It looked as if the black hole landed there. The men studied the promontory and saw movement. Three or four humans were on top of the crag. One of them looked like the woman they sought.

As one, the warriors suddenly remembered why they were all out in the middle of the night.

There was no sportster rocket in sight—Green Lantern had traded that in for a small, silent hover platform with a cloaking shield for the last few miles of his journey so that he would not be detected by any unknown enemies. The near omnipotence that the ring gave him, though, couldn't change the fact that

Kyle was only human—he had neglected to create the shield so stars could shine through.

"Green Lantern!"

To say that Wonder Woman looked very glad to see him would be an understatement. In spite of that, she did not kiss his cheeks or give him a smile as she had done with Flash; instead she grabbed his arm and took him to the spot from where he would be able to see the men's camp most clearly.

"Please rescue him," she said, pointing to Superman lying on the ground. "Watch out for the fire. There is an object in it that shoots light missiles. That's what took him down."

Kyle was shocked at what he saw. Superman was physically the strongest of them all, and to see him lying there hurt was painful. He sorted through his mental scrap file for the appropriate tool in his infinite arsenal, but what he came up with could not have been simpler. He pointed his fist in Superman's direction and willed a green line of energy to shoot out to him. Once there, a giant hand formed out of nothing and grabbed Superman up. Like Fay Wray in King Kong's hairy paw, the Man of Steel looked small and helpless.

When the orb in the fire started shooting missiles, Green Lantern morphed the hand into a protective sphere so Superman wouldn't take any more hits. Then Kyle concentrated on bringing in the unconscious super hero, unmindful of the light missiles that shot at him—in the past his ring's energy had protected him from bigger nuisances than those.

But this orb was not so easily beaten. A red bolt of energy enveloped the green shield, obscuring the caped man inside it. Electric fingers raced up the length of the arm to the man using the ring and spun filaments of pain around him. Kyle screamed. His concentration broke, and Superman dropped to the ground. The red bolt disappeared as soon as Kyle's green projection did.

Green Lantern had to use all of his energy just to remain standing, he was shaken so badly.

"What happened?" Wonder Woman cried as she rushed to give him support. "That thing can't possibly be stronger than your ring!"

Kyle couldn't answer her for a minute. He felt like he had just French kissed a giant light socket.

Ana came up to Green Lantern and took his other arm. Together Wonder Woman and Ana led him to a small boulder so he could sit.

The dazed super hero looked at Ana, deep into her soft brown eyes. Again, he felt like he had been zapped by a thousand volts.

"Who are you?" he managed to croak.

"I'm Ana Lindstadt," she answered. "It is my husband who was lost down here. Are you all right?"

"Yes," Kyle said, after a little consideration. Then, looking embarrassed, he continued, "That's never happened before—I wasn't prepared for the pain. Worse, I feel rotten that I wasn't able to get Superman out of there."

"It was a good try," Wonder Woman said. "I'm sorry—I didn't realize you might get hurt."

The Flash advanced and spoke to Wonder Woman, his face a confusion of disappointment and concern. "You know, Diana, I had a hard time taking the threat of those light missiles seriously, until I saw that just now. If I try to run down and pick up Superman, I stand a good chance of getting zapped, as well. I'm faster than lightning, but I would have to slow down to pick him up."

"I know you want to save him—we all do. But the last thing we need right now is another man down."

"Agreed."

They returned their attentions to Ana and Green Lantern, just as the latter leaned forward and started to stand. But when the color drained from his face he was forced to sit back down.

"Stay put. Have some water," Ana said. She unhooked the water bottle from her belt and gave it to him.

It was just what he needed, but he only drank a little. There was no telling what the water on this island contained, and he seriously doubted if Starbucks had discovered the place yet. His ring could generate a desalinization plant if and when he got his wits back, but in the meantime, rationing the water—and the energy in his ring—seemed the prudent thing to do.

Kyle saw Wonder Woman studying him, looking for any aftereffects of his electric encounter. The young man gave her a big smile, even though he still felt somewhat jangled. The ministrations of the young Brazilian woman helped in that department. He stole glances at her, looking through the mud smeared on her face to admire her cheekbones.

If anyone had asked, Kyle would have had to admit he was taken with Ana. As his head cleared, he noted the ring on her finger. Kyle had a habit of checking out everyone's rings on first meeting—an understandable preoccupation—and resigned himself to worshiping her from afar. He noticed the sad look that lingered in her eyes, but wisely chose not to ask her how *she* was feeling.

"It looks like you wrestled with a cactus and the cactus won," he said, referring to her rips and scratches. "May I help you with those?"

Ana nodded, so Green Lantern created a first-aid kit with his ring that cleaned and patched her scrapes and cuts, then produced a neat green gadget that fused together the most annoying rips in her suit without touching her skin with even the slightest bit of heat. He wanted to use some of the water on a sponge so he could see what she looked like under all that mud she'd smeared on for camouflage, but he resisted the urge.

"Thank you," Ana said when he finished. Then she leaned in to him and planted a kiss on his cheek.

Kyle loved Brazilians.

He noticed Wonder Woman looking at him with one raised eyebrow and knew what that meant. He was back to normal—falling for young women was always a good indicator of that—so they should get back to business. Since they hadn't been able to rescue Superman yet, they needed to brainstorm and come up with another plan of action.

Kyle conjured up a green picnic table with soft

cushions so everyone could get caught up to speed in relative comfort. All that was missing to give the place the feel of a high-priced vacation spot was mood lighting and an unctuous waiter lurking under a palm tree.

Diana started to recount all that had happened by repeating the warnings she'd been given by the oracle on Themyscira, and wrapped up by telling of Superman's fall. In between, she touched on her transport to the other dimension by waterspout, the discovery and transformation of the orb, and its effects on the island men—Henry in particular. Detailing the pictographs in the mountain cave, she noted parallels between the drawings and actual events. Kyle was particularly interested in the cave drawings.

Ana added details of the orb's effects on Wonder Woman, and of how they happened on an antidote.

Flash interrupted. "The remarkable aspect of your love cure is that a pair of males might not have been able to stumble on that remedy, because men are not as open to talking about emotions."

"*Some* men," Kyle corrected, for the benefit of Ana.

"As far as the different ways in which people are affected by the orb, it may be that men react differently than women," Wonder Woman added. "Henry is possessed, but he hasn't changed into a Neanderthal like the other warriors. I was struck by a light missile, but it made me weak and caused me to hallucinate nightmares."

"Or maybe the orb affects those with superpowers differently than others," Green Lantern volunteered.

"Superman was clearly not affected the same as human men were—possibly because he is alien?"

"How is he, Diana? Were you able to tell when you were down there?" Flash asked.

Diana lowered her head."I don't even know if he is alive—when I was close enough to tell, I was under the spell of the orb. And now, ever since Ana dragged me away from the fire, I have been too aware of how easy it would be for that thing to use me to destroy the world. I'm afraid I can't go near him."

Kyle, having felt first-hand the power of the orb, tried to let her know she was not alone. He put an arm around her shoulder and said, "You haven't failed him. The best thing for all concerned was to get you away from danger, since you are key to their plans. One person cannot do all things—that's why we're a team."

Raising her head, Wonder Woman looked gratefully at Green Lantern. He saw her spirits return as she regarded her teammates.

"He's right, Diana," Flash added. "Together, we will be able to save Superman."

"What about Henry?" Ana asked. "If you get him away from the orb, do you think he'll go back to normal?"

"Good question," the Amazon said. "Let's try it and find out. It did wonders for me."

She stood and walked over to where Ana sat, then knelt and took her hand. "We will do everything in our powers to save your husband and stop Ares. We know Henry is more important to you than your own safety, but please remember that you are now important to us."

Kyle smiled, glad that Wonder Woman could so easily put into words what they all felt.

The young Brazilian woman looked at Diana with hope shining in her eyes. "What can I do to help?" she asked.

"Ana, dear," Diana said kindly, "you must wait here. Batman is on his way. It would be a great help if you filled him in on what has happened and help us keep an eye on things from here."

Kyle could see that wasn't what Ana had wanted to hear, but he could tell she would do as they asked.

"All right," she agreed. "Is this Batman as intimidating as his reputation?"

"He's a true gentleman," Kyle said, confidentially. "But don't tell anyone I said so."

That seemed to put Ana at ease. "Then I will keep an eye out for him and tell him what I can when he gets here."

Eager for something to do, Ana remembered her dive light and tore the paper label off her bottle of water. While the trio of super heroes discussed strategies, she fashioned a tiny bat mask around the head of the flashlight's lamp—a little gesture of welcome.

CHAPTER 21

Planning Ahead

Henry, although he didn't think of himself as Henry anymore—the longer he wore the mask the more he began to think of himself as Ares—walked up the mountain trail, followed by his band of idiot brothers. He was angry that none of these warriors had any initiative. They had to be told to blow their noses, for Hades's sake. But, he relented, they would row when he told them to row, kill when he told them to kill, and not one of them would stab him in the back to get his job. Loyal morons.

He thought about the man who'd dropped out of the sky back at the fire. Something seemed familiar about him, but he couldn't pull it forward to his conscious mind. Some vague notion persisted, though, that the man was as powerful as a god. Maybe that was why he had been sent to them. He was supposed to help with their mission—*my mission*, Henry thought. And that's why he needed to visit the cave again. The warriors had taken him to the cave when he'd first arrived on the island. But now that he was the leader, it was time for him to reread the ancient messages in light of recent events. He didn't remember there being a picture of a fallen man on the wall. Henry wanted to see if there was one now, and if so, how was he supposed to help with their plans?

Even though it was only his second trip up the mountain, Henry felt like he'd been there a thousand times. His feet knew every step, his nostrils identified every smell, and the stars looked so very familiar to him—pretty sparkling points of light—shifting positions to make outlines of horses trampling the earth, fire consuming buildings, men raping women . . .

Henry's head was lost in the stars for a while, as dreams of power embedded themselves deeper into his mind, pushing aside memories of his life before he found the island. Everything he'd ever known that didn't have to do with enslaving others and gathering more power was forgotten. He was addicted—"Hello, my name is Henry and I am a god"—and was seriously jonesing for some righteous retribution.

"Damn that whore for escaping," he uttered aloud. "I will make her face every torture of hell here on earth before I send her to Hades for her *eternal* reward."

As he continued up the mountain to the cave, Henry gazed at the stars twinkling over his head as they formed constellations of headless Amazons.

Flash and Kyle listened to Diana's concerns about getting too close to the orb—the bolts it could shoot were dangerous and painful to women and might transform any man into a killing machine. Flash had evaded them before, though, and he was certain he could keep dodging them.

"But as you pointed out," Diana said, "you have to slow to a stop to pick up Superman. Even if it's only for a millionth of a second, that might be enough time for the orb to throw a bolt into you."

"I can try again," Green Lantern suggested. "Now I know what that thing can do . . ."

He trailed off, aware that no one was going to agree to him getting zapped again. And he *didn't* really know yet what the thing was capable of. For all he knew it might be able to raise the dead or paint like Picasso. What they did know, however, was that it had taken down Superman without any trouble at all.

The three super heroes ruminated for a while. Each of them was eager to pull their fallen partner away from the orb, but they all recognized the need to keep from losing another in the process. Kyle picked up a stick and started sketching figures in the dirt while he thought. Just then, Diana's eyes lit up as an idea came to her—something that just might do the trick.

"Mother," Kal-El ventures as they walk along a country lane, arm-in-arm, "why do you look so young? You look younger than I. I remember when we walked along this same lane twenty years ago. I was six and you looked exactly as you do now, except that I looked up at you because I wasn't so tall. And Father—he looks the same as he did when I was young. He looks like he could be my brother."

"*Age is relative, sweetheart,*" Lara says. *She looks up at her son with adoring eyes. "You are our boy, no matter how old you are." They turn down a lane that leads to their house. "Isn't the sky a lovely purple today?"*

"*Shouldn't the sky be blue?*" *he asks, momentarily baffled.*

Lara laughs. "You have an odd sense of humor. If the sky were blue we would be in serious trouble—just ask your father, the scientist." She chuckles some more and hugs his big strong arm. "I'm so glad you never left us. What would we have done if we didn't have you to bring us laughter and love? Your father and I love each other dearly, of course, but having you in our lives has added a fullness neither of us imagined was possible. You are such a good son."

Kal-El blushes at her compliments. Lara never tires of telling him how good he is and how much he is loved; he never tires of hearing it. Picking her up, he swings her around in a wide circle, putting birds and colorful insects to flight around them. He laughs, and his mother giggles with delight. One of her slippers flies off. He sets her down so he can look for it in the tall blue grass. When he finds it, he starts a little because he thinks her shoe is yellow. This shoe is red. As soon as he notes that, it turns to yellow and he immediately forgets that it was red.

He takes the shoe back to his smiling mother, and they continue on down the lane.

Everyone agreed on the plan.

But before they took off they needed to contact Batman so they could fill him in on a few things. Kyle created a bright green virtual computer. With voice command and hand gestures, he drew a map of the island, which they had christened Goon Island. On it he pinpointed the cove, along with the precise number of warships; the promontory, dubbed JLA HQ; and what they had begun to call Boy's Town, where the fire burned and where Superman had gone down. Kyle set it up to fax and told the computer to send.

Then he transformed the computer into a video conferencing terminal. Dialing up Batman took only a second.

"Green Lantern," Batman said. "I got your fax. Good work."

"Nothing to it," the artist replied. "The Flash, Wonder Woman, and I will be heading out in a minute to go get Superman, who is hung up in Boy's Town. We were wondering if you might sabotage a few warships—like, maybe all fifty—before meeting us back here at HQ."

"I'm glad to hear Diana is safe. As for the warships, I'm sure you'll fill me in on the whys and wherefores when I get there."

"Wonder Woman and I are off to alter somebody's plans—too complicated to get into. Ana Lindstadt will fill you in on the details if we aren't back by the time you get here."

Ana stepped in behind Kyle so Batman could get a look at her. She couldn't help but give a little wave and a smile. In the green-tinted virtual monitor, Batman's expression didn't change, which made Ana a bit nervous. But she wasn't the first to react to meeting him like that, nor would she be the last.

"How do you do, Ms. Lindstadt," he said without

apparent interest. Addressing Kyle again he said, "I see the island. I'll be at the ships in 4.5 minutes. Fifty holes in fifty ships might take me another ten depending on their positions, so I'll be at the promontory in under twenty. Over and out."

Kyle looked apologetically at Ana. "He doesn't waste a lot of words."

Ana shrugged her shoulders a little. "Apparently not."

"Let's go," Diana said, stepping up and touching her hand to Kyle's arm.

"You won't be alone here long," Kyle assured Ana.

"Don't worry about me—I can take care of myself."

Kyle saluted her, grinning, then turned to his teammates.

"Meet you back here," Flash said, then zipped out of sight.

Wonder Woman and Green Lantern followed, flying into the dark sky and speeding off toward God Mountain.

Ana blinked, first when Flash turned from a solid human male into a red streak of afterimage, and again at the sight of two people leaping into the air and actually flying. It wasn't the first time she'd seen it, but it still took her breath away.

These people are a trip, she thought. *I'm glad I'm on their side.*

Ana sat on the ground cross-legged, and took up the flashlight so that she could fine-tune the image of the bat in the lamp. Hopefully, Batman would find it amusing.

CHAPTER 22

Sabotage

The Batboat skimmed across the water, faster than most people thought possible for a vessel that didn't have rockets strapped to its hull. The man at the wheel handled it like it had been custom-tailored for him, which it had been.

Batman spotted the glow from Boy's Town, passed the promontory, which was apparently now the JLA's temporary HQ, and rounded Goon Island to find the cove where the warships were anchored. He saw Ana's small powerboat in passing, and noted its location on Kyle's map.

"Oracle, come in," he said aloud, the boat's computer patching him in to his friend.

"Yo," came the voice through the speakers.

"The island looks to be volcanic, possibly active," Batman began. "There are five thousand men on it who are possessed by Ares and intent on invading first Themyscira, then who knows what. Wonder

Woman is safe, the missing man's wife is here and safe, but Superman is down, condition unknown."

"Copy," Oracle said. Batman could hear her entering data in the background.

"I'm going now to destroy their fleet," he explained. "Then I will rendezvous with the Lindstadt woman and possibly the others."

"Will you be able to maintain contact?"

"Unknown," he said. Then, "Were you able to scare off the civilians?"

"Everyone but the U.S. military. They're hard to scare."

"They might come in handy. ETA?"

"Expect choppers in an hour."

"Thanks. Over and out."

The cove containing the ships was easy to reach. Batman expected to find them heavily guarded, but as he slowed his boat to enter the channel that cut through the reef, he couldn't see any sign that anyone was there. Hanging back for a moment to assess the situation, he pulled out his binoculars for a closer look. Nothing. Just fifty boats crafted of wood, large enough to hold a hundred men apiece. Each had holes for fifty pairs of oars on either side. Whoever had made the ships apparently did not have the materials or skills to make sails. Batman noted that the craft were similar in design to those used by the Greeks three thousand years ago. Seaworthy, designed for battle.

Using voice command, Batman instructed the boat's computer to load torpedoes. With his boat maneuvered into position, he lined up his first target, then ordered the computer to fire. The missile sped toward the ship, leaving a silent trail of white under the surface of the water. It hit the boat and exploded. As water rushed into the hole, fire threatened to devour the rest of the ship, but Batman saw it would sink before it would burn.

He set his sights on a second ship, fired, and had similar results. It was a good thing the Batboat was fully stocked for battle. There were more than enough torpedoes to do in the entire fleet.

The routine destruction gave him time to think, so he ticked off facts as he knew them so that he might fit other pieces into the picture as they presented themselves: Ana Lindstadt, whom he had seen on Kyle's video image, was married to the man who had disappeared. This island, which harbored these boats he was destroying, had apparently come from a different dimension. The missing man might have been the trigger that brought the island into existence. Earthquakes were shaking the island constantly, as if a volcano was getting ready to blow. Superman was down and out, but how seriously? Wonder Woman was safe, but the missing man was an unknown. Had he been found and Kyle forgot to mention it?

Finishing off the last of the warships, Batman kept an eye out for trouble, but none came. The cove was now a graveyard of half-submerged and smoking wrecks, cluttered together like old bones in a bathtub. He turned his craft back toward the promontory and hit the throttle, slicing through the channel.

Batman turned to take a look at the smoldering

warships. Through the smoke he saw some figures running—big, hulking brutes that recalled images of yetis. As he continued to stare, however, the shapes melded into the jungle. It was possible the figures were island warriors—he considered going back to round them up—but he was expected at HQ, so he ignored them.

Minutes later Batman pulled up to the beach at the base of the formation. From his Utility Belt he pulled out a grapnel, which he shot to the top of the cliff, stabbing the pronged head deep into the rock. He grasped the handle at the end of line and flipped the switch, the mechanism pulling him up the face of the cliff to the crest of the promontory.

It was an easy feat to climb over the rock face, onto the top of HQ. Looking around, Batman expected to find Ana Lindstadt, but there was no one.

A flashlight lay on the ground. He picked it up and turned it on. It threw a tiny image of a bat onto the rocks.

Green Lantern and Wonder Woman flew to the mouth of the cave without incident. From their vantage point, Wonder Woman spotted Batman's boat heading to the cove to pick off warships. Looking down on the other side of the mountain, Kyle reported the presence of a masked man in a robe, Henry, with a couple of dozen warriors ascending toward them on the trail that led to the cave. At the pace they made, they would probably get to the entrance within a few minutes.

Smoke drifted up from the fire far below, redolent with burning flesh. Not the taste-bud tempting smell of a barbecue, but the stench of seared hair and roasted bowels, and it filled them with sadness. It signaled the first certain death on the island.

As soon as they landed, Wonder Woman grabbed up the torch she'd left on her first trip there, and had Green Lantern ignite it with a flick of a big green cigarette lighter. They raced into the cave to the wall where the pictographs were. Wonder Woman held the torch while Green Lantern created a laser tool that would enable him to sandblast the images. Starting with the picture of Wonder Woman leading the men to Themyscira, he obliterated the rest of the future narrative with a few deft strokes.

Then the earth started to tremble.

The two super heroes traded glances before Kyle started scoping out the interior of the cave. There were no reinforcing beams in sight—it appeared to be a natural formation. Wonder Woman pointed out an airshaft above them they could use as an escape route when the warriors came in, which would happen any minute.

Green Lantern then started *adding* pictographs to the wall with his laser tool. He worked at a speed that was hard to follow with the eye, a hundred times faster than he usually drew—now using the power of his ring. Every image was an excellent counterfeit of the ancient carvings, down to the effects of erosion on the pigment and texture. The first scene he drew showed the Flash running to rescue Superman from the guards posted near the fire. Then he drew Batman swinging through the trees, and members of the JLA rounding up warriors by the thousands. This last image took him a full ten seconds, but only because he drew every single warrior. He also put Ana in the picture, just for fun. Then he added Henry, out of good conscience.

The mountain continued to shake, which actually aided him by adding a realistic crudeness to the counterfeits. Kyle flipped a switch on the laser tool, turning it into an airbrush device. He wanted to make the drawings fit in with the others so that not even an archeologist would know that they differed.

As voices became audible outside the entrance to the cave, Diana whispered urgently, "You'd better wrap it up!"

There was a gap where Green Lantern had erased an image that depicted Ares sitting on the throne of Olympus. He said, "You go! Lemme finish this first—I'll be right behind you!" Kyle prided himself on always meeting his deadlines, but he frequently pushed them to the limits.

Finally, Kyle was using his real talents on the job. He wasn't just using his imagination to create weapons and gadgets, he was drawing scenes that—hopefully—would come to pass. The effort gave him an incredible feeling of power, even more than what he felt when he used the ring to fight.

In the few seconds he was alone in the cave, Kyle felt completely at peace. He was creating images that would help save the world. The sounds of approaching warriors didn't disturb him one bit.

Power surged through his body with each stroke of the ring-chisel on the wall. He didn't know if he would ever be able to go back to producing ordinary illustrations. Doing that used to give him enormous satisfaction, but drawing with the ring on this wall and then drawing with a pencil on a sheet of bristol board would be like stepping out of a Ferrari onto a skateboard. They just weren't in the same class.

Ideas came to him of other things to add to the wall. His hand was poised to start in when he remembered the approaching men. He wasn't afraid of them, but the illusion he was creating would be spoiled if he were caught in the act.

The tools on his ring-hand disappeared. Grabbing up the torch, Green Lantern flew up out of the chimney hole, just in time to miss the advancing warriors.

When Henry entered the cave he noticed there was a light burning inside. Maybe the woman they sought was there. Signaling his men to be quiet, he stole deeper into the cave, ready to do anything to recapture and subdue the woman with her own rope.

Turning a bend, he saw only darkness enveloping the wall of the Fates. Ares must have been here—how else could light in the cave suddenly vanish?

Henry took a torch from one of his men and held it up to the wall. Maybe Ares had elaborated on his plans, offering a clue as to the whereabouts of the missing woman. After all, they needed to find her before they could invade the island of women. The wall had told his men that she would betray her sisters—it should also tell him where to find her.

But when Henry read the pictures on the wall he almost dropped the torch. Was Ares playing a trick on him? Testing his faith and loyalty? Were the Fates having a joke at his expense, or had they changed their plans? Henry was shocked by the story carved on the wall: The woman escapes and joins some friends in odd costumes. One of these people—he looks like a giant bat—destroys the fleet of warships. Another runs to rescue the man who fell from the sky. A figure that seemed to represent Henry is shown with a woman, but not the woman he was seeking. His warriors are rounded up by the flying people and turned back into human men. The mountain explodes, sending clouds of gas and ash pouring down its sides.

This was not what Henry expected to find on the wall. The only other time he had seen it, when he first arrived on the island, the images had resonated with truth. They had mapped out a bright future for Henry and his idiot army. Now he had come hoping to see new information from his god—details, perhaps, that would point him to the missing woman. Instead, he found himself looking at an account of a future completely changed. Previously, the wall depicted their victory over the nations of the world, but now it illustrated their defeat on their own island at the hands of five strangers.

If there was more to the wall of Fates, he couldn't read it, because a massive jolt knocked him off his feet and sent him sprawling onto the floor of the cave with his brothers. If the drawing of the volcano erupting was to come to pass, he didn't want to be in the cave when it happened.

"Run!" he ordered his men—and it was a good thing he told them, because they were so dumb they would have just stood there.

The men ran past huge cracks that split the stone walls. Chunks of rock fell down around them, bouncing off the cave floor and into newly-formed fissures. A fumarole shot hot gas into the narrow passage. The men stumbled over each other to escape entombment in the cave. When the walls collapsed, sealing it off, the men were running down the mountain. Henry ran with them, momentarily forgetting his self-assigned godhood, his robe flapping around him.

When Wonder Woman heard the men approaching, she had propped the torch against a wall. Leaving Kyle to finish his business, she had flown up through the chimneylike passage so she could assess the situation from a ledge overhanging the entrance. She saw the last of the warriors enter the cave.

The mountain wasn't shaking at the moment, but the frequency and increasing violence of the tremors concerned her. Another good jolt could cause an avalanche, or worse. She prayed the men inside the cave would not be trapped.

Kyle shot up through the chimney, flushed with excitement. "That was a *blast*!" he exclaimed. Then he

projected a giant green neon sign into the air, a signal
to the Flash.

"What did you do down there?" Diana asked, unable to disguise the concern in her voice.

"I drew this great scene of the mountain exploding
with a giant volcano. Warriors fleeing, all hell breaking loose—I wish I had a photo of it."

Diana's heart sank. "But Kyle, you were only supposed to draw—" She was cut off by a powerful
quake; the strength and suddenness of it would have
knocked elephants off their feet.

Boulders, dislodged by the jolt, rolled down the
mountain straight toward them. Green Lantern's neon
sign disappeared as he and Wonder Woman flew into
the air above the avalanche of rocks and boulders.

Shouts came from inside the cave. The pair looked
down to see warriors fleeing, followed by Henry with
his robe billowing behind him as he held the mask
tightly over his face.

The cave heaved in on itself, clattering boulders
momentarily drowning out all other sound. When the
jolting stopped and the dust thinned, the super heroes
drifted back down, standing on rubble that used to be
the roof of the cave.

Wonder Woman turned to Green Lantern. "A volcano?!"

"I like drawing explosions. I guess I got carried
away," the young artist confessed.

"Let me tell you how fickle the Fates can be, Kyle,"
Diana said, apprehension creeping into her voice in
spite of her best efforts.

"I guess I don't believe in them," he said, defensively.

"They are hard to comprehend. The best I can do is I don't *not* believe in them," Diana admitted. "Proving they do or don't exist is as impossible as arguing the existence of any number of paradoxical constructs. In other words, there may or may not be a cause-and-effect correlation between the drawings and actual events, but so far, the possibility that they may relate seems very strong, which is why we came up here in the first place—to insure that Flash will be able to rescue Superman safely. It is not wise to tempt fate by introducing an unknown into the equation."

"Huh?"

Diana elaborated: "Because you drew a volcano erupting, we just might have to deal with a volcano, Kyle."

"Oh," he said. "Sorry." Kyle's stomach sank at the possibility that he might have seriously jeopardized their safety. He never would have drawn something so childish on a whim. Some force had made him draw it, but he didn't understand how that could have happened. Then he remembered what he would have drawn next if he hadn't been interrupted by Henry and the warriors. Sweat broke out on his forehead and he lost a little color from his face.

Wonder Woman saw Green Lantern's discomfort so she put her arm around his shoulder to console him, always quick to forgive. "You didn't know. I'm sorry I didn't explain it better before we went in there."

"Listen," Kyle said, "I don't want to sound like I'm making excuses here, but . . ." He paused, searching for the right words. "Something took over my reason in there and made me draw the volcano erupting. I couldn't admit it to myself at first . . ."

Diana's eyes opened wide. "I believe you. If Ares is here—and I believe he is—he could easily have influenced you."

"But then I remembered what I wanted to draw next, and that made me realize something was very wrong."

She steeled herself and asked, "What was it he wanted you to draw next?"

"Ares rising from the mouth of the volcano."

So, Ares planned on making a personal appearance after all—perhaps because a monkey wrench had been thrown into the works. Several monkey wrenches, starting with the formidable Ana.

"Was there anything after that?" Diana asked.

"I'm not sure—this is more of an impression than a real memory," Kyle said. "I think I was supposed to restore the earlier drawings, but in my mind it was because they were historically significant and I shouldn't have altered archeological artifacts. My subconscious was going to town against what I had set out to do."

"That was Ares, not your subconscious. I never should have put you in the position of being exposed to his influence. I think you were vulnerable because you worked directly on one of his magical sites."

"Oh?" Kyle said. He thought about it. Then, "A tattoo artist I know once said that working so intimately on a person's body transfers energy through the contact. A lot of her customers have intense personalities or they're stressed from the pain of the process. She gets pretty uptight after working on skin all day, so she dispels it after work by meditating.

"I wrote it off as jitters from the buzz of her machine, but now I think I get it. Ares got under my skin, so to speak, through my ring."

"There may have been some effect as well from that electrical hit you took earlier," Wonder Woman added.

"You think?" Kyle asked, absently.

The Amazon looked down at the shambles that now filled the cave, then at the collapsed chimney entrance.

"This confirms my suspicion that there is a direct link between the drawings and all these events. We *could* dig down in there and erase the eruption like you did the other drawings, but who knows if it would work, or if it actually needs to be done. The wall probably doesn't exist as such anymore. The future events described on the wall might now be locked in place."

"Too many *ifs*," Green Lantern said.

Diana could sense Kyle's remorse that Ares had influenced him. She was glad, though, that he had told her what had happened down there. Shame could be an impediment, while the free exchange of information helped keep things in perspective. Diana had forgiven him—he would find the time to forgive himself later. Right now there were other things to think about, but that just brought a new concern to the foreground.

"When you drew Flash running in to pick up Superman . . ."

Green Lantern finished her thought. "I didn't show Flash leaving the scene with him. It was something I was going to do, but . . ." He broke off with a heavy sigh, filled with regret and defeat.

"Ares is powerful, Kyle. There was no way you could have known he would manipulate you down there," Diana said, hugging him to show her support.

Looking down at Boy's Town, he said, "I wonder how the Flash is making out."

CHAPTER 23

Snafus

After Flash agreed to meet Wonder Woman and Green Lantern back at HQ, he ran straight down the cliff face. Then he zipped into the jungle, zigging and zagging around trees and brush. He even tripped lightly over some quicksand. *Charming place*, he thought.

The Scarlet Speedster took a roundabout way to Boy's Town so he wouldn't run into any warriors. As he approached the fifty warships, he spotted Batman's boat taking aim at his first target. Halting long enough to watch the fireworks, Flash noticed a pair of warriors jumping at the concussion from the blasts. He assumed they would run to their leader to tell him what happened, but, well, he could run faster.

Soon enough, he was at the perimeter of Boy's Town. The fire still burned, filling the air with a very bad smell. *Barbecued human*, Flash thought.

When he edged closer to the fire, the orb shot light missiles in his direction. They sliced into the night air, disappearing as soon as it was clear they wouldn't hit their target. "Nice to see you again, too," he muttered under his breath.

Parking himself behind a thick palm, Flash could see Superman lying near the fire, and noted that he had changed position slightly. Of course, the guards might have moved him, but the two louts didn't look like they had enough gumption to yawn, let alone move a man who was lying peacefully. Wally's heart thumped a little harder with the certainty that his old friend was alive and that he'd be all right if Flash could cart him away from that malignant little peashooter in the fire.

Flash considered the time. According to Wonder Woman, as soon as Green Lantern redrew the images on the wall of Fates so that there was an image of him rescuing Superman, he would be able to do so safely. They had estimated five minutes to get that much of the job done. To the Flash, five minutes was a long time. Having the ability to move and accomplish things quickly often left him feeling frustrated as he waited for the rest of the world to catch up with him. Still, he knew how to put extra time to good use, so he decided to study the orb further.

A trembler rocked the island. It was mild, maybe a 4.5, but he didn't like the constant seismic activity. It could be a precursor to something greater.

He peered at the orb. When the trembler had shaken the place, it glowed a rich steady red instead of pulsing as it did normally—if normal could be used to describe anything about that orb. When the jarring stopped, it resumed its throbbing. Obviously, there was a connection between the two. If only he could figure out some way to teleport the nasty little pill into some backwater black hole where it would never be seen again. If the real JLA HQ was online, that might have been possible. Maybe they weren't to the point where they could target an object on Earth and place it at a point that far away, but they might have been able to do *something* with it. Flash made a note to himself to talk to the Atom and J'onn about that later.

But now he had to deal with the situation at hand. No use dreaming of tools he didn't have access to for an entity that might not respond, anyway. This thing was magic, and magic didn't work the way regular things worked. Magic cheated.

It hurt the Flash to do so, but he looked at Superman lying by the fire, helpless. He saw the Man of Steel twitch and open one eye to stare into the flames. With a heavy heart, Flash wondered what his old friend was thinking.

Kal-El catches up to Lo-Ess on the common in front of City Hall. Somehow, the scenery doesn't fit in with this place on Krypton, but it is charming anyway. Clapboard and brick buildings with colorful awnings and planters surround the grass-covered square; flags and bunting grace an unoccupied band shell in the center. The grass is blue—at least that part is right. Children throw disks to each other while adults read or sip beverages in the warm afternoon light. Music fills the air, even though there is no apparent source.

Kal-El has caught up to Lo-Ess in other ways, too. No longer her pupil, he is her lover. Somehow, he has grown older than her by a few years, which causes him to wonder how that could happen, but, as his mother always says, age is relative.

"Lo-Ess, how did you get to be so beautiful?" he asks her. He has asked her that a thousand times. She never has an answer for him other than the blush that colors her cheeks.

The slender young woman takes his hand and leads him to the band shell. Trees rustle in the soft breeze, their shiny leaves tinkling delicately against each other like tiny wind chimes. Another perfect day.

She sits on the steps on the shell and pulls him down next to her. They kiss, and it feels as magical as the first time they did so. The sound of tiny hands clapping gradually gets their attention. Looking around, they see children lined up, applauding their love.

Kal-El stands and takes a bow. The children cheer and whistle, some stomp their feet on the blue grass and yell "Encore!" Kal-El pulls Lo-Ess up to him and slips his arm around her waist. It feels so natural, as if the comfort of it connects him to everything he's ever held dear. It links him to his parents, his life on Krypton—it feels like Krypton itself, like a necessary part of him.

The couple wave to all the cheering children and parents, happy to exhibit their natural love that had been out of style on their planet for so long. A red balloon escapes the custody of a little girl. The breeze blows it over to Lo-Ess, who reaches out to take its string. His eyes seeing only the color red, Kal-El suddenly panics and slaps her hand away so that the balloon rises over their heads and sails away.

The spectators gasp. Is this the end of Krypton's most famous love affair?

Lo-Ess rubs her arm where he had slapped it, her face filled with worry and hurt. Kal-El takes her arm and raises it to his lips, covering it in kisses. A smile warms her face; he falls in love all over again.

The children cheer, and their parents heave great sighs of relief.

Kal-El wants to stay in the moment forever.

One thing Wally West had to remind himself of, periodically, was that he was not invincible. Yes, he ran faster than bullets—he could even catch them in his bare hands—but it was still possible, although the chances were next to nil, for things to penetrate his synthetic suit and puncture him.

When another volley of blazing projectiles flew past him, Flash knew he had to take care. As fast as he was, so were they, and it was possible one or more could catch up to him. His success at avoiding them so far might be as much due to luck as talent, so he tried a little experiment.

Flash whipped out an arm from behind the tree. *Zing*—a light bullet whizzed by. Then he flicked out a leg, an arm, more legs and arms—*zing zing zip fssh zoom!* He was fast, but so was the orb. Joe Blow wouldn't have seen a thing as Flash played chicken with the light darts—maybe a flicker of air—but the orb seemed to almost anticipate his moves. *There is intelligence behind it*, Flash thought.

Checking the time, he calculated that Green Lantern

would be almost done redrawing the wall of Fates so that Flash's rescue operation would be successful. Wally didn't know if he believed in such mumbo jumbo but, then again, he wouldn't have believed a red ball could have turned a bunch of passive island guys into an army of bloodthirsty goons. So, assuming that Wonder Woman was right and the drawings channeled some kind of sympathetic magic that made the representations come true, then she could have had Kyle draw the orb turning into a garden snail so they could have called it a day. He wished he'd thought of that earlier, but . . . the unwritten rules of magic might not have allowed it, anyway.

He looked up to the mountain and wondered what was taking Kyle so long. The artist ought to have finished by now but, to make sure, Flash would wait for the signal. A moment passed and then—

A big green neon sign, something that would have looked more appropriate on the strip in Vegas, appeared near the top of the mountain. It read GO MAN GO!

There was no way to time his move to avoid the light darts, so Flash just went for it. In an instant he was kneeling over Superman to pick him up. But instead of getting a little help from his friend, Superman unconsciously backhanded him as if he were swatting a fly that disturbed his slumber. Flash flew into the jungle until a tree stopped his trajectory.

That's when the light from the orb caught up with him.

Ana was terrified, but she knew better than to struggle against her captors. That would only be a waste of energy that she might be able to use later. Besides, there were too many of them—thousands, perhaps. A hundred or more had come swarming over the lip of the promontory like pirates in an old-fashioned swashbuckler, only much bigger and way uglier. Fortunately, they hadn't noticed her knife still strapped to her leg. Hopefully they would keep not noticing until she had a chance to put it to good use. One thing she knew for sure was that if she was to be tortured by a thousand men, she'd rather use it on herself than suffer at the hands of these monsters. The thought wasn't suicidal—it was pragmatic.

"Hey, where are you guys taking me?" she asked no one in particular. "We going to see Henry? I hear he's your leader. You guys sure look like you need one."

Not one of the goons paid her any attention. A buzzing mosquito got more of a reaction than her words did. Ana, on the other hand, felt calmer by talking out loud. None of these men understood a word she said, and they didn't seem to mind, so she kept right on talking.

"Hey, stupid," she called to the man right in front of her. "Yo, Einstein—hey." She nudged him with her foot, and he turned to look at her. "Trying to kill, enslave, and waste people is a real dumb thing to do. Who raised you? Would your mother be proud to see you pumped up like a Muscle Beach steroid boy? No. She'd be wringing her hands, asking you why you didn't finish school and become a dentist like she wanted. Then you'd be home at night instead of tromping around on an island kidnapping innocent women."

Einstein didn't respond. Instead he turned away from her and continued marching toward Boy's Town.

Ana picked on the man carrying her. "Hey, Hercules. I know you think Henry is all that, but you have to stop worshiping him now. Because as soon as he sees me he'll remember how much he loves me and he'll snap back to normal. Beauty tamed the Beast, Prince Charming woke Sleeping Beauty with a kiss, and I will reclaim my Henry. To make it up to you I'll put an ad in the local paper. It'll read, INSANE COMMANDER NEEDED TO LEAD GOONS ON MISSION TO EN-SLAVE HUMANITY. MUST BE OVER 21, PHYSICALLY FIT, AND COMPLETELY OUT OF YOUR GOURD."

Henry wasn't insane. Surely he would remember his Ana and come out of whatever trance he was in as soon as he saw her. After all, talk of love had restored Wonder Woman. When Henry saw the real deal he would remember, and that's all there was to it.

"And even if Henry is brainwashed and doesn't recognize me—which I'm sure will *not* be the case—there are bona fide super heroes on the island who will come and get me as soon as they realize I'm missing. You guys don't stand a chance. They can fly, create machines you've never thought of, and kick your island asses with their super hands tied behind their super backs."

Since not one of the goons understood her, all her words started to sound a little desperate and nutty. Only crazy people talked to themselves, which was essentially what she was doing. Ana decided to save her energy and do what she could to stay calm, instead concentrating on her breathing and studying the captors closest to her.

They stared ahead blankly, moving like dutiful automatons. *They don't look like they have one brain between them,* she thought. Then she realized something. *That's it. They act as if they share one mind.* Ana had seen many species of fish that acted similarly— fusiliers, for instance, schooled in the thousands, hanging in the sea calmly one second, then darting in unison at a sharp angle, as if they had all been goosed. Then they would all stop instantly, hang a bit, and angle off again when the mood struck, a swiftly changing curtain of shimmering fish.

Flocks of birds, hordes of insects, sometimes even mobs of humans acted synchronically in certain circumstances. Somehow she found the warriors a little less frightening when she considered this aspect of their makeup. Their uni-mind would make them easier to fight hand-to-hand, if it came down to that.

Ana searched the sky to see if there was any sign of her new friends. Nothing but a shooting star. Those used to give her a thrill, but now she was disappointed because the star didn't wear a colorful costume and swoop down to save her. She wondered if Henry was looking up at the same sky, and if so, what did he see when he did.

The horde of men trampled the jungle, carrying their trophy back to their leader.

Running past a bullet train in France, Flash salutes a little girl who waves to him from one of the windows.

Through the glass he can see her grin and chatter to her companions who crowd the window to get a look. He slows to keep pace with the train, then turns a dozen cartwheels just to show off. The kids clap and cheer, but he hears none of it.

He hears the pop and crackle of a bonfire.

It is a friendly sound. It reminds him of sitting in front of the fireplace on cold evenings, popping corn with his Aunt Iris, pretending they are on a camping trip. From Wally's swiftly changing perspective, the memory takes on the quality of a still life—he and his aunt seem to move as if they are drugged. As he dwells on the scene, however, he becomes a part of it, sitting cross-legged next to his adoring aunt. But even as he basks in the warmth from the flames, he feels arms lifting him up so he can run. Pumping his legs furiously, he waves good-bye to Aunt Iris and speeds off, through the walls of her house and out again over the rolling hills of the French countryside. It doesn't matter that the sounds of the popping fire don't fit the scenery— Wally's pleasure in running allows him to disregard such niggling details.

He feels most alive when he runs. Perhaps he can speed like this forever. Why stop? The world moves too slowly. It is boring, watching people and objects creep along as they do.

But he is not dull. He is not slow. Flash grins, and pumps his legs even harder.

CHAPTER 24

Inhuman Nature

Batman jumped from tree to tree, covering distance almost as easily as he did in his native Gotham City. He had to take care that his cape didn't snag on branches, but he learned to compensate quickly. He thought of the fictional Tarzan, swinging from tree to tree like a great ape, but he felt more like a flying lemur, spreading his wings and gliding to his next perch.

Catching up to the troop of warriors was fairly easy—they'd be a hard crowd to miss moving en masse as they were. And there was Ana Lindstadt, slung over the shoulder of one of the goons. They were heading straight for Boy's Town. Batman peered up at the mountain, which continued to shake and shiver. He spotted figures moving down the side, maybe twenty-five or thirty men. Sitting in the crotch of a pine tree, Batman reached into his belt and pulled out a small pair of binoculars. Two dozen men, under the apparent command of a man wearing a mask and robe. Interesting. They, too, were probably heading to Boy's Town.

The Dark Knight considered swinging down from the trees and snatching Ana out of their clutches. That would work, but then what? He wouldn't be able to maneuver through the trees well with an extra 130 pounds, which would leave him wide open to attack by several thousand tree-climbing men. He figured, and rightly so, that in any place that had coconut palms and nesting birds, the locals would be adept at shimmying up trees. Catching them off-guard would be helpful, but it was not likely anytime soon.

Batman had no choice for the moment but to follow the men and wait for a better opportunity.

"My ring is fine, I am fine, and you will *not* carry me back to HQ," Green Lantern stated.

"I'm just concerned," Wonder Woman said, "because when you worked on the pictographs, Ares was able to tap into your mind through your ring. It may not be all that safe to use right now."

"No offense, Diana, but if any of the other guys saw you carrying me back to HQ in your arms, I'd never hear the end of it."

"This shouldn't be an issue of pride, Kyle. As a member of the League you have a responsibility to—"

"Look," he said, cutting her off. "I know it's stupid and irresponsible, and I'm just being a male chauvinist jerk, but I *will* get back there on my own steam."

It seemed to Wonder Woman that when any of the team butted heads, it was usually over petty business that should have been resolved by the application of common sense. It would be safer for her to carry Green Lantern back to HQ, but she could see that Kyle would not bend on this point. All she could do was hope for the best and let the Fates weave their will.

"Okay—I'll see you at HQ," Diana said, then took to the air solo.

Green Lantern hadn't let on, but he was also concerned about possible corruption in his ring. Something, maybe it *was* Ares, had gotten control of him when he was in the cave. It had manipulated his mind and, through it, the drawings on the wall. He hadn't intended to draw an erupting volcano—why would he want to do that? While he was drawing it he'd told himself that Wonder Woman's theory was stupid— that it wouldn't matter what he drew on the wall, the only thing it might affect would be what the warriors thought when they saw it. She didn't know for sure if there was cause and effect at work there.

Kyle stopped his thoughts, realizing he was buying back into the same ideas he'd had in the cave. What he should be doing was finding out if the ring had, indeed, been infected by the red bolt or by contact with Ares in the cave of the ancient drawings. And there was only one way to tell.

Concentrating, Kyle visualized an image he'd seen in a magazine. In response, his ring projected a beautiful green actress.

Satisfied, he got rid of the fabrication. Looking at his ring, Kyle noticed it looked a little dull so he huffed on it and rubbed it shiny on his uniform. What a glorious ring.

And who the hell did Wonder Woman think she was? Even *suggesting* she fly him back to HQ was humiliating. He wasn't a bit ashamed to realize that, yes, a lot of that had to do with that fact that she was female. Accepting her as a fighting partner had been difficult, if he remembered rightly. She was a formidable fighter, but she should be leaving the dirty work to the men. Her good looks were spoiled when she threw punches, gritting her pearly whites. Kyle wouldn't take a ride from her unless he absolutely had to. Who the hell did she think she was trying to make him look weak?

Kyle caught himself again. He was being puerile. Wonder Woman was only concerned for his welfare. Well, even he had a right to be childish once in a while. He was under a lot of stress. He would allow himself his feelings.

And since he was in a childish mood, he materialized a prop from his past: a big, cartoony cannon, circus-style. He climbed in, and blasted himself out. He shot by Diana, who was flying gracefully in the predawn sky, and almost forgot there was anything more to the island below than tropical flora and fauna. His animosity toward her disappeared for the moment.

Kyle hurtled toward the promontory and again hoped that Diana was wrong about his ring. Proving her right by splatting on the hard rock surface of the promontory would be a costly way to lose an argument. He visualized a giant green net on top of HQ, and there it was, shooting out ahead of him from that very handy ring. The human cannonball hit the net, bounced like an expert, and took a bow, covering up his look of relief, as Wonder Woman touched down seconds later.

Green Lantern saw tracks all over the plateau, and quickly pieced together the story of what had just happened by which footprint crossed over with the other. His giddiness at emulating an old circus hero vanished.

"Ana's gone!" he said. "It looks like the warriors came up over the side and took her!"

Diana saw the glow from the flashlight with the tiny Bat-Signal fixed on its lamp. She walked over to it and, picking it up, saw familiar footprints. "Batman's gone after her," she told Kyle. "He may not know yet about the orb. He's human, and he's male— it might be able to do to him what it did to Henry."

Kyle bristled at Wonder Woman's implication that men were overly susceptible to the power in the orb. He turned away from her, polishing his ring, which pulsed with a newfound energy.

Since stealth and caution were a matter of routine with Batman, the warriors never saw him as he followed them to Boy's Town. He stayed in the canopy of the trees, clear of the firelight so that no one might pick him out.

He could see a lot from that vantage point, though. Superman was lying on the ground near the fire. He looked asleep, not dead, which was good, but not good. Superman was not the type to sleep on the job—there must have been magic at work. Then, almost concealed behind a copse of trees, Batman saw a man dressed in red, hanging by his arms from a tree so that his feet were a meter above the ground. Actually, Batman had to guess at where the feet were because they were flailing so fast in the air, they were only a blur. *The Flash.* Wind generated by his cycling legs caused nearby brush to bend back as if it was being blown by a powerful fan. If anyone cut the ties that held him suspended, it was possible that he would hit the ground running and never stop. *The Red Shoes*, only for real.

Thousands of warriors milled around the camp as if waiting for orders. Normally, such a large number of men would be divided into groups, each of which would have a leader and a chain of command. Ultimately, one man might run the show, but he would do so through subordinates. On this island, it seemed, there was only one leader for the many thousands of men. Batman followed their stares to see who it was that commanded such an unwieldy army.

The masked man walked into view, carrying his sword and flanked by an entourage of two dozen goons.

Batman knew about masks. Tribal cultures that existed before the ancient Greek city-states formed were known to perform human sacrifice to keep the gods at bay. Greece had its share of volcanoes, earthquakes, floods, and other natural disasters that the ancients credited to the gods. Fearing death, populations offered up human lives to the gods in exchange for peace. Perhaps because of an evolved respect for human life, or maybe less respect for the influence of the gods, sacrifices eventually featured animal, rather than human, victims. Priests directed the citizenry to give their gods the inedible bits of animals—hooves and entrails—while the humans ate the meat. The gods later blamed the fall of the Greeks on their greed with regard to making sacrifices.

But the lines of this mask—with its sepia tints that could only be dried blood—told the Dark Knight that this was a mask that harkened back to the days when the gods were still getting the good stuff—humans.

Just then, the warriors Batman had been following arrived at the camp. The one who bore Ana set her down for the masked man's inspection. Batman watched as the man took off his mask, the better to see her with.

He had long blond hair.

That must be Henry, Batman thought. *Ana's missing husband.*

"Henry!" Ana cried, delirious to see her husband. "I'm so glad you're . . ."

She trailed off, uncertainty invading her as soon as she looked in his eyes. Those were her Henry's eyes—but they weren't. She had never before seen him look at her so cruelly, and a shiver of fear went up her back.

Henry spoke to his men angrily, pointing to Ana with clear contempt. She didn't know what he said because he addressed his men in a foreign language. Still, she got the gist of it: he didn't recognize his own

wife and he was royally pissed off. Wonder Woman
had told her Henry had changed, that Ares possessed
him. But what they had between them was so
strong—maybe she could make him remember her.

"Henry! Henry, my love! I am your Ana. We're on
our honeymoon. We came here to scuba dive, but you
disappeared to this island. Someone has taken your
memories, but you have a life that is full of people
who love you! Come back to me! I can give you love;
this monster Ares can only give you hate! I—"

Before she could finish her plea, Henry walked
closer and slapped her hard across her face. The hard
crack of his hand promised to leave a bruise. Ana
made no sound, but her eyes welled with tears.

"Stop your bleating," Henry said in English. "The
only reason I don't cut off your head right now is because I just thought of a use for you."

Henry put on his mask again and turned to his
men, switching effortlessly to the ancient tongue.

Ana saw him gesture to the man who had carried
her. The man started toward her, hands out as if he
were going to grab her. At the same time, Henry
started lifting his robe. *What's he going to do*, Ana wondered. *Rape me? Show these goons how to do it?*

Ana's head darted around as she looked for her
best chance of escape.

At that instant, a powerful tremor jolted the island.
Most of the men, except Henry or any who could grab
onto a tree, fell. Ana tripped forward, automatically
clutching at her husband for support. As he glared
down at her with searing hatred, Henry's sword arm

cocked above his head as if he would hack her from his side if she did not loosen her grip on his robes. Terror unclenched Ana's hands so she dropped and hit the ground. There she lay, stunned—shaken more by Henry's venomous stare than by striking the hard dirt.

Another violent tremor etched a deep fissure into the earth between Ana and Henry and his men. Boy's Town tore apart as if two giants were rending cloth. Had she not been knocked down already Ana might have fallen into it. Red-orange magma filled the fissure and crept up toward the surface.

Henry stumbled back, self-preservation superseding confidence in his own omnipotence. The earth roared as the fissure deepened and stretched, threatening to cut the island in two. Fire belched up out of the gaping crevice.

Shouting to his men in the ancient tongue, Henry gesticulated wildly to them with his sword, pointing to Ana on the other side of the fissure, and then into the flaming gate to hell.

Ana didn't need an Ancient Greek–English dictionary to know what he was saying. She could feel the goons eyeing her as if she were the proverbial sacrificial virgin, so she picked an escape route and ran.

Warriors scrambled to both ends of the fissure, racing to places over which they could leap, or to limbs that would lead them through the trees. The fissure, about the length of a football field, was twenty feet wide at its middle, but tapered toward its ends. Warriors leaped over these narrower splits and ran toward Ana, shouting and hefting their

weapons. Behind her was the beach, that stone-age
bachelor pad littered with palm fronds and fish guts.
Beyond that was the ocean. Ana was a good swim-
mer, but these men looked strong. If she could only
get to the boat . . . but that was a long race she knew
she wouldn't win.

The knife. Ana reached down and unlatched it
from its sheath. She might not be able to last long, but
she would take as many with her as she could. Positioning herself, Ana took some deep breaths and
waited for the goons.

"Come on, you big imbeciles! The first one to touch
me gets—"

Just then an arrow zinged by her head, close
enough to tickle her short-cropped hair. *Not only are
these men jerks,* she thought, *but they don't fight fair.*
Spears landed within feet of her, and more arrows
sliced the air. Dropping behind a cluster of fallen logs
that served as makeshift benches, Ana prepared for
the onslaught. The warriors ran closer, unafraid of her
six-inch blade. Calculating her chances, she came up
far short of survival. With death looking so certain,
Ana felt two things happen inside her: she became
very calm and, at the same time, was overwhelmed
with enormous regret.

Then, seemingly out of nowhere, a dark figure in a
flowing black cape swung down like Tarzan, snatched
up Ana, and disappeared into the trees.

CHAPTER 25

Kings of Pain

Henry watched the man in the cape and cowl snatch the woman away from his men. The sphere of Ares shot light missiles at the black figure, but throngs of warriors running between the fire and the swinging man took the hits intended for the intruder. Henry's anger at losing the woman faded rapidly—he didn't need her for anything, she was just sport. The man who looked like a bat interested him, though—he might prove to be a valuable addition to his small collection of oddly dressed strangers.

And what might this stranger's reaction to the lightning bolts be, once he was hit? Would he dream, like the running man and the man in the red cape did? Or would he grow strong and hateful, like Henry and his warriors? Was he a man or a god? Henry couldn't wait to find out.

"Catch them! Don't kill them—bring them to me alive!"

At that moment, several warriors ran up to their leader from out of the jungle. He recognized them as the ones he had sent to guard the warships.

"Leader!" one of them shouted. "The warships have all been destroyed!"

Henry almost cut off the man's head at hearing the bad news. But then he remembered that decapitated heads couldn't talk.

"How did that happen?" he asked.

"There is a creature who is half bat and half man. He shot lightning at the boats. They all sank."

Turning to consider the batlike man escaping through the trees, Henry realized he would have to change his plans. Invading the island of women was no longer possible by leading his horde over the sea.

Ares, however, seemed to have delivered Henry other tools with which to conquer his enemies—the man whose skin broke steel, the red running man, and this new one. Once the bat-man was shot by the light missiles, he might become a useful member of Henry's new, smaller army. He didn't quite know how to utilize the creature's skills yet, but that would become clear after his warriors caught him. With a few light missiles and a little coaching, he and the other two that the fire held captivated might just help Henry challenge Ares. After all, why should Ares have all the power when Henry was doing all the work?

The sphere shot a red flame directly into Henry's head. In between screams of pain, Henry could feel it scouring his mind for knowledge. It learned of Henry's last thought and buried a hot poker of pain deep into his brain. Henry collapsed, unable to control his muscles. He twitched and jerked as little bolts and sparks of light popped and sizzled out of his eyeballs and mouth.

When the flame finally dissipated, Henry's feelings were unchanged. Maybe Ares had read his mind and tried to control him with threats of more torture, but the god had only succeeded in turning Henry into a mad man. One who wasn't afraid of more pain.

"Who died and made *you* queen?" Kyle demanded.

The mental picture of her headless mother pumping a river of blood from her neck made Wonder Woman flush. It wasn't what Kyle had meant to evoke with his comment, but the image was too real and recent for Diana to keep quiet in her mind. She calmed herself with a reminder that something was wrong with Green Lantern ever since he'd worked on the pictographs—maybe ever since he'd tried to rescue Superman.

"I'm just saying," Diana said in a low, soothing tone, "that your attitude shift seems to indicate that your ring may have been invaded by some of Ares's energy, and it might be better if you stay here and save your ring for—"

"What! I'm supposed to stay here and knit doilies while you get all the glory of rescuing the other guys?" Kyle began. "That's a little backwards, isn't it? You're just a female. I have more power here," he jutted his middle finger in her face, simultaneously showing off his ring and insulting her, "than you have in your whole body!" Kyle looked her up and down.

"And why do you insist on wearing that slut suit all the time? Cover yourself up, for Christ's sake!"

Diana's concern escalated to certainty that Ares had gotten to Kyle through his ring. Ordinarily, he was one of the most considerate, levelheaded men she knew, but this outbreak put her in the terrible position of possibly having to subdue him.

When she had flown back from the mountain to HQ, she had seen that Superman was still a captive of the orb, as was the Flash. Diana wanted to leave and do something to help the two of them, but Green Lantern was turning into more of a problem by the second. Tying him was always a possibility, but she didn't want to forfeit her weapon before going into battle. So she decided on another tack.

"That's a good suggestion, Kyle. Tell you what—if you give me the ring, I can make myself a robe. Cover myself up."

"No." Kyle immediately hid the ring with his other arm and twisted around so she couldn't grab it.

Diana couldn't help but think of the all-powerful ring of Sauron in *The Hobbit*, which drove any who possessed it to madness. It gave her an idea.

"If you want to keep your ring, you should stay here with it. If you go down to the fire or anywhere else on this island, the others may try to take it from you."

Green Lantern looked at her with suspicion. "Tell me that while you're holding your lasso." He knew she couldn't tell even white lies while holding it.

"All right . . ." Diana unhooked her lasso and held it in front of her. "If you leave the promontory, someone will try to take the ring from you." That was a fact, because she intended to take it from him herself if she had to.

"Okay," he said. "I believe you now. I won't go anywhere."

"Thank you, Kyle." Wonder Woman hooked her lasso back on her hip. She was tempted to have him make his promise while holding onto the golden rope, but decided that wouldn't help the situation. Besides, the young man looked sufficiently freaked out. Her heart ached for him.

"I'm going to see if there's anything I can do for the Flash and Superman. Please stay here."

Glancing back as she took off into the air, Diana saw Kyle hugging the ring—*Precious*—to his chest, rocking back and forth on his haunches.

Keeping his word was not necessary, because he had given it to a woman. Women were dishonest creatures, incapable of acting with honor, so it was all right to lie to them. And why should he believe that someone would take his ring? She had just said that to keep him on the promontory so she could come back and steal it herself.

Suddenly, a rumble and crack shook the island. Instead of leaping into the sky, Green Lantern unlocked his knees and rode it out as if he were on a jitter machine in a fun house. The quakes didn't scare him. In fact, he rather enjoyed them. They felt like power, and he liked power. The quakes made him feel connected to what was going on all over the island.

Shouts from Boy's Town caused Green Lantern to look down from his position on the promontory. Men were running into the jungle, chasing something or someone. He couldn't see what it was, but all of a sudden, Kyle had a burning desire to participate in the chase. After all, those men looked like they were having fun. He had to be careful, though, that the woman wouldn't come back and steal his ring.

Scanning the sky, Kyle located the woman in red and blue flying over the camp. He was glad she was gone—now he could think. Walking over to the edge of the promontory, he could see that Flash was hanging from a tree, but running as if for his life. Superman seemed to be stirring—he probably didn't need to be rescued. And he shouldn't be helped by a woman, anyway. That woman should be kept at home. She shouldn't be flying around, practically naked, fooling men into thinking she wanted them by displaying her skin like that. What a tramp.

Now he could see who the men below were chasing. Another tramp, the one called Ana. Batman was helping her. That pompous, arrogant son of a—

The flying woman was on the other side of the mountain where she wouldn't be able to see him leave the promontory. Feeling emboldened, Green Lantern imagined he was flying, and he was.

"Wow. What do you do for an encore?" Ana asked, looking at the man in black who had just saved her from earth's ultimate barbecue.

Batman didn't answer. Warriors were swarming

beneath them and some were shimmying up the very tree they were in. He pulled a Batarang out of his belt and quickly explained to her how it worked.

"Throw it above and to the right of what you want to hook onto, then pull tight and swing." He threw it for her so she could see how he did it. Then he handed her the end of the rope and said, "Go!"

Ana went. It wasn't exactly smooth sailing—she scraped a few tree limbs on the way—but her tattered and patched dive skin saved her from getting too scratched up. And a few scratches were far easier to take than the alternative.

When her feet touched a limb sturdy enough to hold her, she snapped the rope, which unhooked the Batarang and sent it reeling back to her. As Ana pulled it in she saw Batman close behind her, with hundreds of goons chasing him below. Fortunately, the brush was thick, so the warriors' progress was slowed.

"Go!" Batman shouted.

"Where?"

"My boat is at the base of HQ. We'll have to swim to it."

The trees would only take them so far. They would have to run to the water, then swim. And from what Ana could see of the wave motion, the current would be against them.

That turned out to be a moot point, because there at the edge of the low jungle stood Green Lantern. Ana hooked the end of her Batarang around a limb and swung a last time, leaping into the air, then falling and tumbling on the sand. She ran up to Green Lantern as Batman came in close behind her.

"Can you get us out of here, but quick?" Ana asked, looking back to see warriors gaining ground.

"Sure," Green Lantern answered. Pointing his power ring ahead of him, he created a floating platform. They stepped on and rose so fast that Ana's stomach dropped, as if she were on an express elevator.

"HQ is too easy for the goons to access," Batman said. "Let's go to my boat and get Ana to safety before we do anything else."

Green Lantern nodded, but when the platform started moving, it didn't glide toward the beach, but back toward Boy's Town.

"Kyle, what are you—" Batman looked down and didn't like what he saw.

The platform Green Lantern controlled wasn't green, but red.

CHAPTER 26

Trick or Treason

Wonder Woman flew over Boy's Town low enough to
see what was going on, which meant she was within
range of the light missiles. Several came directly at her,
and she deflected them with her silver bracelets. In between assaults, she got a good look at the situation. Superman looked as if he were coming to—he was
propped up on one arm, looking into the fire—which
made her glad that he was physically all right. *But is he
one of them now?* she wondered. And there was Flash,
churning the air like a propeller as he hung by his wrists
from a tree. Freeing himself from his binds would be
only a matter of vibrating himself through the ropes, so
his mind must have been altered. He was facing the orb
that stilled cooked in the fire. Apparently that was what
was really holding him there.

At one point in her irregular orbit she saw Henry
walk up to Superman and talk to him. It would be nice
to hear what the man said, but she didn't have super-

hearing like the Man of Steel did. Just as she thought that, Superman looked up at her. His eyes flared red and beams shot out. Her wrists deflected the beams without her having to think about it before turning to get out of range. She had engaged in battle with Superman once before and had no desire to do so again. This was bad.

And it got worse. Flying back to HQ to check on Green Lantern, Wonder Woman spotted him with Batman and Ana on a platform that glowed a rich red and was headed straight to Boy's Town. Batman and Ana appeared to be immobilized in some red substance that extended up from their feet to their waists. Wonder Woman flew straight toward the floating red prison, intending to knock out Green Lantern. But as soon as she got close Lantern enveloped the structure in a red force field. Wonder Woman, unable to change her trajectory, hit the shield with a hard thud. The ground rushed up at her, but she was able to recover before she collided with it. Watching her from within his transparent red bubble, Green Lantern sneered.

That was it, Wonder Woman realized. Every other member of the JLA was now captive or under the influence of the orb, along with Ana and Henry. The island was splitting at the seams, the orb looked to be no less powerful than before, and there was no way to rescue her friends without being caught herself. And HQ—the real HQ—was off-line, so getting reinforcements or help from there was a no go. The cave of pictographs was—

Wait!

The oracle in the mountain had said, "What is written comes to pass—what is passed becomes the past."

That's it! Diana thought.

She flew in a wide arc around Boy's Town to avoid colliding with any light missiles. Then Diana headed back to the far side of the rumbling mountain, where the cave had fallen in.

"How are you feeling?" Henry asked in English. He sat on his haunches, looking down through the holes in his mask at the man who could bend steel blades with his skin.

"Wonderful," Superman answered. "Lo-Ess and I are in love . . . we have been for years. Our romance is famous all over the planet. Krypton is beautiful this time of year. My parents, my friends, they love me . . . but . . ." He looked into the fire. There he saw the glowing red orb, but in his mind it was a cool green, a lovely emerald in the solar system it inhabited. "They said something about how the planet is unstable and—"

Superman saw his green home explode into billions of pieces, shooting out in sprays of shrapnel. Those remnants of his planet would become the meteors that could kill him on Earth: kryptonite.

"Lo-Ess! NO! Mother! Father! My home!" Superman cried. He flinched at the exploding fragments, but recovered when the green shards turned out to be as insubstantial as his dreams.

He had just lived an entire alternate life, from boyhood to adult, as Kal-El, beloved son of Jor-El and Lara

on Krypton. Hearing about the demise of his family
and home when he was the adopted child of a loving
couple in Smallville, USA, Planet Earth, was one thing,
but seeing it after he had lived a lifetime there in his
mind was entirely another matter. Everything the orb
had let him see and feel was as real to him as his life on
Earth—perhaps more so because these visions were at
the forefront of his thoughts, pushing aside his old
memories.

"No!" he cried again. In spite of his dazed condition,
his impulse was to grab all the shard figments and re-
shape his beautiful planet—press it back together like a
broken vase and hope the seams didn't show. But the
shattered pieces faded, and Superman was left looking
at—but not seeing—the angry red orb in the fire.

Henry cut into his misery with mocking laughter.
He pointed up at Wonder Woman, who came into
view from behind the tops of trees now and then, deflecting light missiles with her bracelets. "See that flying woman up there? She's the one who blew up
Krypton. You need to teach her a lesson. Do something and bring her to me."

As Superman stared up at his teammate, his eyes
glowed with hatred until hot red beams shot up at
her. His aim was true, and he thought she would
surely catch on fire, but she held up her wrists defensively and reflected the beams out over the jungle
where they did no harm. Superman couldn't believe
how purely evil this woman was—she didn't even
have the courtesy to die when he wanted her to. His
angry eyes followed her even as she disappeared be-

hind treetops. Unlike on Krypton, he could now see through the trees.

"Can you fly, too? I bet you can, considering how you dropped in on us here," Henry said. "If you fly after her and bring her to me, I will reward you with whatever it is your heart desires." He was doing his best imitation of the devil without meaning to. "What is it you would like to have?"

"I want Krypton back. I want my planet and everyone on it to be alive and well."

"And you shall have that," Henry cooed. He leaned in to Superman conspiratorially. "All you have to do is bring me the woman. Don't kill her—that would be bad. Just tie her up and bring her here. Then you can sit in front of the fire and see your parents and all of your old friends again."

Superman almost registered that Henry was offering not life, but the illusion of it. But the influence of the orb was such that reason eluded him, and the false memory of his happy life on Krypton made him ache for its return. He gave a great sigh and looked at the orb in the fire again, hoping to see Krypton.

"All right, I'll bring you the woman."

Then he leaped into the air and headed to the mountain.

Ana strained against the red stuff that bound her to the platform.

"Save your strength, Ana." Batman peered around them, accumulating data. "Right now there's no point in struggling."

"I know you're right," she said, trying to relax. "But I don't think I have ever been this pissed off. I really want to hit something. Or somebody." She eyed Green Lantern, her first target of choice.

The edge of Batman's mouth turned up a bit. Even though he was in a jam, he couldn't help but admire her spirit. "He's possessed, and by the looks of this color shift, I'll bet it's Ares who did it. Green Lantern is one of the kindest people you could hope to meet."

"Yes, I met him before he changed. I think he was even a little sweet on me."

Ana considered Green Lantern again. "Maybe I can use that," she said. "Kyle . . ."

Green Lantern, who now looked like he should be called Red Lantern, turned his head to her. "What?"

"You like me, don't you?" she said teasingly, doing her best to emulate the mating call of a drunken sorority girl on spring break.

"I want you," Green Lantern admitted. That his sexual desires overshadowed his other needs was not surprising—he was, after all, a primal version of himself.

"You can have me if you let down this casing. I want to take off my wedding ring; I consider my marriage to Henry null and void because he tried to have me killed. That is such an unattractive feature in a man. You wouldn't do that to me now, would you? I think not! Maybe I like you because you're not wearing a scary mask and waving a sword around, I dunno, but I do think you look mighty fine in that red and black suit of yours."

Green Lantern slowed the platform's movement to

a stop. The words the woman said intrigued him. He walked over to her and brushed the back of his hand lightly on her cheek.

"In Brazil," Ana toyed, "I would have to fight off the most beautiful women to keep them from getting your attentions. You are *mui belo*."

Batman looked on, obviously struck by Ana's composure.

Ana started talking softly, hypnotically. "I saw how you looked at me before and I can tell you, it made me glad. To see that someone such as yourself could find it in your heart to want me . . . I am so pleased. Just think of the future we could have together, you and I. Making love when the spirit moves us, sharing our love with friends and family . . . I will bear you children who will love you as much as you will love them. Little *crianchinhas* with curly black hair like your own who coo and laugh when you tickle them. Your love for them and me grows with each day. I will love you more deeply than you ever thought possible, healing old wounds and soothing your tired soul. . . ."

Her words had a visible effect on the young man. Kyle's eyes dilated, as if he were watching this idyllic future play out in front of him. The red in his outfit and in the floor of the platform began to turn brown, on its way to green.

"Kyle," Ana said softly, "please let us go and I will throw away this wedding ring. It means nothing to me now."

The hard casing that immobilized Ana evaporated in an instant, although Batman was not surprised to

see he was still imprisoned. The suddenness of the release threw Ana off balance—she had to steady herself to keep from falling. Batman reached out to give
her support, but thought better of it lest Green
Lantern think he was putting a move on her. Green
Lantern reached out for her instead.

"Thank you, Kyle," Ana said, rubbing her legs to
get the blood moving again.

"Do you mean it?" asked Green Lantern, "Will you
love me forever and bear my children?"

Batman saw Ana cross her fingers behind her back,
a sign that she was going to lie.

"Darling man, I can think of no one else I would
rather be with." She ran her fingers along his jawline.
"You are as handsome as Adonis."

"Aren't you going to throw away your ring?" He
looked at her left hand, then into her eyes, as if testing
her for truth.

Ana was superstitious about her ring. She had
promised Henry she would never remove it from her
hand. She truly believed that if she took it off, her
marriage would be in jeopardy. That possibility,
weighed against the certainty that Green Lantern
would revert to Red Lantern and take her and Batman
to Boy's Town, helped her make a decision. Their
lives were worth more than a ring and a superstition.
She grasped her wedding band, a simple platinum
ring with *All my love, Henry* inscribed inside, wriggled
it off her finger, and threw it. A hole opened up in the
force field around the platform allowing the small
symbol of her love to sail out into the low jungle.

Green Lantern watched the ring fall into the brush and smiled. The woman was free, and he was now free to pursue her. She stood close to Batman, whose lower body was still immobilized.

Kyle reached out to Ana and she took his hand. Then he stepped closer to her, which practically put them both in Batman's face. Wrapping his arms around her slender body, he kissed her full on the mouth.

An involuntary shudder ran through Ana's body. Kyle felt it and pushed her back, suddenly aware of how she had tricked him. No one could betray him like that! He instantly visualized imprisoning the traitor in a red box that would squeeze her to death. But—

He fell twenty feet and hit the earth with a hard thud.

The wind knocked out of him, Green Lantern looked around, then up.

Batman was hanging from a tree on the end of a Batarang, suspended like a spider on a thread. He held Ana with his other arm. A tiny glint of starlight reflected off something in his hand. The power ring.

A motor whirred as the Batarang lowered Batman and Ana to the ground. The caped man let Ana drop the last few feet so he could get a better grip on the ring. As soon as his feet touched solid earth he held the Green Lantern's power ring up between his finger and thumb. "I'm going to have to call a time-out, Lantern," he said, before slipping the ring into a pocket on his belt.

Wonder Woman dug furiously at the rocks that sealed the cave. Now that Superman was awake and obviously possessed, she had to work fast. She shoved, threw, and kicked rocks and boulders down the side of the mountain, but there seemed to be an unending supply of them.

Herakles had cleaned the vast and filthy Augean stables—how had he done it? He'd diverted two rivers to wash them clean. Looking around, she could see no tool or instrument of nature she could use, so she went back to clawing at the rocks with her hands.

As she reached in to tug at one large piece of mountain, Wonder Woman sensed—rather than heard—Superman coming in for a strike.

Keeping her back to him and timing her move, she waited until he was almost on her, then she jumped out of the way. Her instincts had been right—Superman smashed into the boulder she had been trying to pry loose. Had she been in front of it, she would have been torn in two. As it was, he shattered the one ton piece of earth into small fragments. *Thank you, my friend,* she thought. Two mighty rivers could not have helped her more—the wall with the pictographs she sought was now open to the air. Turning, she faced her teammate.

"Superman, you are possessed by Ares. He has poisoned you with hatred fed to you by that—"

The Man of Steel sailed in a powerful arc, backlit by thousands of stars in the tropical night, and came at her again with his fists tight in front of him, as if he would batter her flat into the side of the mountain.

Wonder Woman reached for her lasso and made a quick loop, tossing it in the air and twirling it over her head as if she were a cowgirl picking out a steer to bring down. As soon as Superman zoomed to five feet in front of her, she hopped back and slipped the lasso around him.

"Stop fighting!" she commanded him. "Be calm!" Her voice was amplified by fear; there weren't many beings who could take her down. That this one was her old friend made the situation even more terrifying for her.

Superman stopped, as she had told him. He calmed down, which gratified Wonder Woman because she hadn't been sure that her lasso would overpower the hatred he had consumed from the orb. She wondered if he even knew about her lasso. Superman, in his right mind, would never have let himself be trapped so easily.

"I'm so sorry, my friend," Diana said, as she held tightly onto the other end of the lasso that now controlled her comrade. It upset her to use it on him, or anyone she loved. The lasso dominated. Wonder Woman used it only toward good ends, but still, the lasso took from people their own will. It compelled them to be truthful, and to use it on a friend was a violation of that friendship.

Superman, however, was at least partially possessed. She looked at him closely and saw hatred still seething in his eyes.

"Why do you want to kill me?" she asked.

"You destroyed my home. Everyone I know and love was on that planet. I have never known any other home," he cried. "You killed two billion innocent people—everyone on the planet Krypton but me. For that you will die."

Wonder Woman knew how he felt, and that everything he said was true to him. She had watched the orb in the fire and had believed the stories it had shown her, even the future horror of her killing her own mother.

Ana's love potion was going to be in high demand that night.

"You believe that is the truth, but it is a lie. I will help you to remember your real life."

With that, she closed her eyes. She held the lasso tightly in both hands, letting her thoughts travel through it and touch Superman. Images of Lois, Clark's adoptive parents, his friends at the *Daily Planet*; sound bites with Flash, Green Lantern, Batman, and herself—she fed them all through her lifeline to Kal-El. Any memory they shared that had to do with friendship, compassion, or love became fully realized in her mind, then she shared them with Superman through their magical link. Lois was uppermost in her thoughts, how she wisecracked and grinned; how she loved Superman with all her heart. Diana found herself talking and smiling as she spun her remembrances with her old friend.

After a while—she didn't know how long, but the sky was starting to lighten in the east—she heard:

"Diana?"

Wonder Woman opened her eyes to see Superman looking at her. The red glow of hate was gone from his baby blues.

"What happened?" he asked.

In the distant background, the sound of helicopters grew nearer.

CHAPTER 27

The Going Gets Weird

"Run!" shouts a voice.

Flash doesn't think that is necessary—he has never stopped running. Metal hounds race after him, propelled by rockets. Instead of tails they have flames shooting out their backsides. Their barks sound like the screech of metal grinding on metal. When they snap their jaws, sparks fly from their clanging mouths. Their feet don't even touch the ground—they rocket above the earth with their legs tucked under them. Devil dogs. One of them snaps at his heel, but misses.

"Run!" shouts the voice again, this time from within his head.

Okay. It is what he does best, but he is starting to feel dizzy. Food. A body needs food to keep going, just like those devil dogs need gas hoses up their butts to keep them fueled. When was the last time he'd put away a tray of hamburgers? It seems like a year ago.

He runs past a burger joint, a doughnut shop, a row of

taco stands and fast-food huts. Not fast enough. The robot dogs are gaining on him. No time to stop and eat or they will eat him. Their sharp fangs can devour him in half a minute, even though they can't digest his flesh. Does he have any meat left on him? He looks down, but all he can see is the ground whizzing by underneath him. His yellow shoes are just a blur.

Green Lantern—his suit indeed green again—lunged at Batman, furious that he had stolen his ring. Ana gasped, Batman ducked, and Green Lantern landed on his comrade's back. When Batman stood, Green Lantern hooked an arm around the older man's throat and tried to choke him. Batman took a step forward, reached up to hold Kyle's arm with both of his, and snapped forward, throwing him down to the ground like a sack of rice.

Kyle sat there stunned for a moment, then got up to battle again for his ring. The hatred in his eyes was plain—he would kill anyone to get his ring back.

Batman flipped open a compartment on his belt and pulled out a small black pellet. Activating the air filter in his mask, he cracked the pellet's casing with a flick of his thumb, then lobbed it in front of Green Lantern. The gas that spilled out of the little bomb penetrated the young man's system immediately, dropping him first to his knees, then to the ground. Unfortunately, he hadn't been able to warn Ana to hold her breath and she passed out as well.

Batman stood over the unconscious pair and looked around, considering his options. There were warriors approaching, still hunting them. He reached into his belt for another pellet—this time a stink bomb of rotting vegetable matter. He popped it open and waved it in the air to mask any scent they might be emitting. Then he spread his great cape over his fallen companions and crouched next to them, hidden like a black hole.

Warriors came within 10 feet of them, sniffed the air, and moved on.

When Wonder Woman was satisfied that Superman had regained his sense of self, she loosened her lasso. Sitting close to him on the rocky side of the mountain, she hooked an arm around his broad shoulders and pecked his cheek with a kiss that expressed her relief at his recovery.

"I was worried about you, my friend. I felt so helpless when there was nothing I could do to get you away from that orb. Its magic is powerful and must be respected."

"I won't argue with that," Superman said. He looked up into the early morning sky, picking out the constellation from which he had come as a baby. There was longing in that look. "I lived my whole life on Krypton while down there. The orb created my planet and all the people on it just to seduce me into becoming its slave."

"The orb's power was helped along by your own imagination and desires," Wonder Woman explained. "I saw things in the fire that hypnotized me with loveliness when it wasn't showing me horrors, using my fear against me." She looped the lasso and hooked it back on her hip. "Flash is caught by the orb now, running for his life."

Superman started to rise. Wonder Woman grabbed his hand to stop him as she jumped up, blocking him.

"That's not the way. We have to fight magic with magic."

"How? We are not magical beings."

"No, but we can use Ares's own magic against him," she said. "We must clear out these rocks so that wall there is exposed." She pointed out the top of the wall that was tattooed with pictographs.

The moonless sky was still dark, but Superman saw what she wanted. He didn't ask for any explanations, but started heaving boulders out of the caved-in hole like a machine. The two of them worked faster and more effectively than Herakles's two rivers.

The chop of helicopter blades grew louder as they worked. Wonder Woman prayed they could resolve their problem before the military arrived. Otherwise more innocent people might be put in danger.

Henry searched the sky, waiting for the man with the S on his chest to return with the woman who wore the W. Then he looked out toward the dark jungle where a man with a bat over his heart had scooped up the dark-haired woman. He lifted the mask and took off his robe so he could look down at his own chest. Aside from the piece of coral that hung from his neck, it was rather plain. Its bulk was impressive, yes, but maybe an A carved in blood might inspire more fear. It just might give him the power of Ares.

Henry drew the blade of his sword down diagonally across his torso. There was pain, but he welcomed it. Then he started, remembering that the orb could hear him plot. But it pulsed quietly in the fire, apparently unconcerned with Henry's thoughts of emulating Ares. It had been his thought of usurping power that had triggered the painful red flame. With that realization, Henry carved the other side of the bold A, and then, as he finished it off, an image of Ares sitting on the throne of Olympus filled his mind. He smiled. Blood dripped down his chest, striping him with Ares's favorite color. He pictured himself sitting at his lord's side. Truthfully, he'd rather be sitting in the throne—

A red flame leaped out of the fire and licked the wounds on his chest.

Sitting next to Ares is good enough for me, he thought, shutting his eyes tight so he could fix the image in his mind. The red flame retreated. Henry thanked Ares for his compassion by spreading his arms out and arching back so that his god might see the tribute gouged in his chest. Then he prayed for strength.

When Henry opened his eyes he looked into the blotchy shadows of the jungle. The man with the bat on his chest and the black-suited woman would be delivered to him soon. Between that night creature— once the orb made a real man out of him—and the flying man with the red cape, he would have some interesting lieutenants.

Henry looked over to the running man hanging from the tree. A lightning bolt blazed on his chest, a symbol of Zeus. And the little bolts on his cap reminded him of Hermes's wings. Those two symbols disturbed Henry. The man was garbed in red, Ares's color. To whom did this man belong? If Henry abused him, would one of these other gods come to avenge him? All he wanted to do, really, was find a use for him. So far the runner displayed no skills that would be useful in combat. What good was running? That was what cowards excelled at. Henry supposed he could execute people by placing their heads underneath the running man's feet—they would be trampled to death in seconds. That would be fun to watch, but kind of a hazardous operation. The man's legs were pumping so fast they could not be seen. Henry briefly considered hacking the binds that held him suspended, just to watch him shoot away. The whirring sound his legs made was starting to get on Henry's nerves . . . but the man might run to Zeus or Hermes and tell those gods what Ares was up to.

Except for the red eggbeater man who hung by his wrists from the tree, Henry was alone in Boy's Town. And that shouldn't have been. By this time, warriors should have brought him the bat-man and the muddy woman in black. The flying man should have brought him the flying whore. There should be people for him to command. There should be—

Suddenly the ground beneath his feet began to shake again.

The rumbling mountain tumbled more rocks and boulders down into the excavation, but Wonder

Woman and Superman were faster than nature, if the tremors were, indeed, natural. Parts of the wall were completely exposed now. Superman understood immediately how the images related to the events that had happened on the island. *And if Wonder Woman says the wall is magic,* he thought, *then it's magic.*

She had passed along what the oracle on her island had told her:

What is written comes to pass—what is passed becomes the past.

"The original images carved by Ares's agent and the ones redrawn later by Kyle came true," Wonder Woman explained. "Kyle wiped out future events and replaced them with images favorable to us—at least until Ares infected his thoughts through Kyle's power ring. But Kyle *was* able to alter future history. What we didn't realize at the time was what the second part of the oracle's message meant, 'what is passed becomes the past.' If we had, I would have asked Kyle to erase the image of the orb then and there."

"You passed by the drawings of things that had already happened, so they became the past," Superman mused. "The past, then, is not immutable here."

"We need to wipe out the image of Henry bringing the orb out of the water," Wonder Woman said.

Superman used his laser vision to eradicate the pictograph, sweeping his red gaze over the chiseled rock, smoothing it out as if with a sandblasting tool. As soon as the last outline of the orb was gone—

CHAPTER 28

Tropical Paradox

The color leached out of everything, leaving nothing to see but stark bright blankness. A column of white light stormed down from the heavens into the top of the mountain. The mountain didn't just shake—it exploded.

Henry looked around, dazed, as if awakened from a very scary nightmare. His eyes were drawn to a dwindling cook fire where, in his dream, a roaring bonfire had burned. Hadn't there been something in the fire that gave him power?

Looking at the top of the mountain with only a passing interest, it occurred to him that he might live longer if he ran to the ocean. But death looked certain. He could be scorched alive by the coming heat blast, or boiled alive when the volcano's fury reached the sea.

So Henry decided to watch the horrible cloud race down the mountain to consume him.

"Hey, you!"

Henry turned his head. The red eggbeater man stood near the edge of the encampment. But he wasn't running. Should he be?

"Are you Henry Lindstadt?"

"Yes."

The man in red zipped over, pausing long enough to lift Henry without harming him. Then he sped off into the jungle, away from the oncoming cloud of gas and death.

The explosion blew Wonder Woman and Superman half a mile away before they recovered enough to fly back into it. The air was hot, and stank of poison.

"What just happened?" Superman shouted. "Did erasing the orb send us back in time?"

Diana looked at the shift in the skyscape. It was four degrees shifted from where it had been before the blast. "No!" she called back. "It sent us back in *place*. We are now back in the dimension that this island started out in."

"So any history that happened as a result of the orb being discovered is now in an alternate reality?"

"That, or it didn't happen at all, I don't know." Wonder Woman checked her memory. Her recent experiences seemed as if she had dreamed them. She concentrated on recalling every detail she could so they wouldn't be lost, the way unremembered dreams were.

Superman, on the same wavelength, did likewise. Those who forget the past are doomed to repeat it, but neither of these beings was about to let that happen. They flew in silence, mentally logging their experiences.

Batman was about to rouse Ana and Green Lantern with yet another pellet from his belt when the sky turned white again. He guessed, correctly, that they were jumping to another dimension, possibly back to the one from which the island had originally come, but not necessarily. A glint on the ground caught his eye. Ana's ring. He pocketed it while he studied the sky.

Seconds later, when the top of the mountain blew, he fell back down, covering his companions with his dark cloak.

He knew that the persistent and escalating tremors indicated that a pyroclastic eruption might be occurring. If that were so, searing clouds of hot ash would be rolling down the mountainside in clouds big enough to wipe out entire sections of the island. Millions of tons of ash, the stuff that built this island in the first place, could be dumped on them.

Batman popped a capsule under Green Lantern's nose. He woke, woozy, but obviously himself again. "Where am I?"

He was tented under Batman's protective cape and couldn't see a thing. Batman pulled out the power ring from his Utility Belt and pushed it at Green Lantern. "Put it on, quick! We need a force field around as much of the island outside of the mountain as you can generate!"

Kyle didn't ask why, he just did it. An impenetrable force field appeared, arching over the island from the beaches to the base of the mountain like the top half of a big green doughnut. And just in time—ash and rock started pouring down on the field, creating a thunderous roar and clatter.

Henry looked up to see an avalanche of cloud tumbling down toward them at what must have been 100 miles an hour. This man who carried him moved far faster than that. That was interesting. Still, it looked like it was time to die.

"I had a dream and you were in it," said the man in red. "You weren't exactly on the side of the angels, so you won't mind if I don't trust you, will you?"

The boiling red, black, and gray cloud of ash and debris was almost on them. Henry just looked at the running man as if he were an unusual bug.

In spite of carrying Henry's weight, the man outran the roaring demon cloud, even though he looked as if he'd been running all night. And then, suddenly, there was no reason to keep running. The roar became muted, as if they were in a shelter. Looking up, Henry could see that they were. Above them was a huge green protective shield. Rocks and boulders banged and thudded on the hard, semitransparent surface.

The man in red put Henry down and regarded him. "What do you remember about tonight?" he asked.

Henry tried to think, but the roar from above made it hard to concentrate. Just moments ago he had been almost as powerful as a god. Warriors obeyed his every command, although they were a rather stupid lot. Weren't they going to . . . something about an island of women . . . a terrible weapon . . .

But his mind devoured the memories as quickly as morning eats nightmares.

"Nothing," Henry replied.

The man in red looked into his eyes, apparently searching for something Henry didn't have. Then he picked him up in his arms again and sped further into the jungle.

Looking up at the rocks and ash piling up outside the shield, Henry wondered how long the thing could hold up. Then he looked at the running man and thought, *What's the hurry?*

Wonder Woman saw the green shield go up over the island. "Thank Hera," she murmured.

Then, in the thick rising cloud of ash and heat, she saw a form taking shape. "Ares! He's finally showing himself! We've got to get to the orb before he does!"

Superman heard her. His eyes resolved the shifting and swirling contours of the cloud until he saw the god, only partially substantiated as yet. "Any ideas?" he asked. Diana knew Superman deferred to her when it came to Greek deities. She definitely had more experience with this fellow than he.

"Ares must be violently angry to show himself like this. He is a coward, willing to let others fight for him, and reluctant to put himself at risk. But, Kal," she said, remembering Ares's sphere, "he's only a problem right now because the orb still exists. When you erased it from the cave wall it wasn't destroyed—we merely nullified the act of Henry bringing it to the island. It is probably back in the place where he first found it, in the ocean. We have to find that thing before we forget what happened!"

As they circled the erupting volcano, Wonder Woman realized she couldn't remember where on the reef they had first found the orb. "Kal," she said, "your eyes will be able to find it, probably within a hundred feet of the shoreline."

Superman started scanning the reef that girded the island, his search for a hot spot in the ocean confused by a multitude of superheated boulders ejected from the volcano.

"You say it affected Henry when he touched it— made him stronger and more hateful," Superman said. "Do you think, since fire activated it, that freezing would do the opposite?"

"It's our best shot," Wonder Woman agreed. "I hope this dimension has poles with ice caps—that it's a whole world, rather than a detail existing in a void."

"There's only one way to find out," Superman said, "providing I can withstand contact with the orb long enough to fly it away." He pointed to a spot in the reef that lay directly in line with an approaching flow of hot ash. "There it is."

They both flew toward it.

"If I'm right about its having been put back in its place before Henry retrieved it, the orb is currently in its less active state, but it's still dangerous. Be careful, Kal."

Superman looked over to his friend and smiled grimly. "I'll see if I can bring you back some hot sauce from the north pole."

A huge cloud of hot ash was rolling over Green Lantern's protective shield and into the water, causing it to churn and boil, sending steam up into the already thick air. In minutes, the superheated volcanic debris could activate the orb again and make it impossible to disarm. As Wonder Woman pulled out of the dive, unable to help her friend from that point, Superman plunged into the warm water in a race against the spilling, burning ash.

Cutting through the hot ash cloud over the reef, Wonder Woman knew it could set her hair on fire, sear the skin off her bones, or even kill her if she stayed in it long enough. She flew high to escape, but even outside the cloud the air was full of foul mixes she couldn't see. Since volcanic eruptions were triggered by buildups of magma and gasses, eruptions often spewed out hazardous chemical cocktails such as sulfur dioxide, hydrogen sulfide, or hydrogen chloride. These gasses irritate skin and lung tissue, making it difficult to breathe. Although not nearly as dangerous as the superheated air in the hydroclastic clouds, Wonder Woman held her breath as long as she could.

Finally, having pushed herself to the limit, Diana gave in, pulling in a lungful of the worst air she'd ever tasted. Her lungs burned. Below, heat from the ash flow had caused a chemical reaction in the seawater, creating a puffy white plume of hydrochloric acid. Through it she could see—just barely—that the ash spill was almost on top of where Superman and the orb were located, 60 feet below. Biting her lip, Wonder

Woman prayed to Hera that the orb hadn't seduced him again with its lies. If he didn't get Ares's sphere out of there before the molten ash reached it—

Diana scanned the horizon, hoping to see Superman burst out of the water with the orb. But the sky was too thick with steam and debris.

Speculation was useless. The thing to do now was to face down Ares. Looking up, she saw his shape congealing from the thick vapor of cloud and ash that towered over the broken mountain.

Giving it everything she had, Wonder Woman flew into the air, rising high on the hot clouds. It was time to greet the God of War.

CHAPTER 29

Shake and Bake

"Gather the island men to one area!" Green Lantern shouted to Ana and Batman. "I can't keep this large a shield up forever!"

Ana looked skyward and decided that had to be an understatement. The shield, a transparent green skin that extended as far as she could see in the dim light, was being bludgeoned by rocks and heavy ash from the volcano. The thundering barrage echoed in the protective chamber, making it sound like the world was falling down on them.

Glimpsing a streak of red through the trunks of pines and palm trees, Ana stood dumbly as Flash ran up to the group, saluted his mates, and deposited Henry in front of her, as if he were delivering a package.

The last time Ana had seen Henry, he had ordered his men to kill her. She shrank back a little when she saw him, but could see right away that he was different. He wasn't her true-blue loopy loving Henry, but at least he wasn't the cold-blooded general she had seen earlier. The Brazilian woman waved a hand in front of his face. He blinked, but didn't register any curiosity about what she was doing.

"Henry?" she asked. "Honey, are you back?"

There was no reply from the man. Batman took Ana aside and gently suggested they tie Henry's hands, just in case. The thought pained her, but Ana agreed it would be best. They had a lot to do.

The prospect of rounding up the goons didn't appeal to Ana. The brutes had tried to kill her, and then some. Besides, they looked like evil animals with those Neanderthal brows and hairy chests and . . .

A warrior stood very still next to a tree, watching her. His sun-browned skin camouflaged him so that he looked like another tree trunk. But he was normal, not huge and muscle-bound. His face was even and smooth, his eyes a clear brown instead of fiery red.

Ana saw that Batman was also looking at the man.

"If he is any indication of what happened to all of the others," Batman said, "the orb has been deactivated. The men are as they probably were before it was triggered."

"Will I get my Henry back?" Ana asked. "All the way back?"

"We'll see," the Dark Knight said.

Ana didn't like the answer, but she appreciated Batman's reluctance to give false hope.

"Hey!" Green Lantern shouted. "Get the goons to Boy's Town! Now!"

"But none of us speak their language!" Ana said.

She looked at Henry to see if he remembered that part
of his life as a demigod. *Maybe,* she thought, *he can
help us communicate with the island men.* But Henry just
stared ahead blankly, prompting her to ask another
question. "And how do we know they still don't want
us dead?"

"The orb is gone," Flash said. "It's not in the fire. I
can just barely remember that it had been there. . . ."

He stopped. To Ana it looked like he was trying to
dig deeper for fading memories.

"From what I gleaned from Henry here, its disappearance seems to have reverted some things to the
way they were before it was discovered. The island
men never got supercharged because Henry never
found the orb. They ought to be as peaceful as they
were before this all started."

"Then why isn't Henry back to normal?" Ana
asked.

"I seem to remember something Wonder Woman
said about how he acted when she first got here, like
Henry was in a trance. Whatever was causing it then
is still in effect."

Ana searched her own memory, but found that recollections were hazy until she reached back to the time before Henry found the orb. Yes, even then he had been
acting strangely, as if he were a puppet controlled by
strings. It was a big step up from global terrorist, but
Ana prayed she would see her own, true Henry before
she met her end on the godforsaken island.

"I'm shrinking the size of the shield," Kyle said
though gritted teeth. "I've split it on the other side of

the mountain and I'm decreasing its area slowly enough for the men to keep ahead of the outer boundaries. Go to Boy's Town!"

Batman nodded his head. Addressing Flash and Ana he said, "That's the best area to collect everyone because of the open space. The rest of us can't talk to those men, but we can point them in the right direction. Once we're all together, we'll see if Green Lantern has enough energy left to get us off the island in a boat or something."

Ana heard Green Lantern grunt as he shut his eyes in concentration. She couldn't imagine the strain he was under—holding up a canopy that was being crushed by millions of tons of debris. And the number of lives at stake probably wasn't making his job any easier. In a flash, as if they had been in a dream together, she remembered having tricked him. Shame colored her cheeks as she watched the young man wince with pain under the enormous weight he bore.

When Ana looked up, Batman and Flash had disappeared into the darkening jungle. She speculated they were positioning themselves in places where the warriors were likely to pass, in order to herd them toward Boy's Town. Ana took charge of Henry, whose hands were tied behind his back, directing him by holding onto his arm. It felt good, touching him. She could almost pretend he was his old self again.

Total darkness consumed them as the protective shield became buried under millions of tons of ash and rock. Ana remembered her flashlight.

"Flash!" she called out.

The Scarlet Speedster appeared at her side in an instant. "Yes, m'lady?"

"Before the shield is withdrawn from HQ—can you fetch my flashlight?"

Not pausing long enough to answer, Flash zipped out of sight. A second later, he returned with the light.

Ana flipped the switch and illuminated the way for Henry and herself. It had been left on most of the night so she used it only intermittently, to conserve its batteries.

Ahead, men were running away from the closing walls of the green shield. Ana imagined they had no idea what was happening, having never seen a volcano erupt. Even though she had a vague memory of them trying to throw her into a burning pit, her heart went out to them.

All at once she could see flares positioned through the jungle like lights on a landing strip. Apparently, Batman had supplied the instruments, and Flash had used his superspeed to line them up, pointing the way to Boy's Town. Silhouettes of men stumbling past the lights toward the still-burning fire at the camp gave Ana hope. Then she saw—barely—a red streak passing back and forth through the jungle. *The Flash*, she thought, *carrying men to Boy's Town*. She knew the flares wouldn't burn for long, but between those and the Flash, maybe they would succeed in gathering everyone together. They had to condense the safety area for Kyle's sake.

Ana pointed her light at the young man. As soon as she did, she wished she hadn't—his face was con-

torted with pain, his teeth clenched, sweat pouring
down in small rivers. She left Henry for a moment,
taking the water bottle out of her belt so she could
dab some of the liquid onto Kyle's parched lips. If he
noticed, he didn't make a sign. Ana watched as he
crouched under the load he bore, putting one foot in
front of the other, advancing on Boy's Town.

Ana talked to him, telling Kyle how strong and
brave he was, how close he was to the camp, how she
knew he could do it. She had no idea if her words had
any effect on him until she looked up and found they
had made it.

The fire that burned in the center of the camp was
nearly out. Because Henry had never found the orb,
the island men had never stoked the flames into a
bonfire. Ana realized that, as much as she would like
to see more of what was around her, fire would consume too much oxygen in the enclosed space. From
the sounds of breathing and the stench of bodies in
the air, though, she believed everyone on the island
had made it to the protected space.

Everyone, Ana thought, *except Wonder Woman and
Superman.*

Superman had found the throbbing monster easily
enough. After calculating the best route for escape, he
pulled the orb from its crusty coral bed.

Touching it filled him with pangs of longing and
loneliness. Memories of his virtual life on Krypton
came back to him: first glimpses of boyhood adventures with his friends or his father, then snatches of

scenes with his beautiful mother baking him sweets or teaching him about his planet. Kal-El knew these were false memories, manufactured by the orb so that it could control him, but as he hefted the orb in both hands, the scenes from his illusory life on Krypton took on more solidity. Still, he sped away from the advancing blob of heat before it could ignite the orb into being a fully operational dimensional transporter and hate generator. As he did so, he could almost feel his mother and father, smell the crisp air, hear the sounds of insects and flying reptiles as he walked with his parents in the cool light of the red dwarf sun.

What am I doing here? Superman asked himself. He hung in the water at about 40 feet below the surface, holding the orb away from the churning ash flow that heated the water to boiling. Wasn't he supposed to take it somewhere? If he wanted to see more of his home planet he should take the orb over to the ash flow and throw it in where it could burn. If he took the orb away from the island—away from the heat it needed—he would never see his loving parents, his friends, or his beautiful planet again. Krypton would be destroyed, once and for all. That crushing feeling of loss and pain would return. Superman didn't think he could live through that much grief one more time. The memory of seeing his planet shatter into nothingness came back to him, as strong as it was when the orb showed it to him the first time.

Some instinct made him look not at, but *into* the throbbing red center of the orb. There he saw the opposite of what the orb had put into his mind. Not the

purple skies of Krypton, but the red burning ski[e]
Hades. This sphere didn't hold all the people
things he loved, it was filled with hate.

Instantly, Superman snapped out of the trance
had been lulled into, just as the superheated ash flo[w]
threatened to burst the orb's shell with its foul energy.

The Man of Steel pushed up, away from the heat,
and burst out of the water like a missile, holding the
orb in front of him, ascending into the ugly reddish
black cloud. The throbbing idiot tool of Ares tried to
hypnotize him with thoughts of power and of things
lost, but Superman concentrated on flying as fast and
as high as he could. He was half a mile above the
earth, heading for cooler air, when another explosion
rocked the island. A huge cloud of hot ash and rock
flew right at him, tumbling over itself in puffy folds
that looked harmless, but would boil the skin off a
human in seconds. It could also ignite the orb. He
shifted his course to fly more laterally until he was
out of range of the volcano. As the air cooled, the
throbbing in the sphere subsided.

Looking back over at the huge new cloud of pestilence, Superman saw what the second explosion had
brought up—Ares.

CHAPTER 30

Ares

Wonder Woman peered down at the green force field—what she could see of it anyway, the air was so thick with pulverized mountain—and saw that it was shrinking in what appeared to be a controlled manner. *Good*, she thought, *Kyle is conserving the ring's energy.* She hoped he would be able to protect himself and the others for a while longer. If she could disarm or defeat Ares, they would all have a chance. If Ares defeated her, it wouldn't matter how much energy Kyle had left—Ares would destroy them all.

One thing Wonder Woman knew about the God of War was that when he was mad—and this would be one of those instances—he lost his ability to reason well, a shortcoming that had held him back for many millennia. Ares planned his operations when he was calm and collected, so his schemes were usually rather clever. But when it came time to implement them, hot passion often made him get in his own way.

Wonder Woman had sometimes taken advantage of his volatile temper to trick the rogue god, but knew that he was more unpredictable—and therefore dangerous—when he was upset. Also, she knew that Ares was not completely mad, and that he had put an end to more than one campaign after listening to reason. The trick was to figure out if he could be defeated by making him angrier, or by appealing to his better self. Diana hoped it was the latter, since she always preferred diplomacy to fighting.

Princess Diana considered the colossal God of War as he materialized out of the polluted cloud that billowed up from the volcano's crater. Mammoth legs straddled the mouth of the caldera, threatening to collapse more of the mountain underneath him. Ares wore his full battle uniform, body armor strapped around his massive torso, shin and arm guards laced tight over bulging muscles, his dark cape flapping and undulating on the currents of hot air. His crested helmet was Ares's most impressive piece of equipment, though. Except for eye slits through which one could only see red blazing points of light, it concealed his face in horned and studded metal forged in the bowels of the Earth by Hephaestus, the god of fire.

If looks could kill, we'd all be dead already, Wonder Woman thought as she rose to meet Ares's eyes. Her hand went to her Lasso of Truth, not to use it yet, but to connect with its power and beauty. Hope surged into her when she touched it and a small smile graced her face.

"Ares!" she called. "Your plot to use me to get to

my people has failed. Through the gods, we received fair warning that foul deeds were in our future."

Ares reached up a gauntleted arm to grab her, but Wonder Woman slipped easily out of harm's way.

"Mortal fool! The contest has just begun! I will bury your island of infidels yet!"

With that, he reached down and grabbed up huge handfuls of burning rocks. He threw them down onto the place where the green shield protected the island's inhabitants. Wonder Woman winced, hoping Green Lantern's will would be able to withstand the onslaught.

In an effort to distract the god from destroying the shield, she flew close by his hands so he would grab at her. He did, but she eluded his grasp, then looped and tumbled through the air in a disorienting display that made Ares forget about the shield as he tried vainly to catch her. But instead of snagging Wonder Woman, he clutched only hot air and frustration.

The Amazon had neither the desire nor the powers necessary to destroy the god—he was, after all, immortal—she only hoped to keep him from doing more damage and to send him back to where he came from. Once his plans were aborted, she knew, he would need time to lick his wounds before he plotted more mischief.

But how could she do that? Once he gave up on grabbing her, he stood over the fuming mouth of the volcano, coaxing more of the destructive mix out of it. Diana knew that Green Lantern would not be able to protect the humans and wildlife on the island for much longer, so she tried to reason with the surly god.

"You keep starting wars, causing grief and disruption in human lives. But for what? More power? You are powerful enough already. There has never been a time in human history when you have not had a hand in cultures falling, brothers warring, sisters grieving. You bring disease, famine, and despair to so many already. What more does that gain you?"

"More," he answered, as if it were obvious to a child. "I get bored with the memories of wars past. I want a new war, with new weapons to make the music that delights me. Piercing screams, thudding bombs, wailing sirens, moaning wounded—they build into a symphony that soothes me."

"You've got rotten taste in music," Wonder Woman muttered to herself.

The orb pulsed and throbbed, sending Superman false memories of Jor-El and Lara freezing to death. If he continued on his mission, the parents he had never really known would die again, this time by his hand.

"Kal-El," pleaded the phantom voice of his biological mother. *"I'm so cold I feel like I'm on fire from the pain! Please turn back! We raised you to be a loving, caring boy, not some heartless murderer."*

"Please, son," the voice of Jor-El joined in. *"Krypton is in danger. If it gets any colder here, we will all die. You will have the death of an entire planet on your conscience."*

"Turn back," they said together. *"Turn back."*

Superman flew higher, determined to quiet the voices in the orb. The voices resonated within him, but the colder the air became, the less he trusted them. He noticed how the orb's throbbing subsided as he flew closer to his goal. But instead of feeling victorious, the realization that he was annihilating the voices he had come to love threatened to break Kal-El's heart.

Resisting the urge to save the ghosts from extinction, the man who was also known as Clark Kent reached into his real past for recollections of the loving couple who had raised him, Jonathan and Martha Kent. He remembered the patience and good humor with which his adoptive father taught him how to drive the tractor. Delicious smells of homemade bread and cherry pies from Martha's kitchen warmed Superman's heart, even as he flew the orb into colder climes. He mined those memories for the strength to keep going, for the courage to silence the voices of his might-have-been parents forever.

Superman's plan was simple: he would deposit the orb in a glacier at the Arctic Circle where the sub-zero temperatures would render it impotent. Once it was put on ice, Superman would be able to return to the island to help his teammates. The orb wouldn't be safe in deep freeze forever—Ares or some other malcontent might be able to find and retrieve it—but destroying the sphere or taking it to a distant asteroid would have to wait.

Just when Superman could make out ice floes on the horizon, feeling like he had the problem licked, something started to pull the orb away from him—as if a giant magnet was attracting the sphere to it. The attractor was behind him, back where the island lay. Superman pushed and, forced to turn around as the orb resisted his efforts, pulled, but to no good end. Something was wrenching the abomination back to the Bermuda Triangle. Superman could do nothing but hold on as the orb returned them back to the island from which they had come.

"Kal-El, you betrayed us," Jor-El said to him.

"But we forgive you," Lara said. *"We love you."*

"Help us get our strength back and we will be together forever, on a perfect world in a perfect time."

Superman was shaken when he realized a small part of him was glad he hadn't been able to neutralize the orb. Further attempts to reverse or slow the progress of the speeding agent of Ares proved useless, so he applied himself to remembering his real parents, the Kents of Planet Earth.

Ares summoned the orb back to him. That was easy enough to do—he had created the tool so it would obey him, even though there were thousands of miles between them. Once the entity was within his reach he could ignite the forces within again, using the tremendous heat from the volcano. The island would go back to the dimension of humankind, hatred would overcome his warriors, and his able general, Henry, would again lead the attack. The green and black man with the ring would again be his, which meant that all of his costumed friends would belong to Ares, as well.

"How did you know what to do with the cave drawings?" Ares asked Wonder Woman, calm now that he had located his missing messenger of hate. "Who told you of their power?"

"The gods told me through their oracle," the Princess answered. "The gods are not disposed to help simple minds, so they couch their help in riddles:

What is written comes to pass—what is passed becomes the past."

"So you figured out that what you ignored became real only by virtue of your not changing it. Very clever."

Wonder Woman didn't like the way this was going. Ares seemed too relaxed, as if he were sure of an outcome favorable to himself.

"But what now, Ares? The drawings on the wall did not include events that have taken control of this night out of your hands."

"I agree with you there, mortal. Only the Fates know what lies in store for us."

"You may as well retire, Lord," Wonder Woman said, respectfully. "We have shown you before that interference in humankind's destiny would lead to their total destruction—that your source of power would be eliminated if your greed for power was not limited."

The thought occurred to her that, rather than Ares controlling the orb, the orb controlled Ares. He was, after all, a god who would occasionally listen to reason. Not acting in his own best interest wasn't like him. "How do you know that you created the orb? It creates fantasies, hallucinations. Perhaps it produced an illusion for you."

"Don't be absurd," the god said. Diana could not see through his mask, but she sensed he was smiling contemptuously.

"Where did it come from, Ares?" Diana asked.

Clouds of gases roiled up around the bulk of the fearsome being, causing his cloak to billow and flap in the foul air.

"You ask too many questions, child!" the god roared.

He was angry, much like harried parents become irritated by the incessant questions of their offspring, yet Ares himself was starting to act like a child. He stomped his foot, but since he straddled the crater of the volcano, he only succeeded in smashing one wall inward. Choking clouds of ash and gas shot up into his face, as he struggled to maintain his balance. The master of war paused, as if annoyed by his own lack of control. Then, bellowing that the blunder had been Wonder Woman's fault, he swung a giant fist at her.

Dodging the blow was easy—the Amazon zipped out of the way like a hummingbird eluding a cat. Defensive moves would not resolve anything, though, and she knew it. One way she had dealt with Ares in a past encounter had been to lasso him. Her Golden Lasso of Truth compelled even an immortal god to listen to reason and to respond in kind.

Diana unhooked the lasso and spun a large loop off to her side. If Ares showed one moment of carelessness, she would throw the loop over his head and shoulders. Then she would be able to make him stop the volcanic activity so that she might save her friends and the men on the island.

Ares, however, did not give Wonder Woman a chance to follow through with that plan. He batted away the lasso if it came too near him, or tried to grab it so he might use it against her.

"Why, Ares?" Diana asked once again. "Why leave your promises behind to try and destroy those who are only struggling to live in peace?"

"Shut up, fool!" Ares bellowed. "You are just a woman—a mortal woman! I will not lower myself to answer your idiotic questions any longer!"

This was unlike Ares. He usually liked to brag and bluster—show how cunning he was. And even though he was a belligerent creature, he liked women, and especially respected Diana's skills as a warrior.

Diana circled around the massive god, suddenly tired of dealing with his hopelessly arrogant schemes. She cast about for something to distract him, but there was nothing. If they hadn't been cast back into the orb's dimension, they might have been able to get some help from the military and the rescue teams that had been on their way to the erupting volcano.

There, though, over the horizon, was a speck. And it was coming closer—

—Superman.

CHAPTER 31

Domed

The wait was terrible.

Ana watched the Green Lantern as millions of tons of ash and rock continued to rain down on the dome he'd constructed. True, the area he had to protect was smaller—a couple of acres, at most—but she could see the strain of holding up the field when more material was pounding down on it must be enormous. The Emerald Warrior was on his knees, his teeth clenched in concentration. Sweat poured down his face in hot streams.

The protected space was pitch black, ash and rock completely covering the green shield, blocking out whatever sunlight might have existed beyond the volcanic cloud. The Flash had put out the fire in Boy's Town to conserve oxygen. Ana kept her flashlight off for the time being, not knowing when they would really need it. Batman told her he had two remaining flares and a lighter in his Utility Belt, but he wanted to

save them for an emergency. Ana had to wonder what
his definition of "emergency" was.

The young Brazilian woman, exhausted from a
full night of danger and adrenaline rushes, listened
as Batman and Flash made sure the island men—for
they were no longer warriors—stayed in a pack.
They constructed a crude fence of palm fronds and
branches that defined an area so the island men
would stay out of the way. The fence was by no
means a jail—the men were as docile as sheep. They
were so compliant, in fact, that they'd been pro-
moted from "goons" to "drones." The heavy ridges
over their eye sockets were now regular brows, all
were of normal height and weight, and not one had
a nasty red gleam in his eyes. Before the light had
disappeared they had seemed to be fairly ordinary.
Hopefully they would stay that way.

Ana tried out her talk-of-love therapy on Henry,
but with no success. This brought her close to weeping—the one person she'd expected to be able to help
was her own husband, her soul mate. Even if they
were going to die, she would rather die with the man
she loved, not this empty shell. Henry didn't resist
her effort, he just didn't react at all. She had even un-
tied his hands, he was so passive.

An increasing load of debris pressed down on top
of the dome. Every muscle in Green Lantern's body
strained to keep the shield up. Finally, though, a crack
ripped along the thin green shield. Ana heard a spout
of hot gas erupt through the small fissure. It wasn't
enough to harm anyone, but if the opening grew . . .

The temperature inside Green Lantern's protective field rapidly rose.

In the absence of light, other senses work overtime to supply information, which was how Ana overheard Batman discuss possible escape plans with the Flash.

"We could ask Green Lantern to cut a hole in the dome nearest where the Batboat is anchored," Batman murmured.

It sounded to Ana like he was about ten feet away. She wondered if he knew she was within earshot.

"But that won't work," the Dark Knight continued. "You and I would be able to make it out, but the Lindstadts and the drones wouldn't stand a chance."

"Green Lantern is going to need help very soon," Flash added in a low voice.

Ana felt her way over to where the two heroes talked, pulling Henry along with her, and offered them her bottle of water. She had accepted the fact that they might die, and decided to spend what might be her last moments talking to people who talked back.

"I wanted to give some of this to Kyle, but I'm afraid of breaking his concentration. It's unbelievable what he's doing," she said.

Ana couldn't see Batman nod, but she heard Flash's comment:

"That ring enables him to have enormous power . . . but sometimes we forget the price he pays for the privilege."

"Kyle is strong," Batman agreed, "but even he has his limitations."

"Yeah, it's too bad there isn't a recharger that would work on him like the one that works on his ring."

Flash's comment struck Ana with a sudden bolt of inspiration. At first she was afraid to voice the thought because it sounded so far-fetched, but she quickly realized it was worth a try.

"Listen, guys," she said. "I have an idea."

CHAPTER 32

The Truth About Bats and Orbs

"Ares!" Wonder Woman shouted. "Is the orb even your own creation?"

The God of War didn't respond to her question. He looked down at the dome of ash that made an unsightly lump on his ruined island, shifting his position on the edge of the crater, as if considering whether he should smash it in. Wonder Woman flew into his field of vision to distract him.

"How did you create the entity? Or did it make you think *you* were in control?"

Ares's posture momentarily gave away that he wasn't certain. His stubborn arrogance, though, would never let him admit it.

"Impudence!"

With that the God of War swung a sledgehammer fist at the Amazon Princess. She could see that his fury was fuddling his senses. Flying around to the back of his horned mask, she threw the lasso over his gigantic head, then pulled it tight around his neck.

"Stop!" she commanded. Her heart was pounding. It was no small thing to give orders to a god.

Ares quit struggling.

"Listen here—the orb has been controlling *you!* How did you find it?"

The giant god responded as if in a trance. "The red sphere fell from space into the ocean. Poseidon found it and banished the thing to this dimension, not wanting the unknown power to disturb his realm. When I learned of the orb I came to see if it had potential as a weapon.

"Upon finding the object, I was inspired to create the island and the men. I put the pictographs in the cave so that they would know what to do when the time was right. For some reason, Morpheus claimed me and I slept. When I awoke, the island was as a dream. It stayed forgotten until it was accidentally found by that man."

One quality of the Lasso of Truth Diana appreciated was that Ares's recovered memory of what he had just told her would stay with him even after the golden rope was removed. Unlike the orb, which clouded minds with lies, the truth remained clear in the psyche of those who touched the lasso.

"Thank you, Ares," the Amazon Princess said. "I apologize to you, and humbly beg forgiveness of all the gods for using my lasso on you." She released him from his bond.

Ares glowered at Wonder Woman, furious that she had tricked him, but angrier still at having to acknowledge that he had been used by the orb.

Diana kept her lasso at the ready, just in case. Then, beyond the huge figure of Ares, she saw Superman flying closer.

As the orb pulled the Man of Steel to the island from which it had been torn, the voices from within spoke more clearly, more seductively.

"*We forgive you, Kal-El,*" the voice that was Lara said. "*You were under the influence of that woman in the obscene outfit. But remember that she doesn't know what is best for you—only your family and friends on Krypton do. Help us be stronger and your rewards will be many.*"

"*Yes, son,*" Jor-Al's voice joined in. "*Your fidelities lie with us, not with these weak and needy humans on Earth.*"

Superman visualized Lois. So that he wouldn't confuse her with the identical Lo-Ess of his Krypton hallucinations, he concentrated on specific events in their lives: the magical moment they met at the *Daily Planet*, her excitement the first time he took her flying with him, their wedding in the company of all their friends and family, the first time they made love.

When Lo-Ess spoke to him from the orb, he was able to ignore her.

As Superman stared at the ugly sphere he clung to, he recalled Wonder Woman's account of a previous battle with Ares. There was a magical disk created by the god that had been used against humans; when confronted, Diana had been able to use the object to disable Ares. That the weapons gods create could be used against them reassured Superman—how else could they be kept at bay when they had mischief in mind?

He wondered if the orb might be used against Ares. And if so, how?

Shifting his focus to what lay ahead, Superman saw clouds over the Bermuda Triangle, the stuff of active volcanoes. As the orb sped him closer, he saw the giant figure of Ares towering over the crater on the island. And—flying around him like an annoying insect as the god tried to swat her away—Wonder Woman.

The orb, asserting its powers more strongly as the air warmed, continued to send him messages through its long-dead emissaries. Superman, understanding that the force inside might be able to seduce him again, felt the urge to blast the orb to bits with his laser vision. Reason told him that doing so might unleash new, even more powerful dangers, and that continuing to hold onto the orb would destroy his mind and rob him of his will.

He took a deep breath and let go of the pulsing sphere as it plummeted toward Ares.

"Pray?" Batman asked Ana. He took her aside so no one else would hear. "I'm afraid you'll have to leave me out of this operation."

"We need you," Ana insisted. "We need every mind in this enclosure. Yours is a strong, vital force—please think of something you can do to help."

Batman only believed in that which could be proven; he was not one for prayer. Those who did pray to gods had his respect—Wonder Woman, for instance—but the only higher power he had ever consulted in his lonely years as a crime fighter had been the spirits of his beloved mother and father. In rare moments of moral confusion, in times of conflict, he pondered what they might do. And their answers had never been wrong. Reluctant as Batman was to direct his thoughts to a being who had allowed his parents to be murdered in front of his eyes, he knew he could commune with *their* memories, touching his mind to their spirits for reinforcement.

"Okay," he told Ana. "I can join you."

Ana, apparently forgetting how intimidating the man had seemed to her at first, leaped up and kissed him on the cheek.

Another crack formed in the green shield, sending a screeching rip of sound through the interior of the dome, as if giant fingernails scraped a blackboard. Everyone, including Batman, cringed.

Ana tried her best to ignore it. She held the flashlight in her teeth, pointing it on her hands. Lit by the two remaining flares from Batman's belt, she mimicked prayer to the former warriors, showing them what to do. Then she reached out both hands to clasp those of Batman, standing next to her, and the Green Lantern, stooped under the weight of the world. The island men raised their heads in prayer and held hands, just as Ana had hoped they would.

Batman and Flash had pulled down the makeshift fence, positioning the island men in a tightly wound coil, like a watch spring. The outer end of the line led to Green Lantern, just a foot away from Ana. He was still on his knees, apparently unconscious of anything around him as he put all of his mental energies into

keeping the dome from caving in under the tremendous pressure.

As Ana's flashlight dimmed—the tired batteries
giving up the ghost—the young woman almost lost
her faith that what they were trying would work. She
dropped the light from her mouth and called out,
"Pray! Pray to God or Zeus or Ares or Allah! Pray to
whoever you want—just *pray!*"

The flares expired, but it didn't matter—every eye
was closed in prayer. The island men chanted as they focused their minds, probably still for Ares's sake, but it
didn't matter. Energy built and multiplied as concentrated thoughts flowed from one man to another, their
linked hands turning them into a giant generator of positive thought and power. The energy flowed through
them in a dynamic wave, accumulating more with each
mind that added to it. The wave reached the Flash, then
Batman, and finally Ana, who was praying to her own
private Idaho. She was filled with so much energy she
thought she would be lifted off the ground. Her hand
clasped Kyle's and fed him everything that passed through
her. She didn't need light to know it was working.

The screeching in the dome stopped, and the protective barrier became solid again, devoid of seams
and cracks.

Prayers of hope were transformed into, and became compounded by, prayers of thanks.

If Ana had been able to see Kyle in the darkness,
she would have been elated by the joy on his sweat-
streaked face.

CHAPTER 33

Clean Sweep

Wonder Woman saw the orb speeding toward Ares, followed by Superman. She kept her lasso spinning at her side in case she might have to loop it around the speeding sphere, a tricky target indeed. The God of War ignored the Amazon, watching only the pulsing red ball of hate.

"I despise trickery," the god said, as if to himself. "Now I loathe the thing that tricked me."

"What will you do with the orb?" Wonder Woman asked. "The power it wields is great and devious."

"Silence!"

She wasn't surprised the god was still angry with her—she had helped him, and Ares didn't particularly like being helped. In fact, Diana wondered if he might try to kill her, just so no one would learn of how he had been duped.

The orb streaked through the morning sky like a meteor, leaving a scar of red vapor in its wake.

Superman flew behind and below the object, looking like he was trying to avoid the angry trail. Wonder
Woman gestured to him, hoping he would tell her
what to do with the approaching sphere.

"Don't try to stop it!" Superman shouted.

The red ball swooshed by Wonder Woman, temporarily filling her with dread and loathing, and feelings of despair. The effect was as strong as a blow to
the body—she flew backward as if she'd been
punched. Keeping her eye on the hateful thing, she
watched as it flew straight to Ares.

The god caught the orb as easily as a pitcher
catches a lazy pop fly. Then, without a word to either
of the super heroes, he vanished with it into thin air.

The air, though, wasn't exactly thin. It was clogged
with poisons and ash, and was still dangerously hot.
The volcano had stopped emitting more material, but
what hung in the air still threatened to kill their
friends below.

That was another one of Ares's flaws, Wonder
Woman remembered: he never cleaned up after him-
self. *And where*, she wondered, *did he go with the orb*?
Unfortunately, there was no time to think about that.
She and Superman had work to do.

The Man of Steel took in a huge lungful of air and
blew the poisonous clouds into the upper atmos-
phere, spreading them as thinly as possible. Wonder
Woman knew the chemicals in the clouds would return to earth in the form of acid rain—they would
have to deal with that after they rescued their friends.
If, she thought, *they are still alive.*

The pyroclastic ash flows had changed the shape of the island. There were now several more acres of beach-front property, although most of it would be too hot to enjoy for several months. Since the island's shape no longer mirrored that of Themyscira, Diana had a hard time picking out where the dome had been located.

"I see them!" Superman called as he pointed to a lumpish mound at the base of the volcano.

Diana offered a small prayer of thanks to the gods for her friend's excellent X-ray vision.

"And I hear thousands of hearts beating down there! They're alive!"

Diana held her breath as she waited for the Man of Steel to use his powerful eyes to fuse together the ash and rock that covered Green Lantern's dome. As she waited she looked around at the damage done to the island, now that she could see it clearly. Almost two-thirds of the surface was covered in ash. This was the same kind of rubble and muck that had buried Pompeii and broiled its citizens. Parts of the jungle that hadn't been entombed were burning, including the men's houses. Diana prayed to her goddesses to send rains.

After congealing the material over the dome into a solid surface, Superman flew over the sea and blew on the water so that vast sprays fell on hot spots, cooling them. Then he took the last of the air and blew the more noxious clouds away from the island.

Diana sniffed the air, testing it for poisons, and found it to be clean enough. "Is it time to ventilate that dome?"

"Kyle might still be holding up the shield," Superman replied. "We have to signal him to let it down before we can get in there."

Wonder Woman flew to fetch a boulder from the side of the volcano. Handing it over to Superman, she asked, "Do you know Morse code?"

Her friend smiled. "My buddies in Smallville used to play spy games after school. Guess who was quick at decoding?"

Heaving the boulder down on the now-solid dome, Superman tapped out ALL CLEAR. Then he paused, listening.

"I just heard a whoop of joy, and a big sigh of relief out of Kyle. Let's go."

Within seconds, Superman and Wonder Woman had punched a hole in the dome, letting in light and relief to the thousands inside.

A cheer erupted when Superman and Wonder Woman flew into Boy's Town. It might have been on account of their arrival, or for the brand new skylight and fresh air. *Or maybe all of the above*, Wonder Woman thought.

At any rate she was heartened by the cheers. It told her a couple of things: First, many people, if not all, had survived the volcano's deadly blast. Also, the island men, who formerly had made the Terminator look talkative, were now expressing themselves like normal folks.

Her eyes adjusted quickly to the dim light as she picked out Green Lantern. He was limp from his effort, crouching down on his hands and knees. Even the strain of maintaining that position looked unbearable.

Superman flew over to him and said, "You can take a break now, G.L." Then he flew out through the hole in the dome so he could continue fighting the fires in the jungle.

Green Lantern opened his eyes, which immediately filled with tears of relief. Then he collapsed, unable to hold a single muscle in place any longer.

Wonder Woman flew over and caught him before he hit the ground. Scooping him up in her strong arms, she took him to a patch of grass and set him down.

Kyle gazed at her and smiled. "Has anyone ever told you you're beautiful?"

Diana smiled and kissed him on the forehead. He immediately shut his eyes and dropped off to sleep.

Turning to find her comrades, Diana spotted Ana. And Henry. They were hugging each other and looking only into each other's eyes, oblivious to the thousands of unwashed island men surrounding them.

Flash appeared at Diana's side in the blink of an eye. "Cute couple, eh?" he said, nodding his head at the newlyweds.

Diana smiled. "This is very good news, Flash. If Henry is back to the man he was when Ana fell in love with him, then Ares has taken the orb out of this dimension to a place where it won't affect any of these people again."

"Do you think he took it to our dimension, or made a new one just to store the thing?"

"I hope we never find out. Ares may have taken possession of the orb again, but since he didn't create it and doesn't understand how it works, he may not be able to keep it contained forever."

"Where did the orb come from?" Flash asked.

"Space," Diana said. "Whether it came here by accident or by design is anyone's guess. But because the orb used Ares—and he hates being used—he's probably taken it someplace cold, to neutralize it."

"Good. It seems like a bad dream now, but that thing had me running for my life."

Diana, recalling snatches of what the orb had conjured up in her mind, shuddered.

"What's the matter?"

"Maybe I'll tell you about it later." She gave Flash a warm hug. "It's good to see you alive and well."

"You, too, babe," he said with a wink.

Instantly, Flash ran up the inside of the dome and out the hole so he could help Superman put out the fires.

Wonder Woman walked through a crowd of bewildered, milling men and over toward Ana and Henry.

"Henry Lindstadt, I presume?" Diana asked, her hand held out to greet the man she'd already met under less than favorable conditions.

Henry turned to her and gaped. "Wonder Woman!" he gulped. "Wow! Honey, look it's—" he stammered. "I mean, Green Lantern and Flash . . . and wasn't that *Superman?*"

Ana smiled. "Yes, I've been meeting some very interesting people lately."

The young man became lost for words. Ana

grinned at Diana, and Diana winked back. Then Batman joined the group.

Henry looked like he would pop with excitement. "Wow!"

Batman took the young man's hand and shook it in greeting. "Welcome back, Mr. Lindstadt," he said.

Then Batman took Ana's hand, pressing it in both of his, before he turned to join his friends in their firefighting efforts. When Ana opened her hand, Wonder Woman saw it held her wedding ring.

Ana looked at her and smiled as she slipped the ring on her finger. "I'll tell you about it later," she promised.

Wonder Woman turned to Henry, taking his hand and looking into his eyes, where she saw the real Henry once again. "What do you remember of your time on this island?" she asked.

At her warm touch and soothing voice, Henry calmed down. "Not much," he said. "I know something happened to me, but it's like a far-off dream."

He looked at his feet, bare and dirty, and then returned his eyes to Diana's, unable to tell her anything but the truth. "I think I killed a man."

Ana's expression changed from one of joy to worry and dread. "No!" she cried. "You wouldn't—"

"If you killed someone," Diana interjected, "it was not you who did it, but the force that occupied the orb. Do you remember the name of the man you supposedly killed?"

Henry tried to think. "Something that started with a P, I think," he finally said.

"Pelias?"

"Yes!" Henry said. "I'm surprised you know the name. Does that mean it's true?" He shuffled his feet nervously.

Diana looked around the dome. All of the men were still inside until the fires in the jungle were safely contained. Running through the thousands of men, she called out, "Pelias!"

The island's inhabitants, formerly known as drones, goons, and warriors, were now simply men. Their former mien of robotic conformity had disappeared with the orb. They were now singular people, and would have all the problems of living in society that individuals have. No more one-size-fits-all communal living—they were now on the verge of learning competition and selfishness, along with creative thought and expression. A new world was opening up to them in spite of the fact that they were still isolated in this dimensional backwater.

They were also, now that their sponsor had abandoned them, mortal. They were prey to illness, aging, and death. Diana felt both happy and sorry for them at the same time.

Their faces still looked similar—but not identical—to one another, a quality that would change with time as the curse of individuality gave them character. For now, though, Diana could still remember Pelias's face and voice, since she had met him before Henry had found the orb. Her memories of those hours on the island were crystal clear.

Scanning the faces, she couldn't find him. Just because Pelias's murder had been erased didn't mean he survived the volcano blast. If she couldn't find him,

Henry and Ana might be split apart by fears of murder that hadn't really been committed. Desperate to find him, Wonder Woman called out Pelias's name. There was no response.

Continuing her search, face by face, she finally came upon a clutch of men sitting on the ground, a group she hadn't spotted among the standing, milling men. Diana stopped in front of the group, addressing one of them.

"Pelias?" she asked.

The man looked up. It was he.

Diana swept Pelias up in her arms, gave him a kiss on the cheek, and flew him the short distance over to Ana and Henry. He did not look pleased by her attentions.

The Amazon set him down in front of the couple.

"This is the man you thought you killed," she said to Henry in English.

"Pelias," she said, switching to Ancient Greek, "this is Henry and Ana. They are very pleased to meet you."

In spite of Pelias's newfound individuality and mortality, he still had the manners of a goat. He ignored Henry's outstretched hand and walked away to rejoin his brothers.

Ana started giggling out of sheer relief. "Oh, Henry! I'm so glad nothing really bad happened while you were . . ."

Henry took her close to him and smoothed her hair, distracting her from unpleasant thoughts. Then he covered Ana in kisses, making her blush and laugh with joy.

Diana, touched by their happiness, felt her eyes tearing up. Then, feeling like an intruder, she left the couple to help her teammates put the island in order.

CHAPTER 34

All True Isms

The men wanted to stay on the island. They had lived there for so long that relocating was unthinkable. That meant they would stay in this dimension that existed solely to support their island home.

Wonder Woman translated their desires and questions for the benefit of the other JLA members and the Lindstadts, who sat around a small campfire roasting fish in the late afternoon. Everyone had ideas on how to make life comfortable—or at least doable—for the men. They would have to be taught how to clean their fish to keep from being poisoned by bacteria. They had been immune from disease before, but now it would be an ongoing concern. Sanitation was another bugaboo.

Henry surprised everyone with an announcement. "I want to live here—at least part-time—so I can teach the men how to take care of themselves. They will need antibiotics, methods to collect clean water—a lot of things they never needed when they were immortal."

Ana looked at him, interested. "You want me to help?" she asked.

"If you really want to. Being the only woman on the island would be awkward, at best, and lonely at worst, but it would just be part-time—we have jobs and family at home we're not going to abandon. But I need to help these people . . . I feel like I owe it to them for what I did."

Earlier, Henry had asked, so Diana told him the basics of what had happened. The young man was clearly bothered by his part in the scheme and felt like he should repay the men he had treated with such contempt.

"I must admit," he added, "I have some pretty selfish reasons for wanting to help, too. From what Ana and Wonder Woman have described, there's some really great diving in these waters and I wouldn't miss that for the world."

"Watch out for the sharks," Wonder Woman cautioned.

Ana wasn't displeased with his admission—she loved the fact that Henry knew how to enjoy life. This was further proof that he was back to normal. As if it were a longtime dream of theirs, they started brainstorming things to teach the men and what kind of equipment they would need.

"I envy you two," said Green Lantern. "You sound like you're starting out on a great, lifelong honeymoon."

"What about the dimensional portal? How do we know it's still there?" Flash asked.

"Good question," Batman said.

They had been so busy dealing with the aftermath of the eruption and the relocation of the men that they had forgotten they had to get back to "the real world" on their own steam.

Wonder Woman got up and flew to where Ana had told her the thermocline lay. She dove into the water, ignoring the thousands of brightly colored fish, and swam away from the island. Passing though a wall of cold water, she surfaced and looked around. There were several military helicopters and ships looking for a phantom volcanic island, but no island. Before anyone could spot her she took a few deep breaths and dove under to swim back the way she came.

"The portal is still there," she said, to the relief of all. "Since it didn't close when Ares took the orb away, it is probably a permanent fixture.

"There are military craft looking for this island. It was in that dimension last night and is now missing. With luck, since no one from the outside world actually saw it, they will conclude that it was a mirage of sorts caused by the strange energy fluctuations here in the Triangle."

"That would be good," Henry said. "The last thing these islanders need is to be invaded by too much modern culture all at once."

"I couldn't agree more," Diana said. "Since I speak their language, I can tell the men enough about sanitation so they'll be all right for however long it takes you to get back with supplies. I have a friend who has created software that translates modern English into

Ancient Greek, which will help you communicate with them."

"That's wonderful!" Ana said, obviously excited by the adventure she and Henry were about to share.

A short discussion followed in which Green Lantern volunteered to create a submarine that would take everyone who wanted a ride through the underwater portal, back to their own dimension. He would outfit it with a cloaking device so that it would appear to be a whale to any of the military personnel patrolling the area. It was essential for the sake of the men not to give away the existence of the island.

"Can you create enough cargo space to accommodate the Batboat?" Batman asked. "Not being submersible, I can't pilot it through the portal."

"Can do," Green Lantern replied, always willing to be of service.

Ana remembered Henry's and her rental boat. "Oh dear," she said. "I'm afraid the boat I arrived in didn't make it. We'll have to buy a new craft to replace the one that was buried by the volcano. I don't know if we can afford it."

"If you're going to live here part-time, you'll also need one boat for each side of the portal," Batman said. "Submit a proposal to the Wayne Foundation of Gotham City for the boats and whatever supplies you'll need. The foundation's head, Bruce Wayne, is a philanthropist who will probably think highly of your desire to help the men here."

"Can he be trusted to keep the island location a secret?" Ana asked.

"I'll have someone talk to him."

Ana jumped to her feet and planted another kiss on the Dark Knight's cheek.

This time, Batman almost smiled.

Within an hour, everyone was back in the dimension of fast food, air pollution, global conflict, and uncertain futures.

"Home, sweet home!" Flash said, before he galloped back full steam to Keystone City, hoping he wouldn't have to visit any island paradises for a good long while.

Kyle went on with Batman to Gotham City, dropping him off with the Batboat. From there the Emerald Warrior flew to New York, ready for a few nights of rest and relaxation to unwind from his taxing experience in the tropics.

Oracle, after a hard night of being in the dark, was happy to hear that everyone was all right and relayed the good news to the other members of the Justice League.

Overhead, Superman flew straight to Metropolis and his soul mate, Lois Lane. Seeing Ana and Henry so in love had reminded him how much he missed his wife's good humor and terrible cooking.

While the honeymoon couple waited in Miami for a plane to take them home, Wonder Woman discussed their plans for helping the island men.

"Your ideas sound well thought out and considerate."

Ana beamed. "Rather than try to teach the men

English, we're going to learn Ancient Greek. We want to respect their culture as much as possible; we don't want to shove our way of doing things down their throats."

"Well," Henry said, "we're probably going to have to introduce a *few* English words to their vocabulary. 'Soap,' 'antibiotics,' and 'get your own wife' come to mind."

Wonder Woman smiled. "I wish you both the best of luck. You'll be dealing with the familiar in L.A., but venturing into the unknown when you're living on the island. It's not always easy reconciling two lives that are so different."

"We'll manage," Ana said. "One thing I'd like to take from our world into theirs, though, would be a camera so we could film the rich undersea life in that dimension. Down there is how our own seas would look if we didn't overfish and pollute the oceans. Nations could learn so much about conservation and respect for nature if we showed them how things could be."

"But we're sure if we did film it," Henry said, "the worst of our fellow humans would find a way to follow us so they could poach all the fish. They would be followed by hawkers, gawkers, and evangelists, until the island looked like every other tourist trap on the cruise ship routes."

"In other words," Wonder Woman asked, "you'll be leaving your video cameras at home?"

"Exactly."

"Please come to visit us in L.A., or on the island," Ana asked.

"Of course," the Amazon Princess said. "You are my friends, and I like to maintain my friendships. But for now," she continued, "I need to return home to see my mother and sisters. Be well, you two, and cherish each other."

"Thank you for returning my husband to me," Ana said.

"Thank you, Ana," Diana said as she kissed the Brazilian woman's cheeks. "Thank you for your stories of love. They saved my life."

Ana and Henry watched as Wonder Woman flew away, until she disappeared into a cloud.

"So," Henry said, "what were those stories of love you told Wonder Woman?"

Ana grinned at her husband and kissed him, which told him all he really needed to know.

CHAPTER 35

Paradise Island

"Why Henry Lindstadt?" Hippolyta asked. "From what you said, he's not Greek, nor is he religious."

The Princess sat with her mother on a white marble terrace, watching the sun set over the sea. A table held a bowl of fresh fruits and glasses of vintage wine. Freshly cut flowers filled the space with pleasant perfumes, and pleasing shapes and colors. Diana, dressed in a simple silk gown, couldn't remember any time when she had been happier to be on Themyscira, her home.

"Ana told me that Henry first began acting strangely when he saw underwater video of the area on a nature program," Diana said. "I think he was ensnared before that."

"Oh?"

"Henry wore a piece of coral around his neck. I noticed it when I first met him, but thought nothing of it at the time. Later, when he was back to normal, I asked him about it. He said he picked it up last year while diving in Belize. That's a long way from the Triangle, but not that far when you consider how currents and storms move things around."

"And you think this piece of coral was somehow connected to the orb?" Hippolyta asked.

"Yes. Either it fell from the orb and traveled through the portal on the currents, or Ares, under the influence of the orb, deliberately left the piece in Man's World to draw someone to the place. Either way, Henry picked it up and found the coral attractive because of its shape—a man's profile. Wearing it close to his heart transmitted a miniscule amount of the orb's residual energy into him—just enough to make him recognize its parallel location when he saw the footage on the documentary."

"So it was just bad luck that he happened to pick up that particular piece of coral?"

"I believe so. But maybe it was Fate," Diana said.

"Let's not get into that," the Queen cautioned, rolling her eyes.

"We have since neutralized that piece of coral, but . . . what do you think Ares did with the orb?"

"I doubt he destroyed it—from what you told me, I don't know if it *can* be destroyed," her mother answered. "I just *hope* he took it to one of the poles and buried it in permafrost."

"Ares fancies weapons," Diana mused. "He may not be able to control it, but he would want to have it, regardless. Since it is indestructible, I'm afraid we may live to see it gain control of him again, as soon as he forgets how it used him."

"That's possible," Hippolyta agreed, sadly. "Ares finds delight in the ugliest things."

"With the exception of Aphrodite, of course," Diana said.

"Of course." Hippolyta reached for a grape from a tray on the table. "I hear she peels all his grapes for him. Can you imagine?"

"Speaking of food," said the famished Amazon, "what's on the menu tonight?"

"The usual roasted something-or-other. But this time you will tell all. Our sisters have been in their battle gear on full alert, and they will appreciate knowing it was for good cause."

"I won't be happy to tell them the details of my hallucinations—they still fill me with horror. They were so real."

Hippolyta saw the sudden distress in Diana's eyes. Taking her daughter's hand in hers, she squeezed it.

"Talking about it will help you release the horrors. Your sisters will take some of the burden from you just by being there to listen. We are all well. We all love you with all our hearts. Artemis, Chloe, Hermione, Polyxena—they are waiting for you to give their thanks and their love. Their beauty and strength will vanquish your nightmares. Your visions will fade in time, Diana."

"I understand, but sometimes it's hard to believe."

Hippolyta rose and took both her daughter's hands, pulling her to her feet. Reaching out to smooth her flowing black hair, she said, "I know, dear. I know."

The sounds of celebration floated up to the open terrace. As the Queen slipped her arm through Diana's, they went to join their sisters.

Epilogue

The cavern was cold.

Good, Ares thought. *The thing doesn't like cold.*

Sheets of ice coated the walls in glistening milky white layers. Bony fingers of frozen water hung down, as if pointing the way to Hades. But Ares moved forward, ignoring the icy directions. Clouds of breath with a life span of seconds preceded him on the path. The God of War detested the low temperature, but it was a discomfort he would have to tolerate while visiting the newest addition to his collection.

Knowing the orb was in the arctic prison made Ares feel victorious, as if he had conquered his foe and made it his slave. He knew that wasn't true—the orb could easily get the best of him if he let down his guard—but the rogue son of Zeus wasn't going to let that happen. Today, as he had done several times before, he was just going to sit with the sphere so he could hear the screams and the voices inside. Maybe he'd be lucky and see the spectacular scenes of carnage it occasionally showed him. His breath came out in smaller, quicker puffs as he strode down the frigid corridor, eager for his audience with the alien globe.

A cumbersome gate of English oak barred his way. Heaving it open, the god held his torch at the entrance to the small chamber that held the red jewel. Ares checked the flame to make sure it didn't give off too much heat, but it was all right. Then he looked to the stone platform on which he'd set the orb.

It was gone.

Ares's anger echoed down the frozen chambers, causing icicles to break off and drop, adding delicate crystalline chimes to the god's booming eruption. "Thieves! Betrayers! Whoever took the orb will pay dearly!"

Raging and bellowing, he smashed his fists against walls and kicked the massive oak door to splinters. His threats bounced from wall to wall until they faded to nothing—no one was there to hear them.

Finally, Ares stopped his tantrum and sat down to sort out the mystery. Not a soul—not even his troublesome offspring—knew of the orb's existence. He had created the ice cavern himself, to ensure its secrecy. His were the only eyes that had seen the orb since he took it away from the island of fools.

Thinking back to the last time he'd seen it, the God of War recalled the joy he'd felt when he saw humans being tortured and killed at his command. The scene hadn't yet happened—it was a promise of events to come if Ares did as the orb had directed.

He stopped breathing for a moment so he could dig further into his memory. It was like trying to recollect dreams—snatches became available, but only if he concentrated.

An image came to Ares in which he was holding the orb, admiring it closely. Then he sent it somewhere. Possibly someplace warm.

Had he really done that? Ares hit the side of his helmet forcefully, as if trying to kick-start his memory. He had no idea if the scene in his head was real or imagined. All he knew was: the orb was gone.

Ares left the cavern, determined to find it. He half wondered if, someday, the orb might find him instead.

Either way, it would be only a matter of time.

About the Author

CAROL LAY, creator of the weekly cartoon strip "Story Minute," has been writing and drawing comics for more than twenty-five years. Her work has appeared in an array of publications, from underground comix and *MAD* Magazine to *The New Yorker* and *The Wall Street Journal*. She currently lives in Los Angeles with her husband/dive buddy, Allen Murdock.